# THE LIGHTED WAY

# THE LIGHTED WAY

E. PHILLIPS OPPENHEIM

**WILDSIDE PRESS**

**THE LIGHTED WAY**

This edition published 2005 by Wildside Press, LLC.
www.wildsidepress.com

# CHAPTER I

## AN INVITATION TO DINNER

Mr. Samuel Weatherley, sole proprietor of the firm of Samuel Weatherley & Co., wholesale provision merchants, of Tooley Street, London, paused suddenly on his way from his private office to the street. There was something which until that second had entirely slipped his memory. It was not his umbrella, for that, neatly tucked up, was already under his arm. Nor was it the *Times*, for that, together with the supplement, was sticking out of his overcoat pocket, the shape of which it completely ruined. As a matter of fact, it was more important than either of these — it was a commission from his wife.

Very slowly he retraced his steps until he stood outside the glass-enclosed cage where twelve of the hardest-worked clerks in London bent over their ledgers and invoicing. With his forefinger — a fat, pudgy forefinger — he tapped upon a pane of glass, and an anxious errand boy bolted through the doorway.

"Tell Mr. Jarvis to step this way," his employer ordered.

Mr. Jarvis heard the message and came hurrying out. He was an undersized man, with somewhat prominent eyes concealed by gold-rimmed spectacles. He was possessed of extraordinary talents with regard to the details of the business, and was withal an expert and careful financier. Hence his hold upon the confidence of his employer.

The latter addressed him with a curious and altogether unusual hesitation in his manner.

"Mr. Jarvis," he began, "there is a matter — a little matter — upon which I — er — wish to consult you."

"Those American invoices —"

"Nothing to do with business at all," Mr. Weatherley interrupted, ruthlessly. "A little private matter."

"Indeed, sir?" Mr. Jarvis interjected.

"The fact is," Mr. Weatherley blundered on, with considerable awkwardness, for he hated the whole affair, "my wife — Mrs. Weatherley, you know — is giving a party this evening — having some friends to dinner first, and then some other people coming to bridge. We are a man short for dinner. Mrs. Weatherley told me to get some one at the club — telephoned down here just an hour ago."

Mr. Weatherley paused. Mr. Jarvis did his best to grasp the situation, but failed. All that he could do was to maintain his attitude of intelligent interest.

"I don't know any one at the club," continued his employer, irritably. "I feel like a fish out of water there, and that's the truth, Mr. Jarvis. It's a good club. I got elected there — well, never mind how — but it's one thing to be a member of a club, and quite another to get to know the men there. You understand that, Mr. Jarvis."

Mr. Jarvis, however, did not understand it. He could conceive of no spot in the city of London, or its immediate neighborhood, where Mr. Samuel Weatherley, head of the firm of Messrs. Weatherley & Co., could find himself among his social superiors. He knew the capital of the firm, and its status. He was ignorant of the other things which counted — as ignorant as his master had been until he had paid a business visit a few years ago, in search of certain edibles, to an island in the Mediterranean Sea. He was to have returned in triumph to Tooley Street and launched upon the provision-buying world a new cheese of astounding quality and infinitesimal price — instead of which he brought home a wife.

"Anything I can do, sir," began Mr. Jarvis, a little vaguely, —

"My idea was," Mr. Weatherley proceeded, "that one of my own young men — there are twelve of them in there, aren't there?" he added, jerking his head in the direction of the office — "might do. What do you think?"

Mr. Jarvis nodded thoughtfully.

"It would be a great honor, sir," he declared, "a very great honor indeed."

Mr. Weatherley did not contradict him. As a matter of fact, he was of the same opinion.

"The question is which," he continued.

Mr. Jarvis began to understand why he had been consulted. His fingers involuntarily straightened his tie.

"If I could be of any use personally, sir, —"

His employer shook his head.

"My wife would expect me to bring a single man, Jarvis," he said, "and besides, I don't suppose you play bridge."

"Cards are not much in my line," Mr. Jarvis admitted, "not having, as a rule, the time to spare, but I can take a hand at loo, if desired."

"My wife's friends all play bridge," Mr. Weatherley declared, a little brusquely. "There's only one young man in the office, Jarvis, who, from his appearance, struck me as being likely."

"Mr. Stephen Tidey, of course, sir," the confidential clerk agreed. "Most suitable thing, sir, and I'm sure his father would accept it as a high compliment. Mr. Stephen Tidey Senior, sir, as you may be aware, is next on the list for the shrievalty. Shall I call him out, sir?"

Mr. Weatherley looked through the glass and met the glance, instantly lowered, of the young man in question. Mr. Stephen Tidey Junior was short and stout, reflecting in his physique his aldermanic father. His complexion was poor, however, his neck thick, and he wore a necktie of red silk drawn through a diamond ring. There was nothing in his appearance which grated particularly upon Mr. Weatherley's sense of seemliness. Nevertheless, he shook his head. He was beginning to recognize his wife's point of view, even though it still seemed strange to him.

"I wasn't thinking of young Tidey at all," he declared, bluntly. "I was thinking of that young fellow at the end of the desk there — chap with a queer name — Chetwode, I think you call him."

Mr. Jarvis, human automaton though he was, permitted himself an exclamation of surprise.

"Young Chetwode! Surely you're not in earnest, sir!"

"Why not?" Mr. Weatherley demanded. "There's nothing against him, is there?"

"Nothing against him, precisely," Mr. Jarvis confessed, "but he's at the lowest desk in the office, bar Smithers. His salary is only twenty-eight shillings a week, and we know nothing whatever about him except that his references were satisfactory. It isn't to be supposed that he would feel at home in your house, sir. Now, with Mr. Tidey, sir, it's quite different. They live in a very beautiful house at Sydenham now — quite a small palace, in its way, I've been told."

Mr. Weatherley was getting a little impatient.

"Send Chetwode out for a moment, anyway," he directed. "I'll speak to him here."

Mr. Jarvis obeyed in silence. He entered the office and touched the young man in question upon the shoulder.

"Mr. Weatherley wishes to speak to you outside, Chetwode," he announced. "Make haste, please."

Arnold Chetwode put down his pen and rose to his feet. There was nothing flurried about his manner, nothing whatever to indicate on his part any knowledge of the fact that this was the voice of Fate beating upon his ear. He did not even show the ordinary interest of a youthful employee summoned for the first time to an audience with his chief. Standing for a moment by the side of the senior clerk in the middle of the office, tall and straight, with deep brown hair, excellent features, and the remnants of a healthy tan still visible on his forehead and neck, he looked curiously out of place in this unwholesome, gaslit building with its atmosphere of cheese and bacon. He would have been noticeably good-looking upon the cricket field or in any gathering of people belonging to the other side of life. Here he seemed almost a curiously incongruous figure. He passed through the glass-paned door and stood respectfully before his employer. Mr. Weatherley — it was absurd, but he scarcely knew how to make his suggestion — fidgetted for a moment and coughed. The young man, who, among many other quite unusual qualities, was possessed of a considerable amount of tact, looked down upon his employer with a little well-assumed anxiety. As a matter of fact, he really was exceedingly anxious not to lose his place.

"I understood from Mr. Jarvis that you wished to speak to me, sir," he remarked. "I hope that my work has given satisfaction? I know that I am quite inexperienced but I don't think that I have made any mistakes."

Mr. Weatherley was, to tell the truth, thankful for the opening.

"I have had no complaints, Chetwode," he admitted, struggling for that note of condescension which he felt to be in order. "No complaints at all. I was wondering if you — you happened to play bridge?"

Once more this extraordinary young man showed himself to be possessed of gifts quite unusual at his age. Not by the flicker of an eyelid did he show the least surprise or amusement.

"Bridge, sir," he repeated. "Yes, I have played at — I have played occasionally."

"My wife is giving a small dinner-party this evening," Mr. Weatherley continued, moving his umbrella from one hand to the other and speaking very rapidly, "bridge afterwards. We happen to be a man short. I was to have called at the club to try and pick up some one — find I sha'n't have time — meeting at the Cannon Street Hotel to attend. Would you — er — fill the vacant place? Save me the trouble of looking about."

It was out at last and Mr. Weatherley felt unaccountably relieved. He felt at the same time a certain measure of annoyance with his junior clerk for his unaltered composure.

"I shall be very much pleased, sir," he answered, without hesitation. "About eight, I suppose?"

Again Mr. Weatherley's relief was tempered with a certain amount of annoyance. This young man's *savoir faire* was out of place. He should have imagined a sort of high-tea supper at seven o'clock, and been gently corrected by his courteous employer. As it was, Mr. Weatherley felt dimly confident that this junior clerk of his was more accustomed to eight o'clock dinners than he was himself.

"A quarter to, tonight," he replied. "People coming for bridge afterwards, you see. I live up Hampstead way — Pelham Lodge — quite close to the tube station."

Mr. Weatherley omitted the directions he had been about to give respecting toilet, and turned away. His youthful employee's manners, to the last, were all that could be desired.

"I am much obliged to you, sir," he said. "I will take care to be punctual."

Mr. Weatherley grunted and walked out into the street. Here his behavior was a little singular. He walked up toward London Bridge, exchanging greetings with a good many acquaintances on the way. Opposite the London & Westminster Bank he paused for a moment and looked searchingly around. Satisfied that he was unobserved, he stepped quickly into a very handsome motor car which was drawn up close to the curb, and with a sigh of relief sat as far back among the cushions as possible and held the tube to his mouth.

"Get along home," he ordered, tersely.

*     *     *

Arnold Chetwode, after his interview with his employer, returned unruffled to his place. Mr. Jarvis bustled in after him. He was annoyed, but he wished to conceal the fact. Besides, he still had an arrow in his quiver. He came and stood over his subordinate.

"Congratulate you, I'm sure, Chetwode," he said smoothly. "First time any one except myself has been to the house since Mr. Weatherley's marriage."

Mr. Jarvis had taken the letters there one morning when his employer had been unwell, and had waited in the hall. He did not, however, mention that fact.

"Indeed?" Chetwode murmured, with his eye upon his work.

"You understand, of course," Mr. Jarvis continued, "that it will be an evening-dress affair. Mrs. Weatherley has the name of being very particular."

He glanced covertly at the young man, who was already immersed in his work.

"Evening dress," Chetwode remarked, with a becoming show of interest. "Well, I dare say I can manage something. If I wear a black coat and a white silk bow, and stick a red handkerchief in underneath my waistcoat, I dare say I shall be all right. Mr. Weatherley can't expect much from me in that way, can he?"

The senior clerk was secretly delighted. It was not for him to acquaint this young countryman with the necessities of London life. He turned away and took up a bundle of letters.

"Can't say, I'm sure, what the governor expects," he replied, falsely. "You'll have to do the best you can, I suppose. Better get on with those invoices now."

Once more the office resounded to the hum of its varied labors. Mr. Jarvis, dictating letters to a typist, smiled occasionally as he pictured the arrival of this over-favored young man in the drawing-room of Mrs. Weatherley, attired in the nondescript fashion which his words had suggested. One or two of the clerks ventured upon a chaffing remark. To all appearance, the person most absorbed in his work was the young man who had been singled out for such especial favor.

# CHAPTER II

## RUTH

In the topmost chamber of the last of a row of somber gray stone houses in Adam Street a girl with a thin but beautiful face and large, expectant eyes sat close to the bare, uncurtained window, from which it was possible to command a view of the street below. A book which she had apparently been reading had fallen neglected onto the floor. Steadfastly she watched the passers-by. Her delicate, expressive features were more than once illuminated with joy, only to be clouded, a moment later, with disappointment. The color came and went in her cheeks, as though, indeed, she were more sensitive than her years. Occasionally she glanced around at the clock. Time dragged so slowly in that great bare room with its obvious touch of poverty!

At last a tall figure came striding along the pavement below. This time no mistake was possible. There was a fluttering handkerchief from above, an answering wave of the hand. The girl drew a sigh of inexpressible content, moved away from the window and faced the door, with lifted head waiting for the sound of footsteps upon the stairs. They arrived at last. The door was thrown open. Arnold Chetwode came hastily across the room and gripped the two hands which were held out to him. Then he bent down and kissed her forehead.

"Dear little Ruth!" he exclaimed. "I hope you were careful crossing the landing?"

The girl leaned back in her chair. Her eyes were fixed anxiously upon his face. She completely ignored his question.

"The news at once!" she insisted. "Tell me, Arnold!"

He was a little taken aback.

"How did you know that I had any?"

She smiled delightfully.

"Know, indeed! I knew it directly I saw you, I knew it every time your foot touched the stairs. What is it, Arnold? The cheeses didn't smell so bad today? Or you've had a rise? Quick! I must hear all about it."

"You shall," Arnold replied. "It is a wonderful story. Listen. Have you ever heard the fable of Dick Whittington?"

"Married his employer's daughter, of course. What's she like, Arnold? Have you seen her? Did you save her life? When are you going to see her again?"

Chetwode was already on his knees, dragging out an old trunk from underneath the faded cupboard. Suddenly he paused with a gesture of despair.

"Alas!" he exclaimed. "My dream fades away. Old Weatherley was married only last year. Consequently, his daughter —"

"He can't have one," she interrupted, ruthlessly. "Tell me the news at once?"

"I am going to dine with old Weatherley," he announced.

The girl smiled, a little wistfully.

"How funny! But you will get a good dinner, won't you, Arnold? Eat ever so much, dear. Yesterday I fancied that you were getting thin. I do wish I could see what you have in the middle of the day."

"Little mother!" he laughed. "Today I gorged myself on poached eggs. What did Isaac give you?"

"Mutton stew and heaps of it," the girl replied, quickly. "Tonight I shall have a bowl of milk as soon as you are gone. Have you everything you ought to have to wear, Arnold?"

"Everything," he declared, rising to his feet with a sigh of relief. "It's so long since I looked at my clothes that to tell you the truth I was a little bit anxious. They may be old-fashioned, but they came from a good man to start with."

"What made Mr. Weatherley ask you?" she demanded.

"Wanted one of his clerks to fill up and found that I played bridge," Arnold answered. "It's rather a bore, isn't it? But, after all, he is my employer."

"Of course you must go and behave your very nicest. Tell me, when have you to start?"

"I ought to be changing in a quarter of an hour. What shall we do till then?"

"Whatever you like," she murmured.

"I am coming to sit at the window with you," he said. "We'll look down at the river and you shall tell me stories about the ships."

She laughed and took his hand as he dragged a chair over to her side. He put his arm around her and her head fell naturally back upon his shoulder. Her eyes sought his. He was leaning forward, gazing down between the curving line of lamp-posts, across the belt of black river with its flecks of yellow light. But Ruth watched him only.

"Arnie," she whispered in his ear, "there are no fairy ships upon the river tonight."

He smiled.

"Why not, little one? You have only to close your eyes."

Slowly she shook her head.

"Don't think that I am foolish, dear," she begged. "Tonight I cannot look upon the river at all. I feel that there is something new here — here in this room. The great things are here, Arnold. I can feel life hammering and throbbing in the air. We aren't in a garret any longer, dear. It's a fairy palace. Listen. Can't you hear the people shout, and the music, and the fountains playing? Can't you see the dusky walls fall back, the marble pillars, the lights in the ceiling?"

He turned his head. He found himself, indeed, listening, found himself almost disappointed to hear nothing but the far-off, eternal roar of the city, and the melancholy grinding of a hurdy-gurdy below. Always she carried him away by her intense earnestness, the bewitching softness of her voice, even when it was galleons full of treasure that she saw, with blood-red sails, coming up the river, full of treasure for them. Tonight her voice had more than its share of inspiration, her fancies clung to her feverishly.

"Be careful, Arnold," she murmured. "Tonight means a change. There is something new coming. I can feel it coming in my heart."

Her face was drawn and pale. He laughed down into her eyes.

"Little lady," he reminded her, mockingly, "I am going to dine with my cheesemonger employer."

She shook her head dreamily. She refused to be dragged down.

"There's something beating in the air," she continued. "It came into the room with you. Don't you feel it? Can't you feel that you are going to a tragedy? Life is going to be different, Arnold, to be different always."

He drew himself up. A flicker of passion flamed in his own deep gray eyes.

"Different, child? Of course it's going to be different. If there weren't something else in front, do you think one could live? Do you think one could be content to struggle through this miserable quagmire if one didn't believe that there was something else on the other side of the hill?"

She sighed, and her fingers touched his.

"I forgot," she said simply. "You see, there was a time when I hadn't you. You lifted me out of my quagmire."

"Not high enough, dear," he answered, caressingly. "Some day I'll take you over to Berlin or Vienna, or one of those wonderful places. We'll leave Isaac to grub along and sow red fire in Hyde Park. We'll find the doctors. We shall teach you to walk again without that stick. No more gloominess, please."

She pressed his hand tightly.

"Dear Arnold!" she whispered softly.

"Turn around and watch the river with me, little one," he begged. "See the lights on the barges, how slowly they move. What is there behind that one, I wonder?"

Her eyes followed his finger without enthusiasm.

"I can't look out of the room tonight, Arnold," she said. "The fancies won't come. Promise me one thing."

"I promise," he agreed.

"Tell me everything — don't keep anything back."

"On my honor," he declared, smiling. "I will bring the menu of the dinner, if there is one, and a photograph of Mrs. Cheesemonger if I can steal it. Now I am going to help you back into your room."

"Don't bother," she begged. "Open the door and I can get there quite easily."

He set the door open and, crossing the bare stone landing, opened the door of another room, similar to his. They were somber apartments at the top of the deserted house, which had once been a nobleman's residence. The doors were still heavy, though blistered with time and lack of varnish. There were the remains of paneling upon the wall and frescoes upon the ceiling.

"Come and see me before you go," she pleaded. "I am all alone. Isaac has gone to a meeting somewhere."

He promised and returned to his own apartment. With the help of a candle which he stuck upon the mantelpiece, and a cracked mirror, he first of all shaved, then disappeared for a few minutes behind a piece of faded curtain and washed vigorously. Afterwards he changed his clothes, putting on a dress suit produced from the trunk. When he had finished, he stepped back and laughed softly to himself. His clothes were well cut. His studs, which had very many times been on the point of visiting the pawnbroker's, were correct and good. He was indeed an incongruous figure as he stood there and, with a candle carefully held away from him in his hand, looked at his own reflection. For some reason or other, he was feeling elated. Ruth's words had lingered in his brain. One could never tell which way fortune might come!

He found her waiting in the darkness. Her long arms were wound for a moment around his neck, a sudden passion shook her.

"Arnold — dear Arnold," she sobbed, "you are going into the storm — and I want to go! I want to go, too! My hands are cold, and my heart. Take me with you, dear!"

He was a little startled. It was not often that she was hysterical. He looked down into her convulsed face. She choked for a moment, and then, although it was not altogether a successful effort, she laughed.

"Don't mind me," she begged. "I am a little mad tonight. I think that the twilight here has got upon my nerves. Light the lamp, please. Light the lamp and leave me alone for a moment while you do it."

He obeyed, fetching some matches from his own room and setting the lamp, when it was lit, on the table by her side. There were no tears left in her eyes now. Her lips were tremulous, but an unusual spot of color was burning in her cheeks. While he had been dressing, he saw that she had tied a piece of deep blue ribbon, the color he liked best, around her hair.

"See, I am myself now. Good night and good luck to you, Arnold! Eat a good dinner, mind, and remember your promise."

"There is nothing more that I can do for you?" he asked.

"Nothing," she replied. "Besides, I can hear Uncle Isaac coming."

The door was suddenly opened. A thin, undersized man in worn black clothes, and with a somber hat of soft black felt still upon his head, came into the room. His dark hair was tinged with gray, he walked with a pronounced stoop. In his shabby clothes, fitting loosely upon his diminutive body, he should have been an insignificant figure, but somehow or other he was nothing of the sort. His thin lips curved into a discontented droop. His cheeks were hollow and his eyes shone with the brightness of the fanatic. Arnold greeted him familiarly.

"Hullo, Isaac!" he exclaimed. "You are just in time to save Ruth from being left all alone."

The newcomer came to a standstill. He looked the speaker over from head to foot with an expression of growing disgust, and he spat upon the floor.

"What livery's that?" he demanded.

Arnold laughed good-naturedly.

"Come, Isaac," he protested, "I don't often inflict it upon you, do I? It's something that belongs to the world on the other side, you know. We all of us have to look over the fence now and then. I have to cross the borderland tonight for an hour or so."

Isaac threw open the door by which he had entered.

"Get out of here," he ordered. "If you were one of us, I'd call you a traitor for wearing the rags. As it is, I say that no one is welcomed under my roof who looks as you look now. Why, d — n it, I believe you're a gentleman!"

Arnold laughed softly.

"My dear Isaac," he retorted, "I am as I was born and made. You can't blame me for that, can you? Besides, —"

He broke off suddenly. A little murmur from the girl behind reminded him of her presence. He passed on to the door.

"Good night, Isaac," he said. "Look after Ruth. She's lonely tonight."

"I'll look after her," was the grim reply. "As for you, get you gone. There was one of your sort came to the meeting of Jameson's moulders this afternoon. He had a question to ask and I answered him. He wanted to know wherein wealth was a sin, and I told him."

Arnold Chetwode was young and his sense of humor triumphant. He turned on the threshold and looked into the shadowy room, dimly lit with its cheap lamp. He kissed his hands to Ruth.

"My dear Isaac," he declared, lightly, "you are talking like an ass. I have two shillings and a penny ha'penny in my pocket, which has to last me till Saturday, and I earn my twenty-eight shillings a week in old Weatherley's counting-house as honestly as you earn your wage by thundering from Labor platforms and articles in the *Clarion*. My clothes are part of the livery of civilization. The journalist who reports a Lord Mayor's dinner has to wear them. Some day, when you've got your seat in Parliament, you'll wear them yourself. Good night!"

He paused before closing the door. Ruth's kiss came wafted to him from the shadows where her great eyes were burning like stars. Her uncle had turned his back upon him. The word he muttered sounded like a malediction, but Arnold Chetwode went down the stone steps blithely. It was an untrodden land, this, into which he was to pass.

# CHAPTER III

## ARNOLD SCENTS MYSTERY

From the first, nothing about that evening was as Arnold had expected. He took the tube to Hampstead station, and, the night being dry, he walked to Pelham Lodge without detriment to his carefully polished patent shoes. The neighborhood was entirely strange to him and he was surprised to find that the house which was pointed out to him by a policeman was situated in grounds of not inconsiderable extent, and approached by a short drive. Directly he rang the bell he was admitted not by a flamboyant parlormaid but by a quiet, sad-faced butler in plain, dark livery, who might have been major-domo to a duke. The house was even larger than he had expected, and was handsomely furnished in an extremely subdued style. It was dimly, almost insufficiently lit, and there was a faint but not unpleasant odor in the drawing-room which reminded him of incense. The room itself almost took his breath away. It was entirely French. The hangings, carpet and upholstery were all of a subdued rose color and white. Arnold, who was, for a young man, exceedingly susceptible to impressions, looked around him with an air almost of wonder. It was fortunate, perhaps, that the room was empty.

"Mr. and Mrs. Weatherley will be downstairs in one moment, sir," the man announced. "Mr. Weatherley was a little late home from the city."

Arnold nodded and stood upon the hearthrug, looking around him. He was quite content to spend a few moments alone, to admire the drooping clusters of roses, the elegance with which every article of furniture and appointment of the room seemed to fit into its place. Somehow or other, too, nothing appeared new. Everything seemed subdued by time into its proper tone. He began to wonder what sort of woman the presiding genius over such perfection could be. Then, with a quaint transition of thought, he remembered the little counting-house in Tooley Street, the smell of cheeses, and Mr. Weatherley's half-nervous invitation. His lips twitched and he began to smile. These things seemed to belong to a world so far away.

Presently he heard footsteps outside and voices. The door was opened but the person outside did not immediately enter. Apparently she had turned round to listen to the man who was still some distance behind. Arnold recognized his employer's voice.

"I am sorry that you are displeased, my dear Fenella, but I assure you that I did the best I could. It is true that the young man is in my office, but I am convinced that you will find him presentable."

A peal of the softest and most musical laughter that Arnold had ever heard in his life effectually stopped Mr. Weatherley's protestations. Yet, for all its softness and for all its music, there was a different note underneath, something a little bitter, unutterably scornful.

"My dear Samuel, it is true, without doubt, that you did your best. I do not blame you at all. It was I who was foolish to leave such a matter in your hands. It was not likely that among your acquaintances there was one whom I would have cared to welcome to my house. But that you should have gone to your employees — that, indeed, is funny! You do amuse me very much. Come."

The door was pushed fully open now and a woman entered, at the sight of whom Arnold forgot all his feelings of mingled annoyance and amusement. She was of little over the medium height, exceedingly slim — a slimness which was accentuated by the fashion of the gown she wore. Her face was absolutely devoid of color, but her features were almost cameolike in their sensitive perfection. Her eyes were large and soft and brown, her hair a Titian red, worn low and without ornament. Her dress was of pale blue satin, which somehow had the effect of being made in a single piece, without seam or joining. Her neck and throat, exquisitely white, were bare except for a single necklace of pearls which reached almost to her knees. The look in Arnold's face, as she came slowly into the room, was one of frank and boyish admiration. The woman came towards him with a soft smile about her lips, but she was evidently puzzled. It was Mr. Weatherley who spoke. There was something almost triumphant in his manner.

"This is Mr. Chetwode, dear, of whom I was speaking to you," he said. "Glad to see you, Chetwode," he added, with ponderous condescension.

The woman laughed softly as she held out her hand.

"Are you going to pretend that you were deaf, to forgive me and be friends, Mr. Chetwode?" she asked, looking up at him. "One foggy day my husband took me to Tooley Street, and I did not believe that anything good could come out of the yellow fog and the mud and the smells. It was my ignorance. You heard, but you do not mind? I am sure that you do not mind?"

"Not a bit in the world," Arnold answered, still holding the hand which she seemed to have forgotten to draw away, and smiling down into her upturned face. "I was awfully sorry to overhear but you see I couldn't very well help it, could I?"

"Of course you could not help it," she replied. "I am so glad that you came and I hope that we can make it pleasant for you. I will try and send you in to dinner with some one very charming."

She laughed at him understandingly as his lips parted and closed again without speech. Then she turned away to welcome some other guests, who were at that moment announced. Arnold stood in the background for a few minutes. Presently she came back to him.

"Do you know any one here?" she asked.

"No one," he answered.

She dropped her voice almost to a whisper. Arnold bent his head and listened with a curious pleasure to her little stream of words.

"It is a strange mixture of people whom you see here," she said, "a mixture, perhaps, of the most prosaic and the most romantic. The Count Sabatini, whom you see talking to my husband, is my brother. He is a person who lives in the flood of adventures. He has taken part in five wars, he has been tried more than once for political offenses. He has been banished from what is really our native country, Portugal, with a price set upon his head. He has an estate upon which nothing grows, and a castle with holes in the roof in which no one could dwell. Yet he lives — oh, yes, he lives!"

Arnold looked across at the man of whom she was speaking — gaunt and olive-skinned, with deep-set eyes and worn face. He had still some share of his sister's good looks and he held himself as a man of his race should.

"I think I should like your brother," Arnold declared. "Will he talk about his campaigns?"

"Perhaps," she murmured, "although there is one about which you would not care to hear. He fought with the Boers, but we will not speak of that. Mr. and Mrs. Horsman there I shall say nothing about. Imagine for yourself where they belong."

"They are your husband's friends," he decided, unhesitatingly.

"You are a young man of great perceptions," she replied. "I am going to like you, I am sure. Come, there is Mr. Starling standing by the door. What do you think of him?"

Arnold glanced across the room. Mr. Starling was apparently a middle-aged man — clean-shaven, with pale cheeks and somewhat narrow eyes.

"An American, without a doubt," Arnold remarked.

"Quite right. Now the lady in the gray satin with the wonderful coiffure — she has looked at you already more than once. Her name is Lady Blennington, and she is always trying to discover new young men."

Arnold glanced at her deliberately and back again at his hostess.

"There is nothing for me to say about her," he declared.

"You are wonderful," she murmured. "That is so exactly what one feels about Lady Blennington. Then there is Lady Templeton — that fluffy little thing behind my husband. She looks rather as though she had come out of a toy shop, does she not?"

"She looks nice," Arnold admitted. "I knew —"

She glanced up at him and waited. Arnold, however, had stopped short.

"You have not yet told me," he said, "the name of the man who stands alone near the door — the one with the little piece of red ribbon in his coat?"

It seemed to him that, for some reason, the presence of that particular person affected her. He was a plump little man, sleek and well-dressed, with black hair, very large pearl studs, black moustache and imperial. Mrs. Weatherley stood quite still for a moment. Perhaps, he thought, she was listening to the conversation around them.

"The man's name is Rosario," she replied. "He is a financier and a man of fashion. Another time you must tell me what you think of him, but I warn you that it will not be so easy as with those others, for he is also a man of schemes. I am sorry, but I must send you in now with Mrs. Horsman, who is much too amiable to be anything else but dull. You shall come with me and I will introduce you."

Dinner was announced almost at that moment. Arnold, keen to enjoy, with all the love of new places and the enthusiasm of youth in his veins, found every moment of the meal delightful. They took their places at a round table with shaded lights artistically arranged, so that they seemed to be seated before a little oasis of flowers and perfumes in the midst of a land of shadows. He found his companion pleasant and sympathetic. She had a son about his age who was going soon into the city and about whom she talked incessantly. On his left, Lady Blennington made frank attempts to engage him in conversation whenever an opportunity arose. Arnold felt his spirits rise with every moment. He laughed and talked the whole of the time, devoting himself with very little intermission to one or the other of his two neighbors. Mr. Weatherley, who was exceedingly uncomfortable and found it difficult even to remember his few staple openings, looked across the table more than once in absolute wonder that this young man who, earning a wage of twenty-eight shillings a week, and occupying almost the bottom stool in his office, could yet be entirely and completely at his ease in this exalted company. More than once Arnold caught his hostess's eye, and each time he felt, for some unknown reason, a little thrill of pleasure at the faint relaxing of her lips, the glance of sympathy which shone across the roses. Life was a good place, he thought to himself, for these few hours, at any rate. And then, as he leaned back in his place for a moment, Ruth's words seemed suddenly traced with a finger of fire upon the dim wall. Tonight was to be a night of mysteries. Tonight the great adventure was to be born. He glanced around the table. There was, indeed, an air of mystery about some of these guests, something curiously aloof, something which it was impossible to put into words. The man Starling, for instance, seemed queerly placed here. Count Sabatini was another of the guests who seemed somehow to be outside the little circle. For minutes together he sat sometimes in grim silence. About him, too, there was always a curious air of detachment. Rosario was making the small conversation with his neighbor which the occasion seemed to demand, but he, too, appeared to talk as one who had more weighty matters troubling his brain. It was a fancy of Arnold's, perhaps, but it was a fancy of which he could not rid himself. He glanced towards his employer and a curious feeling of sympathy stirred him. The man was unhappy and ill at ease. He had lost his air of slight pomposity, the air with which he entered his offices in the morning, strutted about the warehouse, went out to lunch with a customer, and which he somehow seemed to lose as the time came for returning to his home. Once or twice he glanced towards his wife, half nervously, half admiringly. Once she nodded back to him, but it was the nod of one who gathers up her skirts as she throws alms to a beggar. Then Arnold realized that his little fit of thoughtfulness had made a material difference to the hum of conversation. He remembered his duty and leaned over toward Lady Blennington.

"You promised to tell me more about some of these people," he reminded her. "I am driven to make guesses all the time. Why does Mr. Starling look so much like an unwilling and impatient guest? And where is the castle of the Count Sabatini which has no roof?"

Lady Blennington sighed.

"This table is much too small for us to indulge in scandal," she replied. "It really is such a pity. One so seldom meets any one worth talking to who doesn't know everything there is that shouldn't be known about everybody. About Count Sabatini, for instance, I could tell you some most amusing things."

"His castle, perhaps, is in the air?" Arnold inquired.

"By no means," Lady Blennington assured him.

"On the contrary, it is very much upon the rocks. Some little island near Minorca, I believe. They say that Mr. Weatherley was wrecked there and Sabatini locked him up in a dungeon and refused to let him go until he promised to marry his sister."

"There are a good many men in the world, I should think," Arnold murmured, "who would like to be locked up on similar conditions."

She looked at him with a queer little smile.

"I suppose it is inevitable," she declared. "You will have to go through it, too. She certainly is one of the loveliest women I ever saw. I suppose you are already convinced that she is entirely adorable?"

"She has been very kind to me," Arnold replied.

"She would be," Lady Blennington remarked, dryly. "Look at her husband. The poor man ought to have known better than to have married her, of course, but do you think that he looks even reasonably happy?"

Arnold was beginning to feel rather uncomfortable. He was conscious of a strong desire not to discuss his hostess. Yet his curiosity was immense. He asked one question.

"Tell me," he said, "if she came from this little island in the Mediterranean, why does she speak English so perfectly?"

"She was educated in England," Lady Blennington told him. "Afterwards, her brother took her to South America. She had some small fortune, I believe, but when she came back they were penniless. They were really living as small market gardeners when Mr. Weatherley found them."

"You don't like her," he remarked. "I wonder why?"

Lady Blennington shook her head.

"One never knows," she replied. "I admire her, if that is anything."

"But you do not like her," he persisted.

She shrugged her shoulders slightly.

"I am afraid it is true," she agreed.

"You admit that and yet you are willing to be her guest?"

She smiled at him approvingly.

"If there is one masculine quality which I do appreciate," she said, "it is directness. I come because I love bridge and because I love my fellow-creatures and because my own friends are none too numerous. With the exception of those worthy friends of our host and his wife who are seated upon your right — Mr. and Mrs. Horsman, I believe they are called — we are all of the same ilk. Mr. Starling no one knows anything about; Count Sabatini's record is something awful."

"But there is Rosario," Arnold protested.

"Rosario goes into all the odd corners of the world," she replied. "Sometimes the corners are respectable and sometimes they are not. It really doesn't matter so far as he is concerned. Supposing, in return for all this information, you tell me something about yourself?"

"There isn't anything to tell," Arnold assured her. "I was asked here to fill up. I am an employee of Mr. Weatherley's."

She turned in her chair to look at him. Her surprise was obvious.

"Do you mean that you are his secretary, or something of that sort?" she demanded.

"I am a clerk in his office," Arnold told her.

She was evidently puzzled, but she asked him no more questions. At that moment Mrs. Weatherley rose from her place. As she passed Arnold she paused for a moment.

"You are all coming in five minutes," she said. "Before we play bridge, come straight to me. I have something to say to you."

He bowed and resumed his seat, from which he had risen quickly at her coming. Mr. Weatherley motioned to him to move up to his side. His face now was a little flushed, but his nervousness had not disappeared. He was certainly not the same man whom one met at Tooley Street.

"Glad to see you've made friends with the wife, Chetwode," he said. "She seems to have taken quite a fancy to you."

"Mrs. Weatherley has been very kind," Arnold answered.

"Enjoying yourself, I hope?" Mr. Weatherley asked.

"Very much indeed," Arnold declared. "It has been quite a treat for me."

Sabatini and Starling were talking earnestly together at the other side of the table. Rosario, bringing his wine down, came and sat at his host's other side.

"Beautiful vintage, this, Mr. Weatherley," he said. "Excellent condition, too."

Mr. Weatherley, obviously pleased, pursued the subject. In a way, it was almost pathetic to see his pleasure in being addressed by one of his own guests. Arnold drew a little away and looked across the banks of roses. There was something fascinating to him in the unheard conversation of Sabatini and Starling, on the opposite side of the table. Everything they said was in an undertone and the inexpressive faces of the two men gave no indication as to the nature of their conversation. Yet the sense of something mysterious in this house and among these guests was growing all the time with Arnold.

# CHAPTER IV

## THE FACE AT THE WINDOW

Mr. Weatherley laid his hand upon his young companion's arm as they crossed the hall on their way from the dining-room.

"We are going to play bridge in the music-room," he announced. "Things are different, nowadays, than when I was a boy. The men and the women, too, have to smoke cigarettes all the time while they play cards. A bad habit, Chetwode! A very bad habit indeed! I've nothing to say against a good Havana cigar in the dining-room or the smoking-room, but this constant cigarette smoking sickens me. I can't bear the smell of the things. Here we are. I don't know what table my wife has put you at, I'm sure. She arranges all these things herself."

Several guests who had arrived during the last few minutes were already playing at various tables. Mrs. Weatherley was moving about, directing the proceedings. She came across to them as soon as they entered, and, laying her hand upon Arnold's arm, drew him on one side. There was a smile still upon her lips but trouble in her eyes. She looked over her shoulder a little nervously and Arnold half unconsciously followed the direction of her gaze. Rosario was standing apart from the others, talking earnestly with Starling.

"I want you to stay with me, if you please," she said. "I am not sure where you will play, but there is no hurry. I myself shall not sit down at present. There are others to arrive."

Her brother, who had been talking languidly to Lady Blennington, came slowly up to them.

"You, Andrea, will wait for the baccarat, of course?" she said. "I know that this sort of bridge does not amuse you."

He answered her with a little shrug of the shoulders and, leaning towards her, spoke a few words in some tongue which Arnold did not at once recognize. She looked again over her shoulder at Rosario and her face clouded. She replied in the same tongue. Arnold would have moved away, but she detained him.

"You must not mind," she said softly, "that my brother and I talk sometimes in our native language. You do not, by chance, know Portuguese, Mr. Chetwode?"

"Not a word," he replied.

"I am going to leave all these people to amuse themselves," she continued, dropping her voice slightly. "I want you to come with me for a moment, Mr. Chetwode. You must take care that you do not slip. These wooden floors are almost dangerous. I did give a dance here once," she continued, as they made their way across the room, talking a little vaguely and with an obvious effort. "I did not enjoy it at all. To me the style of dancing in this country seems ungraceful. Look behind, Mr. Chetwode. Tell me, is Mr. Rosario following us?"

Arnold glanced over his shoulder. Rosario was still standing in the same place, but he was watching them intently.

"He is looking after us, but he has not moved," Arnold announced.

"It is better for him that he stays there," Mrs. Weatherley said softly. "Please come."

At the further end of the apartment there was a bend to the left. Mrs. Weatherley led the way around the corner into a small recess, out of sight of the remainder of the people. Here she paused and, holding up her finger, looked around. Her head was thrown back, the trouble still gleamed in her eyes. She listened intently to the hum of voices, as though trying to distinguish those she knew. Satisfied, apparently, that their disappearance had not occasioned any comment, she moved forward again, motioned Arnold to open a door, and led him down a long passage to the front of the house. Here she opened the door of an apartment on the left-hand side of the hall, and almost pushed him in. She closed the door quickly behind them. Then she held up her finger.

"Listen!" she said.

They could hear nothing save the distant murmur of voices in the music-room. The room which they had entered was in complete darkness, through which the ivory pallor of her arms and face, and the soft fire of her eyes, seemed to be the only things visible. She was standing quite close to him. He could hear her breathing, he could almost fancy that he heard her heart beat. A strand of hair even touched his cheek as she moved.

"I do not wish to turn the light up for a moment," she whispered. "You do not mind?"

"I mind nothing," Arnold answered, bewildered. "Are you afraid of anything? Is there anything I can do?"

A sense of excitement was stirring him.

"Just do as I ask, that is all," she murmured. "I want to look outside a moment. Just do as I ask and keep quiet."

She stole from him to the window and, moving the curtain a few inches, knelt down, peering out. She remained there motionless for a full minute. Then she rose to her feet and came back. His eyes were becoming more accustomed to the gloom now and he could see the outline of her figure as she moved towards him.

"Take my place there," she whispered. "Look down the drive. Tell me whether you can see any one watching the house?"

He went down on his knees at the place she indicated and peered through the parted curtain. For a few seconds he could see nothing; then, as his eyes grew accustomed to the gloom, he discerned two motionless figures standing on the left-hand side of the drive, partly concealed by a tall laurel bush.

"I believe," he declared hoarsely, "that there are two men standing there."

"Tell me, are they moving?" she demanded.

"They seem to be simply watching the house," he replied.

She was silent. He could hear her breath come and go.

"They still do not move?" she asked, after a few seconds.

He shook his head, and she turned away, listening to some footsteps in the hall.

"Remember," she whispered, "I am standing where I can turn on the light in a moment. If any one comes, you are here to see my South American curios. This is my own sitting-room. You understand?"

"I understand," he assented. "Whatever you tell me to say, I will say."

She seemed to be gathering courage. She laughed very softly, as though amused at his earnestness. There was little enough of mirth in her laughter, yet somehow it gave him heart.

"What do these men want?" he asked. "Would you like me to go out and send them away?"

"No," she replied. "I do not wish you to leave me."

"But they are terrifying you," he protested. "What right have they in your garden? They are here, perhaps, as thieves."

"Hush!"

She sprang away from him. The room was suddenly flooded with light. She was leaning with her arm upon the mantelpiece, a statuette of black ivory in her hand.

"If you are really fond of this sort of thing," she began, "you should come with me to the South Kensington Museum one day — Who is that?"

The door had opened. It was Mr. Weatherley who appeared. Mr. Weatherley was distinctly fussy and there was some return of his pompous manner.

"My dear Fenella!" he exclaimed. "What on earth are you doing in here, with half your bridge tables as yet unarranged? Your guests are wondering what has become of you."

"Has any one fresh turned up?" she asked, setting down the statuette.

"A Lady Raynham has just arrived," Mr. Weatherley replied, "and is making herself very disagreeable because there is no one to tell her at which table she is to play. I heard a young man who came with her, too, asking Parkins what time supper was. I do not wish to criticize the manners of your guests, but really, my dear Fenella, some of them do seem to have strange ideas."

"Lady Raynham," she remarked, coldly, "is a person who should be glad to find herself under any respectable roof without making complaints. Mr. Chetwode," she continued, turning to him, "it is my wish to finish showing you my treasures. Therefore, will you wait here, please, for a short time, while I go and start another bridge table? I shall return quite soon. Come, Samuel."

Mr. Weatherley coughed. He seemed unwilling to leave Arnold behind.

"I dare say young Chetwode would like a hand at bridge himself, my dear," he protested.

"Mr. Chetwode shall have one later on," she promised. "I think that very likely he will play at my table. Come."

They left the room together. She looked back for a moment before, they disappeared and Arnold felt his heart give a little jump. She was certainly the most beautiful creature he had ever seen, and there was something in her treatment of him, the subtle flattery of her half appealing confidence, which went to his head like wine. The door closed and he was left alone. He listened to their departing footsteps. Then he looked around him, for the first time forming some idea of his surroundings. He was in a very charming, comfort-able-looking apartment, with deep easychairs, a divan covered with luxu-rious cushions, numbers of little tables covered with photographs and flowers, a great bowl of hot-house roses, and an oak cabinet with an oak back-ground in the further corner of the room, which was packed with curios. After his first brief inspection, however, he felt scarcely any curiosity as to the contents of the room. It was the window which drew him always towards It. Once more he peered through the chink of the curtains. He had not cared to turn out the lights, however, and for several moments everything was indistinguishable. Then he saw that the two figures still remained in very nearly the same position, except that they had drawn, if anything, a little closer to the house.

A tiny clock upon the mantelpiece was ticking away the seconds. Arnold had no idea how long he remained there watching. Suddenly, however, he received a shock. For some time he had fancied that one of the two figures had disappeared altogether, and now, outside on the windowsill, scarcely a couple of feet from the glass through which he was looking, a man's hand appeared and gripped the windowsill. He stared at it, fascinated. It was so close to him that he could see the thin, yellow fingers, on one of which was a signet ring with a blood-red stone; the misshapen knuckles, the broken nails. He was on the point of throwing up the window when a man's face shot up from underneath and peered into the room. There was only the thickness of the glass between them, and the light from the gas lamp which stood at the corner of the drive fell full upon the white, strained features and the glittering black eyes which stared into the room. The chink of the curtain through which Arnold was gazing was barely an inch wide; but it was sufficient. For a moment he stared at the man. Then he threw the curtains open and stooped to unfasten the window. It was the affair of a few seconds only to throw it up. To his surprise, the man did not move. Their faces almost touched.

"What the devil do you want?" Arnold exclaimed, gripping him by the arm.

The man did not flinch. He inclined his head towards the interior of the room.

"Rosario, the Jew," he answered thickly. "He is in the house there. Will you take him a message?"

"Ring at the door and bring it yourself," Arnold retorted.

The man laughed contemptuously. He stared at Arnold for a moment and seemed to realize for the first time that he was a stranger.

"You are a fool to meddle in things you know nothing of!" he muttered.

"I know you've no right where you are," said Arnold, "and I shall keep you until some one comes."

The intruder made a sudden dive, freeing himself with an extraordinary turn of the wrist. Arnold caught a glimpse of his face as he slunk away. While he hesitated whether to follow him, he heard the door open and the soft rustle of a woman's skirts.

"What are you doing out there, Mr. Chetwode?"

He turned around. Mrs. Weatherley was standing just behind him, leaning also out of the window, with a little halo of light about her head. For a moment he was powerless to answer. Her head was thrown back, her lips parted. She seemed to be listening as well as watching. There was fear in her eyes as she looked at him, yet she made the most beautiful picture he had ever seen. He pulled himself together.

"Well?" she asked, breathlessly.

"I was waiting here for you," he explained. "I looked through the curtains. Then I saw a man's hand upon the sill."

Her hand shot to her side.

"Go on," she whispered.

"I saw his face," Arnold continued. "It was pressed close to the window. It was as though he meant to enter. I threw the curtains back, opened the window, and gripped him by the arm. I asked him what he wanted."

She sat down in a chair and began to tremble.

"He said he wanted Rosario, the Jew," Arnold went on. "Then, when he found that I was a stranger, he got away. I don't know how he managed it, for my fingers are strong enough, but he wrenched himself free somehow."

"Look out once more," she implored. "See if he is anywhere around. I will speak to him."

He stood at the window and looked in every direction.

"There is no one in sight," he declared. "I will go to the corner of the street, if you like."

She shook her head.

"Close the window and bolt it, please," she begged. "Draw the curtains tight. Now come and sit down here for a moment."

He did as he was bidden with some reluctance.

"The man was a villainous-looking creature," he persisted. "I don't think that he was up to any good. Look! There's a policeman almost opposite. Shall I go and tell him?"

She put out her hand and clasped his, drawing him down to her side. Then she looked steadfastly into his face.

"Mr. Chetwode," she said slowly, "women have many disadvantages in life, but they have had one gift bestowed upon them in which they trust always. It is the gift of instinct. You are very young, and I know very little about you, but I know that you are to be trusted."

"If I could serve you," he murmured, —

"You can," she interrupted.

Then for a time she was silent. Some new emotion seemed to move her. Her face was softer than he had ever seen it, her beautiful eyes dimmer. His mind was filled with new thoughts of her.

"Mrs. Weatherley," he pleaded, "please do believe in me, do trust me. I mean absolutely what I say when I tell you there is nothing in the world I would not do to save you from trouble or alarm."

Her moment of weakness was over. She flashed one wonderful smile at him and rose to her feet.

"It is agreed," she declared. "When I need help — and it may be at any moment — I shall call upon you."

"I shall be honored," he assured her, gravely. "In the meantime, please tell me — are we to speak of this to Rosario?"

"Leave it to me," she begged. "I cannot explain to you what all this means, but I think that Mr. Rosario can take care of himself. We must go back now to the bridge-room. My husband is annoyed with me for coming away again."

Mr. Weatherley met them in the passage. He was distinctly irritable.

"My dear Fenella!" he exclaimed. "Your guests do not understand your absence. Mr. Rosario is most annoyed and I cannot imagine what is the matter with Starling. I am afraid that he and Rosario have had words."

She turned her head as she passed, and smiled very slightly.

"I have no concern," she said, "in the quarrel between Mr. Starling and Mr. Rosario. As for the others — Mr. Chetwode and I are quite ready for bridge now. We are going in to do our duty."

# CHAPTER V

## AN UNUSUAL ERRAND

Arnold arrived at the office the next morning punctually at five minutes to nine, and was already at work when Mr. Jarvis appeared ten minutes later.

"Gayety's not upset you, then, eh?" the latter remarked, divesting himself of his hat and overcoat.

"Not at all, thanks," Arnold answered.

"Nice house, the governor's, isn't it?"

"Very nice indeed."

"Good dinners he gives, too," continued Mr. Jarvis. "Slap-up wines, and the right sort of company. Must have been an eye-opener for you."

Arnold nodded. He was not in the least anxious to discuss the events of the previous evening with Mr. Jarvis. The latter, however, came a little nearer to him. He took off his gold-rimmed spectacles and wiped them carefully.

"Now I should like to know," he said, "exactly how Mrs. Weatherley struck you?"

"She appeared to me to be a singularly charming and very beautiful lady," Arnold replied, writing quickly.

Mr. Jarvis was disappointed.

"She's good-looking enough," he admitted. "I can't say that I've seen much of her, mind you, but she gave me the impression of a woman who wasn't above using the powder-puff. She drove down here with the governor one day, and to look at her you'd have thought she was a princess come among the slums."

"She was born abroad," Arnold remarked. "I dare say this atmosphere would seem a little strange to her."

"Sort of half a foreigner, I've understood," Mr. Jarvis continued. "Speaks English all right, though. I can't help thinking," he went on, "that the governor would have done better to have married into one of our old city families. Nothing like them, you know, Chetwode. Some fine women, too. There's Godson, the former Lord Mayor. He had four daughters, and the governor might have had his pick."

"Here he comes," Arnold remarked, quietly.

Mr. Jarvis took the hint and went off to his work. A moment or two later, Mr. Weatherley arrived. He passed through the office and bestowed upon every one his customary salutation. At Arnold's desk he paused for a moment.

"Feeling all right this morning, young man?" he inquired, striving after a note of patronage which somehow or other eluded him.

"Quite well, thank you, sir."

"You found the evening pleasant, I hope? Didn't lose any money at bridge, eh?"

"Mrs. Weatherley was good enough to take on the stakes, sir," Arnold replied. "As a matter of fact, I believe that we won. I enjoyed the evening very much, thank you."

Mr. Weatherley passed on to his office. Jarvis waited until his door was closed.

"So you played bridge with Mrs. Weatherley, eh?" he remarked.

"I did," Arnold admitted. "Have you noticed the shrinkage of weight in these last invoices?"

Mr. Jarvis accepted the papers which his junior passed him, and departed into the warehouse. Arnold was left untroubled with any more questions. At half-past twelve, however, he was sent for into Mr. Weatherley's private office. Mr. Weatherley was leaning back in his chair and he had the air of a man who has come to a resolution.

"Shut the door, Chetwode," he ordered.

Arnold did as he was bidden.

"Come up to the desk here," he was further instructed. "Now, listen to me," Mr. Weatherley continued, after a moment's pause. "You are a young man of discretion, I am sure. My wife, I may say, Chetwode, thought quite highly of you last night."

Arnold looked his employer in the face and felt a sudden pang of sympathy. Mr. Weatherley was certainly not looking as hale and prosperous as a few months ago. His cheeks were flabby, and there was a worried look about him which the head of the firm of Weatherley & Co. should certainly not have worn.

"Mrs. Weatherley is very kind, sir," he remarked. "As to my discretion, I may say that I believe I am to be trusted. I should try, of course, to justify any confidence you might place in me."

"I believe so, too, Chetwode," Mr. Weatherley declared. "I am going to trust you now with a somewhat peculiar commission. You may have noticed that I have been asked to speak privately upon the telephone several times this morning."

"Certainly, sir," Arnold replied. "It was I who put you through."

"I am not even sure," Mr. Weatherley continued, "who it was speaking, but I received some communications which I think I ought to take notice of.

I want you accordingly to go to a certain restaurant in the west-end, the name and address of which I will give you, order your lunch there — you can have whatever you like — and wait until you see Mr. Rosario. I dare say you remember meeting Mr. Rosario last night, eh?"

"Certainly, sir. I remember him quite well."

"He will not be expecting you, so you will have to sit near the door and watch for him. Directly you see him, you must go to him and say that this message is from a friend. Tell him that whatever engagement he may have formed for luncheon, he is to go at once to the Prince's Grill Room and remain there until two o'clock. He is not to lunch at the Milan — that is the name of the place where you will be. Do you understand?"

"I understand perfectly," Arnold assented. "But supposing he only laughs at me?"

"You will have done your duty," Mr. Weatherley said. "There need be no mystery about the affair. You can say at once that you are there as the result of certain telephone messages addressed to me this morning, and that I should have come myself if it had been possible. If he chooses to disregard them, it is his affair entirely — not mine. At the same time, I think that he will go."

"It seems an odd sort of a thing to tell a perfect stranger, sir," Arnold remarked.

Mr. Weatherley produced a five-pound note.

"You can't go into those sort of places without money in your pocket," he continued. "You can account to me for the change later, but don't spare yourself. Have as good a lunch as you can eat. The restaurant is the Milan Grill Room on the Strand — the café, mind, not the main restaurant. You know where it is?"

"Quite well, sir, thank you."

Mr. Weatherley looked at his employee curiously.

"Have you ever been there, then?" he inquired.

"Once or twice, sir," Arnold admitted.

"Not on the twenty-eight shillings a week you get from me!"

"Quite true, sir," Arnold assented. "My circumstances were slightly different at the time."

Mr. Weatherley hesitated. This young man's manner did not invite confidences. On the other hand, he was genuinely curious about him.

"What made you come into the city, Chetwode?" he inquired. "You don't seem altogether cut out for it — not that you don't do your work and all that sort of thing," he went on, hastily. "I haven't a word of complaint to make, mind. All the same, you certainly seem as though you might have done a little better for yourself."

"It is the fault of circumstances, sir," Arnold replied. "I am hoping that before long you will find that I do my work well enough to give me a better position."

"You are ambitious, then?"

The face of the young man was suddenly grim.

"I mean to get on," he declared. "There were several years of my life when I used to imagine things. I have quite finished with that. I realize that there is only one way by means of which a man can count."

Mr. Weatherley nodded ponderously.

"Well," he said, "let me see that your work is well done, and you may find promotion is almost as quick in the city as anywhere else. You had better be off now."

"I trust," Arnold ventured, as he turned toward the door, "that Mrs. Weatherley is quite well this morning?"

"So far as I know, she is," Mr. Weatherley replied. "My wife isn't usually visible before luncheon time. Continental habits, you know. I shall expect you back by three o'clock. You must come and report to me then."

Arnold brushed his hat and coat with extra care as he took them down from the peg.

"Going to lunch early, aren't you?" Mr. Jarvis remarked, looking at the clock. "Not sure that we can spare you yet. Smithers isn't back."

"I am going out for the governor," Arnold replied.

"What, to the bank?" Mr. Jarvis asked.

Arnold affected not to hear. He walked out into the street, lit a cigarette, and had his boots carefully polished at London Bridge Station. Then, as he had plenty of time, he took the train to Charing Cross and walked blithely down the Strand. Freed from the routine of his office work, he found his mind once more full of the events of last night. There was so much that he could not understand, yet there was so much that seemed to be leading him on towards the land of adventures. He found himself watching the faces in the Strand with a new interest, and he laughed to himself as he realized what it was. He was looking all the time for the man whose face he had seen pressed to the windowpane!

# CHAPTER VI

## THE GLEAM OF STEEL

At the Milan, Arnold found himself early for luncheon. He chose a table quite close to the entrance, ordered his luncheon with some care, and commenced his watch. A thin stream of people was all the time arriving, but for the first half-hour there was no one whom he could associate in any way with his commission. It was not until he had actually commenced his lunch that anything happened. Then, through the half-open door, he heard what he recognized instantly as a familiar voice. The manager of the restaurant hurried toward the entrance and he heard the question repeated.

"Is Mr. Rosario here?"

"We have a table for him, madame, but he has not yet arrived," the *maître d'hôtel* replied. "If madame will allow me to show her the way!"

Arnold rose to his feet with a little start. Notwithstanding her fashionable outdoor clothes and thick veil, he recognized Mrs. Weatherley at once as she swept into the room, following the *maître d'hôtel*. She came up to him with slightly upraised eyebrows. It was clear that his presence there was a surprise to her.

"I scarcely expected to see you again so soon," she remarked, giving him her fingers. "Are you lunching alone?"

"Quite alone," Arnold answered.

She glanced half carelessly around, as though to see whether she recognized any acquaintances. Arnold, however, was convinced that she was simply anxious not to be overheard.

"Tell me," she inquired, "has my husband sent you here?"

Arnold admitted the fact.

"I have a message," he replied.

"For Mr. Rosario?"

"For Mr. Rosario."

"You have not seen anything of him yet, then?" she asked quickly.

"He has not been here," Arnold assured her. "I have kept my eyes glued upon the door."

"Tell me the message quickly," she begged.

Arnold did not hesitate. Mr. Weatherley was his employer but this woman was his employer's wife. If there were secrets between them, it was not his concern. It seemed natural enough that she should ask. It was certainly not his place to refuse to answer her question.

"I was to tell him that on no account was he to lunch here today," Arnold said. "He was to go instead to the grill room at Prince's in Piccadilly, and remain there until two o'clock."

Mrs. Weatherley made no remark. Her face was emotionless. Closely though he was watching her, Arnold could not himself have declared at that moment whether indeed this message had any import to her or not.

"I find my husband's behavior exceedingly mysterious," she said thoughtfully. "I cannot imagine how he became concerned in the matter at all."

"I believe," Arnold told her, "that some one telephoned Mr. Weatherley this morning. He was asked for privately several times and he seemed very much disturbed by some message he received."

"Some one telephoned him," she repeated, frowning. "Now I wonder who that person could be."

She sat quite still for a moment or two, looking through the glass-paneled door. Then she shrugged her shoulders.

"In any case," she declared, "I am here to lunch and I am hungry. I will not wait for Mr. Rosario. May I sit here?"

He called a waiter and the extra place was very soon prepared.

"If Mr. Rosario comes," she said, "we can see him from here. You can then give him your message and he can please himself. I should like some Omelette aux Champignons, please, and some red wine — nothing more. Perhaps I will take some fruit later. And now, please, Mr. Arnold Chetwode, will you listen to me?"

She undid her ermine cloak and laid aside her muff. The collection of costly trifles which she had been carrying she threw carelessly upon the table.

"Last night," she continued, softly, "we agreed, did we not, to be friends? It is possible you may find our friendship one of deeds, not words alone."

"There is nothing I ask for more sincerely," he declared.

"To begin with, then," she went on, "I do not wish that you call me Mrs. Weatherley. The name annoys me. It reminds me of things which at times it is a joy to me to forget. You shall call me Fenella, and I shall call you Arnold."

"Fenella," he repeated, half to himself.

She nodded.

"Well, then, that is arranged. Now for the first thing I have to ask of you. If Mr. Rosario comes, I do not wish that message from my husband to be delivered."

Arnold frowned slightly.

"Isn't that a little difficult?" he protested. "Mr. Weatherley has sent me up here for no other reason. He has given me an exact commission, has told me even the words I am to use. What excuse can I possibly make?"

She smiled.

"You shall be relieved of all responsibility," she declared. "If I tell my husband that I do not wish you to obey his bidding, that will be sufficient. It is a matter of which my husband understands little. There are people whose interest it is to protect Rosario. It is they who have spoken, without a doubt, this morning through the telephone, but my husband does not understand. Rosario must take care of himself. He runs his own risks. He is a man, and he knows very well what he is doing."

Arnold looked at her thoughtfully.

"Do you seriously suppose, then," he asked, "that the object of my message is to bid Mr. Rosario keep away from here because of some actual danger?"

"Why not? Mr. Rosario has chosen to interfere in a very difficult and dangerous matter. He runs his own risks and he asks for a big reward. It is not our place to protect him."

She raised her veil and he looked at her closely. She was still as beautiful as he had thought her last night, but her complexion was pallid almost to fragility, and there were faint violet lines under her eyes.

"You have not slept," he said. "It was the fear of last night."

"I slept badly," she admitted, "but that passes. This afternoon I shall rest."

"I cannot help thinking," he went on, "about those men who watched the house last night. They could have been after no good. I wish you would let me go to the police-station. Or would you like me to come and watch myself, tonight or tomorrow night, to see if they come again?"

She shook her head firmly.

"No!" she decided. "It wouldn't do any good. Just now, at any rate, it is Rosario they want."

Their conversation was interrupted for several moments while she exchanged greetings with friends passing in and out of the restaurant. Then she turned again to her companion.

"Tell me," she asked, a little abruptly, "why are you a clerk in the city? You do not come of that order of people."

"Necessity," he assured her promptly. "I hadn't a sovereign in the world when your husband engaged me."

"You were not brought up for such a life!"

"Not altogether," he admitted. "It suits me very well, though."

"Poor boy!" she murmured. "You, too, have had evil fortune. Perhaps the black hand has shadowed us both."

"A man makes his own life," he answered, impulsively, "but you — you were made for happiness. It is your right."

She glanced for a moment at the rings upon her fingers. Then she looked into his eyes.

"I married Mr. Weatherley," she reminded him. "Do you think that if I had been happy I should have done that? Do you think that, having done it, I deserve to know, or could know, what happiness really means?"

It was very hard to answer her. Arnold found himself divided between his loyalty towards the man who, in his way, had been kind to him, and the woman who seemed to be stepping with such fascinating ease into the empty places of his life.

"Mr. Weatherley is very much devoted to you," he remarked.

A shadow of derision parted her lips.

"Mr. Weatherley is a very worthy man," she said, "but it would have been better for him as well as for me if he had kept away from the Island of Sabatini. Tell me, what did Lady Blennington say about us last night?"

His eyes twinkled.

"She told me that Mr. Weatherley was wrecked upon the Island of Sabatini, and that your brother kept him in a dungeon till he promised to marry you."

She laughed.

"And you? What did you think of that?"

"I thought," he replied, "that if adventures of that sort were to be found in those seas, I would like to beg or borrow the money to sail there myself and steer for the rocks."

"For a boy," she declared, "you say very charming things. Tell me, how old are you?"

"Twenty-four."

"You would not look so old if it were not for that line. You know, I read characters and fortunes. All the women of my race have done so. I can tell you that you had a youth of ease and happiness and one year of terrible life. Then you started again. It is true, is it not?"

"Very nearly," he admitted.

"I wonder —"

She never finished her sentence. From their table, which was nearest to the door, they were suddenly aware of a commotion of some sort going on just outside. Through the glass door Rosario was plainly visible, his sleekness ruffled, his white face distorted with terror. The hand of some unseen person was gripping him by the throat, bearing him backwards. There was a shout and they both saw the cloakroom attendant spring over his counter. Something glittered in the dim light — a flash of blue polished steel. There was a gleam in the air, a horrible cry, and Rosario collapsed upon the floor. Arnold, who was already on his feet and halfway to the door, caught one glimpse of the upstretched hand, and all his senses were thrilled with what he saw. Upon the little finger was a signet ring with a scarlet stone!

The whole affair was a matter of seconds, yet Arnold dashed through the door to find Rosario a crumpled-up heap, the cloakroom attendant bending over him, and no one else in the vestibule. Then the people began to stream in — the hall porter, the lift man, some loiterers from the outer hall. The cloakroom attendant sprang to his feet. He seemed dazed.

"Stop him!" he shouted. "Stop him!"

The little group in the doorway looked at one another.

"He went that way!" the cloakroom attendant cried out again. "He passed through that door!"

Some of them rushed into the street. One man hurried to the telephone, the others pressed forward to where Rosario lay on his back, with a thin stream of blood finding its way through his waistcoat. Arnold was suddenly conscious of a woman's arm upon his and a hoarse whisper in his ear.

"Come back! Take me away somewhere quickly! This is no affair of ours. I want to think. Take me away, please. I can't look at him."

"Did you see the man's hand?" Arnold gasped.

"What of it?"

"It was the hand I saw upon your windowsill last night. It was the same ring — a scarlet signet ring. I could swear to it."

She gave a little moan and her whole weight lay upon his arm. In the rush of people and the clamor of voices around, they were almost unobserved. He passed his arm around her, and even in that moment of wild excitement he was conscious of a nameless joy which seemed to set his heart leaping. He led her back through the restaurant and into one of the smaller rooms of the hotel. He found her an easychair and stood over her.

"You won't leave me?" she begged.

He held her hand tightly.

"Not until you send me away!"

# CHAPTER VII

## "ROSARIO IS DEAD!"

Fenella never became absolutely unconscious. She was for some time in a state apparently of intense nervous prostration. Her breath was coming quickly, her eyes and her fingers seemed to be clinging to his as though for support. Her touch, her intimate presence, her reliance upon him, seemed to Arnold to infect the very atmosphere of the place with a thrill of the strangest excitement.

"You think that he is dead?" she faltered once.

"Of course not," he replied reassuringly. "I saw no weapon at all. It was just a quarrel."

She half closed her eyes.

"There was blood upon his waistcoat," she declared, "and I saw something flash through the window."

"I will go and see, if you like," Arnold suggested.

Her fingers gripped his.

"Not yet! Don't leave me yet! Why did you say that you recognized the hand — that it was the same hand you saw upon the windowsill last night?"

"Because of the signet ring," Arnold answered promptly. "It was a crude-looking affair, but the stone was bright scarlet. It was impossible to mistake it."

"It was only the ring, then?"

"Only the ring, of course," he admitted. "I did not see the hand close enough. It was foolish of me, perhaps, to say anything about it, and yet — and yet the man last night — he was looking for Rosario. Why should it not be the same?"

He heard the breath come through her teeth in a little sob.

"Don't say anything at present to any one else. Indeed, there are others who might have worn such a ring."

Arnold hesitated, but only for a second. He chanced to look into her face, and her whisper became his command.

"Very well," he promised.

A few moments later she sat up. She was evidently becoming stronger.

"Now go," she begged, "and see — how he is. Find out exactly what has happened and come back. I shall wait for you here."

He stood up eagerly.

"You are sure that you will be all right?"

"Of course," she replied. "Indeed, I shall be better when I know what really has happened. You must go quickly, please, and come back quickly. Stop!"

Arnold, who had already started, turned back again. They were in a ladies' small reception room at the head of the stairs leading down into the restaurant, quite alone, for every one had streamed across the courtyard to see what the disturbance was. The side of the room adjoining the stairs and the broad passage leading to the restaurant was entirely of glass. A man, on his way up the stairs, had paused and was looking intently at them.

"Tell me, who is that?" demanded Fenella.

Arnold recognized him at once.

"It is your friend Starling — the man from South America."

"Starling!" she murmured.

"I think that he is coming in," Arnold continued. "He has seen you. Do you mind?"

She shook her head.

"No. He will stay with me while you are away. Perhaps he knows something."

Arnold hurried off and met Starling upon the threshold of the room.

"Isn't that Mrs. Weatherley with you?" the latter inquired.

"Yes," Arnold told him. "She was lunching with me in the Grill Room. I believe that she was really waiting for Rosario — when the affair happened."

"What affair?"

Arnold stared at him. It seemed impossible that there was any one ignorant of the tragedy.

"Haven't you heard?" Arnold exclaimed. "Rosario was stabbed outside the Grill Room a few moments ago."

Starling's pallid complexion seemed suddenly to become ghastly.

"Rosario — Rosario stabbed?" he faltered.

"I thought that every one in the place must have heard of it," Arnold continued. "He was stabbed just as he was entering the café, not more than ten minutes ago."

"By whom?"

Starling's words came with the swift crispness of a pistol shot. Arnold shook his head.

"I didn't see. I am just going to ask for particulars. Will you stay with Mrs. Weatherley?"

Starling looked searchingly along the vestibule. The news seemed to have affected him strangely. His head was thrown a little back, his nostrils distended. He reminded Arnold for a moment of a watch-dog, listening.

"Of course," he muttered, "of course. Come back as soon as you can and let us know what has happened."

Arnold made his way through the reception hall and across the court-yard. Already the crowd of people was melting away. A policeman stood on guard at the opposite door, and two more at the entrance of the café. The whole of the vestibule where the affair had happened was closed, and the only information which it was possible to collect Arnold gathered from the excited conversations of the little knots of people standing around. In a few minutes he returned to the small reception room. Fenella and Starling looked eagerly up as he entered. They both showed signs of an intense emotion. Starling was even gripping the back of a chair as he spoke.

"What of Rosario?" he demanded.

Arnold hesitated, but only for a moment. The truth, perhaps, was best.

"Rosario is dead," he replied gravely. "He was stabbed to the heart and died within a few seconds."

There was a queer silence. Arnold felt inclined to rub his eyes. Gone was at least part of the horror from their white faces. Fenella sank back in her chair with a little sob which might almost have been of relief. Starling, as though suddenly mindful of the conventions, assumed a grimly dolorous aspect.

"Poor fellow!" he muttered. "And the murderer?"

"He's gotten clean off, for the present at any rate," Arnold told them. "They seem to think that he reached the Strand and had a motor car waiting."

Again there was silence. Then Mrs. Weatherley rose to her feet, glanced for a moment in the looking-glass, and turning round held out both her hands to Arnold.

"You have been so kind to me," she said softly. "I shall not forget it — indeed I shall not. Mr. Starling is going to take me home in his car. Good-bye!"

Arnold held her hands steadfastly and looked into her eyes. They were more beautiful than ever now with their mist of risen tears. But there were other things in her face, things less easy to understand. He turned away regretfully.

"I am sorry that you should have had such a shock," he said. "Is there any message for Mr. Weatherley?"

She exchanged a quick glance with her companion. Then for the first time Arnold realized the significance of the errand on which he had come.

"Some one must have warned Mr. Weatherley of what was likely to happen!" he exclaimed. "It was for that reason I was sent here!"

Again no one spoke for several seconds.

"It was not your fault," she said gently. "You were told to wait inside the restaurant. You could not have done more."

Arnold turned away with a little shiver. His mission had been to save a man's life, and he had failed!

# CHAPTER VIII

## THE DUTIES OF A SECRETARY

It was twenty minutes to four before Arnold reached the office. Mr. Jarvis looked at him curiously as he took off his hat and hung it up.

"I don't know what you've been up to, young man," he remarked, "but you'll find the governor in a queer state of mind. For the last hour he's been ringing his bell every five minutes, asking for you."

"I was detained," Arnold answered shortly. "Is he alone now?"

Mr. Jarvis nodded.

"I think that you had better go in at once," he advised. "There he is stamping about inside. I hope you've got some good excuse or there'll be the dickens to pay."

The door of the inner office was suddenly opened. Mr. Weatherley appeared upon the threshold. He recognized Arnold with an expression partly of anger, partly of relief.

"So here you are at last, young man!" he exclaimed. "Where the dickens have you been to all this while? Come in — come in at once! Do you see the time?"

"I am very sorry indeed, sir," Arnold replied. "I can assure you that I have not wasted a moment that I know of."

"Then what in the name of goodness did you find to keep you occupied all this time?" Mr. Weatherley demanded, pushing him through into the office and closing the door behind them. "Did you see Mr. Rosario? Did you give him the message?"

"I had no opportunity, sir," Arnold answered gravely.

"No opportunity? What do you mean? Didn't he come to the Milan? Didn't you see him at all?"

"He came, sir," Arnold admitted, "but I was not able to see him in time. I thought, perhaps," he added, "that you might have heard what happened."

Mr. Weatherley had reached the limits of his patience. He struck the table with his clenched fist. For a moment anger triumphed over his state of nervous excitability.

"Heard?" he cried. "Heard what? What the devil should I hear down here? If you've anything to tell, why don't you tell it me? Why do you stand there looking like a —"

Mr. Weatherley was suddenly frightened. He understood from Arnold's expression that something serious had happened.

"My God!" he exclaimed. "Mrs. Weatherley — my wife —"

"Mrs. Weatherley is quite well," Arnold assured him quickly. "It is Mr. Rosario."

"What of him? What about Rosario?"

"He is dead," Arnold announced. "You will read all about it in the evening papers. He was murdered — just as he was on the point of entering the Milan Grill Room."

Mr. Weatherley began to shake. He looked like a man on the verge of a collapse. He was still, however, able to ask a question.

"By whom?"

"The murderer was not caught," Arnold told him. "No one seems to have seen him clearly, it all took place so quickly. He stole out of some corner where he must have been hiding, and he was gone before anyone had time to realize what was happening."

Mr. Weatherley had been standing up all this time, clutching nervously at his desk. He suddenly collapsed into his easychair. His face was gray, his mouth twitched as though he were about to have a stroke.

"My God!" he murmured. "Rosario dead! They had him, after all! They — killed him!"

"It was a great shock to every one," Arnold went on. "Mrs. Weatherley arrived about a quarter of an hour before it occurred. I understood that she was expecting to lunch with him, but when I told her why I was there she came and sat at my table. She was sitting there when it happened. She was very much upset indeed. I was detained looking after her."

Mr. Weatherley looked at him narrowly.

"I am sorry that she was there," he said. "She is not strong. She ought not to be subjected to such shocks."

"I left her with Mr. Starling," Arnold continued. "He was going to take her home."

"Was Starling lunching there?" Mr. Weatherley asked.

"We saw him afterwards, coming up from the restaurant," Arnold replied. "He did not seem to have been in the Grill Room at all."

Mr. Weatherley sat back in his chair and for several minutes he remained silent. His eyes were fixed upon vacancy, his lips moved once or twice, but he said nothing. He seemed, indeed, to have lost the power of speech.

"It is extraordinary how the affair could have happened, almost unnoticed, in such a crowded place," Arnold went on, feeling somehow that it was best for him to talk. "There is nearly always a little stream of people coming in, or a telephone boy, or some one passing, but it happened that Mr.

Rosario came in alone. He had just handed his silk hat to the cloakroom attendant, who had turned away with it, when the man who killed him slipped out from somewhere, caught him by the throat, and it was all over in a few seconds. The murderer seems to have kept his face entirely hidden. They do not appear to have found a single person who could identify him. I had a table quite close to the door, as you told me, and I really saw the blow struck. We rushed outside, but, though I don't believe we were more than a few seconds, there wasn't a soul in sight."

"The police will find out something," Mr. Weatherley muttered. "They are sure to find out something."

"Some people think," Arnold continued, "that the man never left the hotel, or, if he did, that he was taken away in a motor car. The whole hotel was being searched very carefully when I left."

There was a knock at the door. Mr. Jarvis, who had been unable to restrain his curiosity any longer, brought some letters in for signature.

"If you can spare a moment, sir," he began, apologetically, "there is this little matter of Bland & Company's order. I have brought the reports with me."

Mr. Weatherley felt his feet upon the ground again. He turned to the papers which his clerk laid before him and gave them his close attention. When Arnold would have left the room, however, he signed impatiently to him to remain. As soon as he had given his instructions, and Mr. Jarvis had left the room, he turned once more to Arnold.

"Chetwode," he said, looking at him critically, "you appear to me to be a young man of athletic build."

Arnold was quite speechless.

"I mean that you could hold your own in a tussle, eh? You look strong enough to knock any one down who attempted to take liberties with you."

Arnold smiled.

"I dare say I might manage that, sir," he admitted.

"Very well — very well, then," Mr. Weatherley repeated. "Have your desk moved in here at once, Chetwode. You can have it placed just where you like. You'll get the light from that window if you have the easychair moved and put in the corner there against the wall. Understand that from now on you are my private secretary, and you do not leave this room, whoever may come in to see me, except by my special instructions. You understand that, eh?"

"Perfectly, sir."

"Your business is to protect me, in case of anything happening — of any disagreeable visitors, or anything of that sort," Mr. Weatherley declared. "This affair of Mr. Rosario has made me nervous. There is a very dangerous gang of people about who try to get money from rich men, and, if they don't succeed, use violence. I have already come into contact with something of the sort myself. Your salary — what do you get at present?"

"Twenty-eight shillings a week, sir."

"Double it," Mr. Weatherley ordered promptly. "Three pounds a week I will make it. For three pounds a week I may rely upon your constant and zealous service?"

"You may rely absolutely on that," Arnold replied, not quite sure whether he was on his head or his feet.

"Very well, then, go and tell some of the porters to bring in your desk. Have it brought in this very moment. Understand, if you please, that it is my wish not to be left alone under any circumstances — that is quite clear, isn't it? — not under any circumstances! I have heard some most disquieting stories about black-mailers and that sort of people."

"I don't think you need fear anything of the sort here," Arnold assured him.

"I trust not," Mr. Weatherley asserted, "but I prefer to be on the right side. As regards firearms," he continued, "I have never carried them, nor am I accustomed to handling them. At the same time, —"

"I wouldn't bother about firearms, if I were you, sir," Arnold interrupted. "I can promise you that while I am in this office no one will touch you or harm you in any way. I would rather rely upon my fists any day."

Mr. Weatherley nodded.

"I am glad to hear you say so. A strong young man like you need have no fear, of course. You understand, Chetwode, not a word in the outer office."

"Certainly not, sir," Arnold promised. "You can rely entirely upon my discretion. You will perhaps tell Mr. Jarvis that I am to do my work in here. Fortunately, I know a little shorthand, so if you like I can take the letters down. It will make my presence seem more reasonable."

Mr. Weatherley leaned back in his chair and lit a cigar. He was recovering slowly.

"A very good idea, Chetwode," he said. "I will certainly inform Mr. Jarvis. Poor Rosario!" he went on thoughtfully. "And to think that he might have been warned. If only I had told you to wait outside the restaurant!"

"Do you know who it was who telephoned to you, sir?" Arnold asked.

"No idea — no idea at all," Mr. Weatherley declared. "Some one rang up and told me that Mr. Rosario was engaged to lunch in the Grill Room with my wife. I don't know who it was — didn't recognize the voice from Adam — but the person went on to say that it would be a very great service indeed to Mr. Rosario if some one could stop him from lunching there today. Can't think why they telephoned to me."

"If Mr. Rosario were lunching with your wife," Arnold pointed out, "it would be perfectly easy for her to get him to go somewhere else if she knew of the message, whereas he might have refused an ordinary warning."

"You haven't heard the motive even hinted at, I suppose?" Mr. Weatherley asked.

"Not as yet," Arnold replied. "That may all come out at the inquest."

"To be sure," Mr. Weatherley admitted. "At the inquest — yes, yes! Poor Rosario!"

He watched the smoke from his cigar curl up to the ceiling. Then he turned to some papers on his table.

"Get your desk in, Chetwode," he ordered, "and then take down some letters. The American mail goes early this afternoon."

# CHAPTER IX

## A STRAINED CONVERSATION

Arnold swung around the corner of the terrace that evening with footsteps still eager notwithstanding his long walk. The splendid egoism of youth had already triumphed, the tragedy of the day had become a dim thing. He himself was moving forward and onward. He glanced up at the familiar window, feeling a slight impulse of disappointment when he received no welcoming wave of the hand. It was the first time for weeks that Ruth had not been there. He climbed the five flights of stone stairs, still buoyant and light-hearted. Glancing into his own room, he found it empty, then crossed at once the passageway and knocked at Ruth's door. She was lying back in her chair, with her back toward the window.

"Why, Ruth," he exclaimed, "how dare you desert your post!"

He felt at once that there was something strange in her reception of him. She stopped him as he came across the room, holding out both her hands. Her wan face was strained as she gazed and gazed. Something of the beautiful softness of her features had passed for the moment. She was so anxious, so terrified lest she should misread what was written in his face.

"Arnold!" she murmured. "Oh, Arnold!"

He was a little startled. It was as though tragedy had been let loose in the room.

"Why do you look at me like that, dear?" he cried. "Is there anything so terrible to tell me? What have I done?"

"God knows!" she answered. "Don't come any nearer for a moment. I want to look at you."

She was leaning out from her chair. It was true, indeed, that at that moment some sort of fear had drained all the beauty from her face, though her eyes shone still like fierce stars.

"You have gone, Arnold," she moaned. "You have slipped away. You are lost to me."

"You foolish person!" he exclaimed, stepping towards her. "Never in my life! Never!"

She laid her hand upon the stick which leaned against her chair.

"Not yet," she implored. "Don't come to me yet. Stay there where I can see your face. Now tell me — tell me everything."

He laughed, not altogether easily, with a note half of resentment, half of protest.

"Dear Ruth," he pleaded, "what have I done to deserve this? Nothing has happened to me that I will not tell you about. You have been sitting here alone, fancying things. And I have news — great news! Wait till you hear it."

"Go on," she said, simply. "Tell me everything. Begin at last night."

He drew a little breath. It was, after all, a hard task, this, that lay before him. Last night in his mind lay far enough back now, a tangled web of disconnected episodes, linked together by a strangely sweet emotional thread of sentiment. And the girl was watching his face with every sense strained to catch his words and the meaning of them. Vaguely he felt his danger, even from the first.

"Well, I got there in plenty of time," he began. "It was a beautiful house, beautifully furnished and arranged. The people were queer, not at all the sort I expected. Most of them seemed half foreign. They were all very hard to place for such a respectable household as Mr. Weatherley's should be."

"They were not really, then, Mr. Weatherley's friends?" she asked quietly.

"As a matter of fact, they were not," he admitted. "That may have had something to do with it. Mrs. Weatherley was a foreigner. She came from a little island somewhere in the Mediterranean, and is half Portuguese. Most of the people were there apparently by her invitation. After dinner — such a dinner, Ruth — we played bridge. More people came then. I think there were eight tables altogether. After I left, most of them stayed on to play baccarat."

Her eyes still held his. Her expression was unchanged.

"Tell me about Mrs. Weatherley," she murmured.

"She is the most beautiful woman I have ever seen. She is pale and she has strange brown eyes, not really brown but lighter. I couldn't tell you the color for I've never seen anything else like it. And she has real red-brown hair, and she is slim, and she walks like one of these women one reads about. They say that she is a Comtesse in her own right but that she never uses the title."

"And was she kind?" asked Ruth.

"Very kind indeed. She talked to me quite a good deal and I played bridge at her table. It seems the most amazing thing in the world that she should ever have married a man like Samuel Weatherley."

"Now tell me the rest," she persisted. "Something else has happened — I am sure of it."

He dropped his voice a little. The terror was coming into the room.

"There was a man there named Rosario — a Portuguese Jew and a very wealthy financier. One reads about him always in the papers. I have heard of him many times. He negotiates loans for foreign governments and has a bank of his own. I left him there last night, playing baccarat. This morning Mr. Weatherley called me into his office and sent me up to the Milan Restaurant with a strange message. I was to find Mr. Rosario and to see that he did not lunch there — to send him away somewhere else, in fact. I didn't understand it, but of course I went."

"And what happened?" she demanded.

He held his breath for a moment.

"I was to take a table just inside the restaurant," he explained, "and to tell him directly he entered. I did exactly as I was told, but it was too late. Rosario was stabbed as he was on the point of entering the restaurant, within a few yards of where I was sitting."

She shivered a little, although her general expression was still unchanged.

"You mean that he was murdered?"

"He was killed upon the spot," Arnold declared.

"By whom?"

He shook his head.

"No one knows. The man got away. I bought an evening paper as I came along and I see they haven't arrested any one yet."

"Was there a quarrel?" she asked.

"Nothing of the sort," he replied. "The other man seemed simply to have run out from somewhere and stabbed him with one thrust. I saw it all but I was powerless to interfere."

"You saw the man who did it?" she asked.

"Only his arm," Arnold answered. "He kept his body twisted around somehow. It was a blackguardly thing to do."

"It was horrible!" she murmured.

There was an interruption. The piece of tattered curtain which concealed the portion of the room given over to Isaac, and which led beyond to his sleeping chamber, was flung on one side. Isaac himself stood there, his black eyes alight with anger.

"Liar!" he exclaimed. "Liars, both of you!"

They looked at him without speech, his interruption was so sudden, so unexpected. The girl had forgotten his presence in the room; Arnold had never been conscious of it.

"I tell you that Rosario was a robber of mankind," Isaac cried. "He was one of those who feed upon the bones of the poor. His place was in Hell and into Hell he has gone. Honor to the hand which started him on his journey!"

"You go too far, Isaac," Arnold protested. "I never heard any particular harm of the man except that he was immensely wealthy."

Isaac stretched out his thin hand. His bony forefinger pointed menacingly towards Arnold.

"You fool!" he cried. "You brainless creature of brawn and muscle! You have heard no harm of him save that he was immensely wealthy! Listen. Bear that sentence in your mind and listen to me, listen while I tell you a story. A party of travelers was crossing the desert. They lost their way. One man only had water, heaps of water. There was enough in his possession for all, enough and to spare. The sun beat upon their heads, their throats were parched, their lips were black, they foamed at the mouth. On their knees they begged and prayed for water; he took not even the trouble to reply. He kept himself cool and refreshed with his endless supply; he poured it upon his head, he bathed his lips and drank. So he passed on, and the people around died, cursing him. Last of all, one who had seen his wife sob out her last breath in his arms, more terrible still had heard his little child shriek with agony, clutch at him and pray for water — he saw the truth, and what power there is above so guided his arm that he struck. The man paid the just price for his colossal greed. The vultures plucked his heart out in the desert. So died Rosario!"

Arnold shook his head.

"The cases are not similar, Isaac," he declared.

"You lie!" Isaac shrieked. "There is not a hair's-breadth of difference! Rosario earned his wealth in an office hung with costly pictures; he earned it lounging in ease in a padded chair, earned it by the monkey tricks of a dishonest brain. Never an honest day's work did he perform in his life, never a day did he stand in the market-place where the weaker were falling day by day. In fat comfort he lived, and he died fittingly on the portals of a restaurant, the cost of one meal at which would have fed a dozen starving children. Pity Rosario! Pity his soul, if you will, but not his dirty body!"

"The man is dead," Arnold muttered.

"Dead, and let him rot!" Isaac cried fiercely. "There may be others!"

He caught up his cloth cap and, without another word, left the room. Arnold looked after him curiously, more than a little impressed by the man's passionate earnestness. Ruth, on the other hand, was unmoved.

"Isaac is Isaac," she murmured. "He sees life like that. He would wear the flesh off his bones preaching against wealth. It is as though there were some fire inside which consumed him all the time. When he comes back, he will be calmer."

But Arnold remained uneasy. Isaac's words, and his attitude of pent-up fury, had made a singular impression upon him. For those few moments, the Hyde Park demagogue with his frothy vaporings existed no longer. It seemed to Arnold as though a flash of the real fire had suddenly blazed into the room.

"If Isaac goes about the world like that, trouble will come of it," he said thoughtfully. "Have you ever heard him speak of Rosario before?"

"Never," she answered. "I have heard him talk like that, though, often. To me it sounds like the waves beating upon the shores. They may rage as furiously, or ripple as softly as the tides can bring them, — it makes no difference . . . I want you to go on, please. I want you to finish telling me — your news."

Arnold looked away from the closed door. He looked back again into the girl's face. There was still that appearance of strained attention about her mouth and eyes.

"You are right," he admitted. "These things, after all, are terrible enough, but they are like the edge of a storm from which one has found shelter. Isaac ought to realize it."

"Tell me what this is which has happened to you!" she begged.

He shook himself free from that cloud of memories. He gave himself up instead to the joy of telling her his good news.

"Listen, then," he said. "Mr. Weatherley, in consideration not altogether, I am afraid, of my clerklike abilities, but of my shoulders and muscle, has appointed me his private secretary, with a seat in his office and a salary of three pounds a week. Think of it, Ruth! Three pounds a week!"

A smile lightened her face for a moment as she squeezed his fingers.

"But why?" she asked. "What do you mean about your shoulders and your muscle?"

"It is all very mysterious," he declared, "but do you know I believe Mr. Weatherley is afraid. He shook like a leaf when I told him of the murder of Rosario. I believe he thinks that there was some sort of blackmailing plot and he is afraid that something of the kind might happen to him. My instructions are never to leave his office, especially if he is visited by any strangers."

"It sounds absurd," she remarked. "I should have thought that of all the commonplace, unimaginative people you have ever described to me, Mr. Weatherley was supreme."

"And I," Arnold agreed. "And so, in a way, he is. It is his marriage which seems to have transformed him — I feel sure of that. He is mixing now with people whose manners and ways of thinking are entirely strange to him. He has had the world he knew of kicked from beneath his feet, and is hanging on instead to the fringe of another, of which he knows very little."

Ruth was silent. All the time Arnold was conscious that she was watching him. He turned his head. Her mouth was once more set and strained, a delicate streak of scarlet upon the pallor of her face, but from the fierce questioning of her eyes there was no escape.

"What is it you want to know that I have not told you, Ruth?" he asked.

"Tell me what happened to you last night!"

He laughed boisterously, but with a flagrant note of insincerity.

"Haven't I been telling you all the time?"

"You've kept something back," she panted, gripping his fingers frantically, "the greatest thing. Speak about it. Anything is better than this silence. Don't you remember your promise before you went — you would tell me everything — everything! Well?"

Her words pierced the armor of his own self-deceit. The bare room seemed suddenly full of glowing images of Fenella. His face was transfigured.

"I haven't told you very much about Mrs. Weatherley," he said, simply. "She is very wonderful and very beautiful. She was very kind to me, too."

Ruth leaned forward in her chair; her eyes read what she strove yet hated to see. She threw herself suddenly back, covering her face with her hands. The strain was over. She began to weep.

# CHAPTER X

## AN UNEXPECTED VISITOR

Mr. Weatherley laid down his newspaper with a grunt. He was alone in his private office with his newly appointed secretary.

"Two whole days gone already and they've never caught that fellow!" he exclaimed. "They don't seem to have a clue, even."

Arnold looked up from some papers upon which he was engaged.

"We can't be absolutely sure of that, sir," he reminded his employer. "They wouldn't give everything away to the Press."

Mr. Weatherley threw the newspaper which he had been reading onto the floor, and struck the table with his fist.

"The whole affair," he declared, "is scandalous — perfectly scandalous. The police system of this country is ridiculously inadequate. Scotland Yard ought to be thoroughly overhauled. Some one should take the matter up — one of the ha'penny papers on the lookout for a sensation might manage it. Just see here what happens," he went on earnestly. "A man is murdered in cold blood in a fashionable restaurant. The murderer simply walks out of the place into the street and no one hears of him again. He can't have been swallowed up, can he? You were there, Chetwode. What do you think of it?"

Arnold, who had been thinking of little else for the last few days, shook his head.

"I don't know what to think, sir," he admitted, "except that the murderer up till now has been extraordinarily lucky."

"Either that or he was fiendishly clever," Mr. Weatherley agreed, pulling nervously at his little patch of gray sidewhiskers. "I wonder, now — you've read the case, Chetwode?"

"Every word of it," Arnold admitted.

"Have you formed any idea yourself as to the motive?" Mr. Weatherley asked nervously.

Arnold shook his head.

"At present there seems nothing to go on, sir," he remarked. "I did hear it said that some one was trying to blackmail him and Mr. Rosario wasn't having any."

Mr. Weatherley pushed his scant hair back with his hand. He appeared to feel the heat of the office.

"You've heard that, too, eh?" he muttered. "It occurred to me from the first, Chetwode. It certainly did occur to me. You will remember that I mentioned it."

"What did your brother-in-law think of it, sir?" Arnold asked. "He and Mr. Rosario seemed to be very great friends. They were talking together for a long time that night at your house."

Mr. Weatherley jumped to his feet and threw open the window. The air which entered the office from the murky street was none of the best, but he seemed to find it welcome. Arnold was shocked to see his face when he turned around.

"The Count Sabatini is a very extraordinary man," Mr. Weatherley confessed. "He and his friends come to my house, but to tell you the truth I don't know much about them. Mrs. Weatherley wishes to have them there and that is quite enough for me. All the same, I don't feel that they're exactly the sort of people I've been used to, Chetwode, and that's a fact."

Mr. Weatherley had resumed his seat. He was leaning back in his chair now, his hands drooping to his side, looking precisely what he was — an ungraceful, commonplace little person, without taste or culture, upon whom even a good tailor seemed to have wasted his efforts. A certain pomposity which in a way became the man — proclaimed his prosperity and redeemed him from complete insignificance — had for a moment departed. He was like a pricked bladder. Arnold could scarcely help feeling sorry for him.

"I shouldn't allow these things to worry me, if I were you, sir," Arnold suggested respectfully. "If there is anything which you don't understand, I should ask for an explanation. Mrs. Weatherley is much too kind and generous to wish you to be worried, I am sure."

Then the side of the man with which Arnold wholly sympathized showed itself suddenly. At the mention of his wife's name an expression partly fatuous, partly beatific, transformed his homely features. He was looking at her picture which stood always opposite him. He had the air of an adoring devotee before some sacred shrine.

"You are quite right, Chetwode," he declared, "quite right, but I am always very careful not to let my wife know how I feel. You see, the Count Sabatini is her only relative, and before our marriage they were inseparable. He was an exile from Portugal and it seems to me these foreigners hang on together more than we do. I am only too glad for her to be with him as much as she chooses. It is just a little unfortunate that his friends should sometimes be — well, a trifle distasteful, but — one must put up with it. One must put up with it, eh? After all, Rosario was a man very well spoken of. There was no reason why he shouldn't have come to my house. Plenty of other men in my position would have been glad to have entertained him."

"Certainly, sir," agreed Arnold. "I believe he went a great deal into society."

"And, no doubt," Mr. Weatherley continued, eagerly, "he had many enemies. In the course of his commercial career, which I believe was an eventful one, he would naturally make enemies. . . . By the bye, Chetwode, speaking of blackmail — that blackmail rumor, eh? You don't happen to have heard any particulars?"

"None at all, sir," replied Arnold. "I don't suppose anything is really known. It seems a probable solution of the affair, though."

Mr. Weatherley nodded thoughtfully.

"It does," he admitted. "I can quite imagine any one trying it on and Rosario defying him. Just the course which would commend itself to such a man."

"The proper course, no doubt," Arnold remarked, "although it scarcely turned out the best for poor Mr. Rosario."

Mr. Weatherley distinctly shivered.

"Well, well," he declared, "you had better take out those invoices, and ask Jarvis to see me at once about Budden & Williams' account. . . . God bless my soul alive, why, here's Mrs. Weatherley!"

A car had stopped outside and both men had caught a vision of a fur-clad feminine figure crossing the pavement. Mr. Weatherley's fingers, busy already with his tie, were trembling with excitement. His whole appearance was transformed.

"Hurry out and meet her, Chetwode!" he exclaimed. "Show her the way in! This is the first time in her life she has been here of her own accord. Just as we were speaking about her, too!"

Fenella entered the office as a princess shod in satin might enter a pigsty. Her ermine-trimmed gown was raised with both her hands, her delightful nose had a distinct tilt and her lips a curl. But when she saw Arnold, a wonderful smile transformed her face. She was in the middle of the clerk's office, the cynosure of twenty-four staring eyes, but she dropped her gown and held out both her delicately gloved hands. The fall of her skirts seemed to shake out strange perfumes into the stuffy room.

"Ah! you are really here, then, in this odious gloom? You will show me where I can find my husband?"

Arnold stepped back and threw open the door of the inner office. She laughed into his face.

"Do not go away," she ordered. "Come in with me. I want to thank you for looking after me the other day."

Arnold murmured a few words of excuse and turned away. Mr. Tidey Junior carefully arranged his necktie and slipped down from his stool.

"Jarvis," he exclaimed, "a free lunch and my lifetime's gratitude if you'll send me into the governor's office on any pretext whatever!"

Mr. Jarvis, who was answering the telephone, took off his gold-rimmed spectacles and wiped them.

"Some one must go in and say that Mr. Burland, of Harris & Burland, wishes to know at what time he can see the governor. I think you had better let Chetwode go, though."

The young man turned away, humming a tune.

"Not I!" he replied. "Don't be surprised, you fellows, if I am not out just yet. The governor's certain to introduce me."

He knocked at the door confidently and disappeared. In a very few seconds he was out again. His appearance was not altogether indicative of conquest.

"Governor says Burland can go to the devil, or words to that effect," he announced, ill-naturedly. "Chetwode, you're to take in the private cheque book. . . . I tell you what, Jarvis," he added, slowly resuming his stool, "the governor's not himself these days. The least he could have done would have been to introduce me, especially as he's been up at our place so often. Rotten form, I call it. Anyway, she's not nearly so good-looking close to."

Mr. Jarvis proceeded to inform the inquirer through the telephone that Mr. Weatherley was unfortunately not to be found at the moment. Arnold, with Mr. Weatherley's cheque book in his hand, knocked at the door of the private office and closed the door carefully behind him. As he stood upon the threshold, his heart gave a sudden leap. Mr. Weatherley was sitting in his accustomed chair, but his attitude and expression were alike unusual. He was like a man shrinking under the whip. And Fenella — he was quick enough to catch the look in her face, the curl of her lips, the almost wicked flash of her eyes. Yet in a moment she was laughing.

"Your cheque book, Mr. Weatherley," he remarked, laying it down upon the desk.

Mr. Weatherley barely thanked him — barely, indeed, seemed to realize Arnold's presence. The latter turned to go. Fenella, however, intervened.

"Don't go away, if you please, Mr. Chetwode," she begged. "My husband is angry with me and I am a little frightened. And all because I have asked him to help a very good friend of mine who is in need of money to help forward a splendid cause."

Arnold was embarrassed. He glanced doubtfully at Mr. Weatherley, who was fingering his cheque book.

"It is scarcely a matter for discussion —" his employer began, but Fenella threw out her hands.

"Oh! la, la!" she interrupted. "Don't bore me so, my dear Samuel, or I will come to this miserable place no more. Mr. Starling must have this five hundred pounds because I have promised him, and because I have promised my brother that he shall have it. It is most important, and if all goes well it will come back to you some day or other. If not, you must make up your mind to lose it. Please write out the cheque, and afterwards Mr. Chetwode is to take me out to lunch. Andrea asked me especially to bring him, and if we do not go soon," she added, consulting a little jeweled watch upon her wrist, "we shall be late. Andrea does not like to be kept waiting."

"I was hoping," Mr. Weatherley remarked, with an unwieldy attempt at jocularity, "that I might be asked out to luncheon myself."

"Another day, my dear husband," she promised carelessly. "You know that you and Andrea do not agree very well. You bore him so much and then he is irritable. I do not like Andrea when he is irritable. Give me my cheque, dear, and let me go."

Mr. Weatherley dipped his pen in the ink, solemnly wrote out a cheque and tore it from the book. Fenella, who had risen to her feet and was standing over him with her hand upon his shoulder, stuffed it carelessly into the gold purse which she was carrying. Then she patted him on the cheek with her gloved hand.

"Don't overwork," she said, "and come home punctually. Are you quite ready, Mr. Chetwode?"

Arnold, who was finding the position more than ever embarrassing, turned to his employer.

"Can you spare me, sir?" he asked.

Mr. Weatherley nodded.

"If my wife desires you to go, certainly," he replied. "But Fenella," he added, "I am not very busy myself. Is it absolutely necessary that you lunch with your brother? Perhaps, even if it is, he can put up with my society for once."

She threw a kiss to him from the door.

"Unreasonable person!" she exclaimed. "Today it is absolutely necessary that I lunch with Andrea. You must go to your club if you are not busy, and play billiards or something. Come, Mr. Chetwode," she added, turning towards the door, "we have barely a quarter of an hour to get to the Carlton. I dare not be late. The only person," she went on, as they passed through the outer office and Arnold paused for a moment to take down his hat and coat, "whom I really fear in this world is Andrea."

Mr. Weatherley remained for a moment in the chair where she had left him, gazing idly at the counterfoil of the cheque. Then he rose and from a safe point of vantage watched the car drive off. With slow, leaden footsteps he returned to his seat. It was past his own regular luncheon hour, but he made no movement to leave the place.

# CHAPTER XI

## AN INTERRUPTED LUNCHEON

The great car swung to the right, out of Tooley Street and joined the stream of traffic making its slow way across London Bridge. Fenella took the tube from its place by her side and spoke in Italian to the chauffeur. When she replaced it, she turned to Arnold.

"Do you understand what I said?" she asked.

"Only a word or two," he replied. "You told him to go somewhere else instead of to the Carlton, didn't you?"

She nodded, and lay back for a moment, silent, among the luxurious cushions. Her mood seemed suddenly to have changed. She was no longer gay. She watched the faces of the passers-by pensively. Presently she pointed out of the window to a gray-bearded old man tottering along in the gutter with a trayful of matches. A cold wind was blowing through his rags.

"Look!" she exclaimed. "Look at that! In my own country, yes, but here I do not understand. They tell me that this is the richest city in the world, and the most charitable."

"There must be poor everywhere," Arnold replied, a little puzzled.

She stared at him.

"It is not your laws I would complain of," she said. "It is your individuals. Look at him — a poor, shivering, starved creature, watching a constant stream of well-fed, well-clothed, smug men of business, passing always within a few feet of him. Why does he not help himself to what he wants?"

"How can he?" Arnold asked. "There is a policeman within a few yards of him. The law stands always in the way."

"The law!" she repeated, scornfully. "It is a pleasant word, that, which you use. The law is the artificial bogey made by the men who possess to keep those others in the gutter. And they tell me that there are half a million of them in London — and they suffer — like that. Could your courts of justice hold half a million law-breakers who took an overcoat from a better clad man, or the price of a meal from a sleek passer-by, or bread from the shop which taunted their hunger? They do not know their strength, those who suffer."

Arnold looked at her in sheer amazement. It was surely a strange woman who spoke! There was no sympathy in her face or tone. The idea of giving alms to the man seemed never to have occurred to her. She spoke with clouded face, as one in anger.

"Don't you believe," he asked, "in the universal principle, the survival of the fittest? Where there is wealth there must be poverty."

She laughed.

"Change your terms," she suggested; "where there are robbers there must be victims. But one may despise the victims all the same. One may find their content, or rather their inaction, ignoble."

"Generally speaking, it is the industrious who prosper," he affirmed.

She shook her head.

"If that were so, all would be well," she declared. "As a matter of fact, it is entirely an affair of opportunity and temperament."

"Why, you are a socialist," he said. "You should come and talk to my friend Isaac."

"I am not a socialist because I do not care one fig about others," she objected. "It is only myself I think of."

"If you do not sympathize with laws, you at least recognize morals?"

She laughed gayly, leaning back against the dark green upholstery and showing her flawless teeth; her long, narrow eyes with their seductive gleam flashed into his. A lighter spirit possessed her.

"Not other people's," she declared. "I have my own code and I live by it. As for you, —"

She paused. Her sudden fit of gayety seemed to pass.

"As for me?" he murmured.

"I am a little conscience-stricken," she said slowly. "I think I ought to have left you where you were. I am not at all sure that you would not have been happier. You are a very nice boy, Mr. Arnold Chetwode, much too good for that stuffy little office in Tooley Street, but I do not know whether it is really for your good if one is inclined to try and help you to escape. If you saw another man holding a position you wanted yourself, would you throw him out, if you could, by sheer force, or would you think of your laws and your morals?"

"It depends a little upon how much I wanted it," he confessed.

She laughed.

"Ah! I see, then, that there are hopes of you," she admitted. "You should read the reign of Queen Elizabeth if you would know what Englishmen should be like. You know, I had an English mother, and she was descended from Francis Drake. . . . Ah, we are arrived!"

They had lost themselves somewhere between Oxford Street and Regent Street. The car pulled up in front of a restaurant which Arnold had certainly never seen or heard of before. It was quite small, and it bore the name "Café

André" painted upon the wall. The lower windows were all concealed by white curtains. The entrance hall was small, and there was no commission-naire. Fenella, who led the way in, did not turn into the restaurant but at once ascended the stairs. Arnold followed her, his sense of curiosity growing stronger at every moment. On the first landing there were two doors with glass tops. She opened one and motioned him to enter.

"Will you wait for me for a few moments?" she said. "I am going to tele-phone."

He entered at once. She turned and passed into the room on the other side of the landing. Arnold glanced around him with some curiosity. The room was well appointed and a luncheon table was laid for four people. There were flowers upon the table, and the glass and cutlery were superior to anything one might have expected from a restaurant in this vicinity. The window looked down into the street. Arnold stood before it for a moment or two. The traffic below was insignificant, but the roar of Oxford Street, only a few yards distant, came to his ears even through the closed window. He lis-tened thoughtfully, and then, before he realized the course his thoughts were taking, he found himself thinking of Ruth. In a certain sense he was supersti-tious about Ruth and her forebodings. He found himself wondering what she would have said if she could have seen him there and known that it was Fenella who had brought him. And he himself — what did he think of it? A week ago, his life had been so commonplace that his head and his heart had ached with the monotony of it. And now Fenella had come and had shown him already strange things. He seemed to have passed into a world where mysterious happenings were an every-day occurrence, into a world peopled by strange men and women who always carried secrets about with them. And, in a sense, no one was more mysterious than Fenella herself. He asked himself as he stood there whether her vagaries were merely temperamental, the air of mystery which seemed to surround her simply accidental. He thought of that night at her house, the curious intimacy which from the first moment she had seemed to take for granted, the confidence with which she had treated him. He remembered those few breathless moments in her room, the man's hand upon the windowsill, with the strange colored ring, worn with almost flagrant ostentation. And then, with a lightninglike transition of thought, the gleam of the hand with that self-same ring, raised to strike a murderous blow, which he had seen for a moment through the doors of the Milan. The red seal ring upon the finger — what did it mean? A doubt chilled him for a moment. He told himself with passionate insistence, that it was not possible that she could know of these things. Her words were idle, her theories a jest. He turned away from the window and caught up a morning paper, resolved to escape from his thoughts. The first headline stared up at him:

THE ROSARIO MURDER.
SENSATIONAL ARREST EXPECTED.
RUMORED EXTRAORDINARY DISCLOSURES.

He threw the paper down again. Then the door was suddenly opened, and Fenella appeared. She rang a bell.

"I am going to order luncheon," she announced. "My brother will be here directly."

Arnold bowed, a little absently. Against his will, he was listening to voices on the landing outside. One he knew to be Starling's, the other was Count Sabatini's. He closed his ears to their speech, but there was no doubt whatever that the voice of Starling shook with fear. A moment or two later the two men entered the room. Count Sabatini came forward with out-stretched hand. A rare smile parted his lips. He looked a very distinguished and very polished gentleman.

"I am pleased to meet you again, Mr. Chetwode," he said, "the more pleased because I understand from my sister that we are to have the pleasure of your company for luncheon."

"You are very kind," Arnold murmured.

"Mr. Starling — I believe that you met the other night," Count Sabatini continued.

Arnold held out his hand but could scarcely repress a start. Starling seemed to have lost weight. His cheeks were almost cadaverous, his eyes hollow. His slight arrogance of bearing had gone; he gave one a most unpleasant impression.

"I remember Mr. Starling quite well," Arnold said. "We met also, I think, at the Milan Hotel, a few minutes after the murder of Mr. Rosario."

Starling shook hands limply. Sabatini smiled.

"A memorable occasion," he remarked. "Let us take luncheon now. Gustave," he added, turning to the waiter who had just entered the room, "serve the luncheon at once. It is a queer little place, this, Mr. Chetwode," he went on, turning to Arnold, "but I can promise you that the omelette, at least, is as served in my own country."

They took their places at the table, and Arnold, at any rate, found it a very pleasant party. Sabatini was no longer gloomy and taciturn. His manner still retained a little of its deliberation, but towards Arnold especially he was more than courteous. He seemed, indeed, to have the desire to attract.

Fenella was almost bewitching. She had recovered her spirits, and she talked to him often in a half audible undertone, the familiarity of which gave him a curious pleasure. Starling alone was silent and depressed. He drank a good deal, but ate scarcely anything. Every passing footstep upon the stairs outside alarmed him; every time voices were heard he stopped to listen. Sabatini glanced towards him once with a scornful flash in his black eyes.

"One would imagine, my dear Starling, that you had committed a crime!" he exclaimed.

Starling raised his glass to his lips with shaking fingers, and drained its contents.

"I had too much champagne last night," he muttered.

There was a moment's silence. Every one felt his statement to be a lie. For some reason or other, the man was afraid. Arnold was conscious of a sense of apprehension stealing over him. The touch of Fenella's fingers upon his arm left him, for a moment, cold. Sabatini turned his head slowly towards the speaker, and his face had become like the face of an inquisitor, stern and merciless, with the flavor of death in the cold, mirthless parting of the lips.

"Then you drank a very bad brand, my friend," he declared. "Still, even then, the worst champagne in the world should not give you those ugly lines under the eyes, the scared appearance of a hunted rabbit. One would imagine —"

Starling struck the table a blow with his fist which set the glasses jingling.

"D — n it, stop, Sabatini!" he exclaimed. "Do you want to —"

He broke off abruptly. He looked towards Arnold. He was breathing heavily. His sudden fit of passion had brought an unwholesome flush of color to his cheeks.

"Why should I stop?" Sabatini proceeded, mercilessly. "Let me remind you of my sister's presence. Your lack of self-control is inexcusable. One would imagine that you had committed some evil deed, that you were indeed an offender against the law."

Again there was that tense silence. Starling looked around him with the helpless air of a trapped animal. Arnold sat there, listening and watching, completely fascinated. There was something which made him shiver about the imperturbability, not only of Sabatini himself, but of the woman who sat by his side.

Sabatini poured himself out a glass of wine deliberately.

"Who in the world," he demanded, "save a few unwholesome sentimentalists, would consider the killing of Rosario a crime?"

Starling staggered to his feet. His cheeks now were ashen.

"You are mad!" he cried, pointing to Arnold.

"Not in the least," Sabatini proceeded calmly. "I am not accusing you of having killed Rosario. In any case, it would have been a perfectly reasonable and even commendable deed. One can scarcely understand your agitation. If you are really accused of having been concerned in that little contretemps, why, here is our friend Mr. Arnold Chetwode, who was present. No doubt he will be able to give evidence in your favor."

Arnold was speechless for a moment. Sabatini's manner was incomprehensible. He spoke as one who alludes to some trivial happening. Yet even his light words could not keep the shadow of tragedy from the room. Even at that instant Arnold seemed suddenly to see the flash of a hand through the glass-topped door, to hear the hoarse cry of the stricken man.

"I saw nothing but the man's hand!" he muttered, in a voice which he would scarcely have recognized as his own. "I saw his hand and his arm only. He wore a red signet ring."

Sabatini inclined his head in an interested manner.

"A singular coincidence," he remarked, pleasantly. "My sister has already told me of your observation. It certainly is a point in favor of our friend Starling. It sounds like the badge of some secret society, and not even the most ardent romanticist would suspect our friend Starling here of belonging to anything of the sort."

Starling had resumed his luncheon, and was making a great effort at a show of indifference. Nevertheless, he watched Arnold uneasily.

"Say, there's no sense in talking like this!" he muttered. "Mr. Chetwode here will think you're in earnest."

"There is, on the contrary, a very great deal of sound common sense," Sabatini asserted, gently, "in all that I have said. I want our young friend, Mr. Chetwode, to be a valued witness for the defense when the misguided gentlemen from Scotland Yard choose to lay a hand upon your shoulder. One should always be prepared, my friend, for possibilities. You great —"

He stopped short. Starling, with a smothered oath, had sprung to his feet. The eyes of every one were turned toward the wall; a small electric bell was ringing violently. For the next few moments, events marched swiftly. Starling, with incredible speed, had left the room by the inner door. A waiter had suddenly appeared as though by magic, and of the fourth place at table there seemed to be left no visible signs. All the time, Sabatini, unmoved, continued to roll his cigarette. Then there came a tapping at the door.

"See who is there," Sabatini instructed the waiter.

Gustave, his napkin in his hand, threw open the door. A young man presented himself — a person of ordinary appearance, with a notebook sticking out of his pocket. His eyes seemed to take in at once the little party. He advanced a few steps into the room.

"You are perhaps not aware, sir," Sabatini said gently, "that this is a private apartment."

The young man bowed.

"I must apologize for my intrusion, sir and madame," he declared, looking towards Fenella. "I am a reporter on the staff of the *Daily Unit*, and I am exceedingly anxious to interview — you will pardon me!"

With a sudden swift movement he crossed the room, passed into the inner apartment and disappeared. Sabatini rose to his feet.

"I propose," he said, "that we complain to the proprietor of this excitable young journalist, and take our coffee in the palm court at the Carlton."

Fenella also rose and stepped in front of the looking-glass.

"It is good," she declared. "I stay with you for one half hour. Afterwards I have a bridge party. You will come with us, Mr. Chetwode?"

Arnold did not at once reply. He was gazing at the inner door. Every moment he expected to hear — what? It seemed to him that tragedy was there, the greatest tragedy of all — the hunting of man! Sabatini yawned.

"Those others," he declared, "must settle their own little differences. After all, it is not our affair."

# CHAPTER XII

## JARVIS IS JUSTLY DISTURBED

It was fully half-past three before Arnold found himself back in Tooley Street. He hung up his coat and hat and was preparing to enter Mr. Weatherley's room when the chief clerk saw him. Mr. Jarvis had been standing outside, superintending the unloading of several dray loads of American bacon. He laid his hand upon Arnold's shoulder.

"One moment, Chetwode," he said. "I want to speak to you out here."

Arnold followed him to a retired part of the warehouse. Mr. Jarvis leaned against an old desk belonging to one of the porters.

"You are very late, Chetwode," he remarked.

"I am sorry, but I was detained," Arnold answered. "I will explain it to Mr. Weatherley directly I go in."

Mr. Jarvis coughed.

"Of course," he said, "as you went out with Mrs. Weatherley I suppose it's none of my business as to your hours, but you must know that to come back from lunch at half-past three is most irregular, especially as you are practically junior in the place."

"I quite agree with you," Arnold assented, "but, you see, I really couldn't help myself today. I don't suppose it is likely to happen again. Is that all that you wanted to speak to me about?"

"Not altogether," Mr. Jarvis admitted. "To tell you the truth," he went on, confidentially, "I wanted to ask you a question or two."

"Well, look sharp, then," Arnold said, good-humoredly. "I dare say Mr. Weatherley will be getting impatient, and he probably saw me come in."

"I want to ask you," Mr. Jarvis began, impressively, "whether you noticed anything peculiar about the governor's manner this morning?"

"I don't think so — not especially," Arnold replied.

Mr. Jarvis took off his gold-rimmed spectacles and wiped them carefully.

"Mr. Weatherley," he proceeded, "has always been a gentleman of very regular habits — he and his father before him. I have been in the service of the firm for thirty-five years, Mr. Chetwode, so you can understand that my interest is not merely a business one."

"Quite so," Arnold agreed, glancing at the man by his side with a momentary curiosity. He had been in Tooley Street for four months, and even now he was still unused to the close atmosphere, the pungent smells, the yellow fog which seemed always more or less to hang about in the streets; the dark, cavernous-looking warehouse with its gloomy gas-jets always burning. From where they were standing at that moment, the figures of the draymen and warehousemen moving backwards and forwards seemed like phantoms in some subterranean world. It was odd to think of thirty-five years spent amid such surroundings!

"It is a long time," he remarked.

Mr. Jarvis nodded.

"I mention it," he said, "so that you may understand that my remarks to you are not dictated by curiosity or impertinence. Mr. Weatherley's behavior and mode of life has been entirely changed, Chetwode, since his marriage."

"I can understand that," Arnold replied, with a faint smile. What, indeed, had so beautiful a creature as Fenella to do with Samuel Weatherley of Tooley Street!

"Mrs. Weatherley," Mr. Jarvis continued, "is, no doubt, a very beautiful and accomplished lady. Whether she is a suitable wife for Mr. Weatherley I am not in a position to judge, never having had the opportunity of speech with her, but as regards the effect of his marriage upon Mr. Weatherley, I should like you to understand, Chetwode, at once, that it is my opinion, and the opinion of all of us, and of all his business friends, that a marked change for the worse in Mr. Weatherley has set in during the last few months."

"I am sorry to hear it," Arnold interposed.

"You, of course," Mr. Jarvis went on, "could scarcely have noticed it, as you have been here so short a time, but I can assure you that a year or so ago the governor was a different person altogether. He was out in the warehouse half the morning, watching the stuff being unloaded, sampling it, and suggesting customers. He took a live interest in the business, Chetwode. He was here, there and everywhere. Today — for the last few weeks, indeed — he has scarcely left his office. He sits there, signs a few letters, listens to what I have to say, and goodness knows how he spends the rest of his time. Where the business would be," Mr. Jarvis continued, rubbing his chin thoughtfully, "if it were not for us who know the running of it so well, I can't say, but a fact it is that Mr. Weatherley seems to have lost all interest in it."

"I wonder he doesn't retire," Arnold suggested.

Mr. Jarvis looked at him in amazement.

"Retire!" he exclaimed. "Why should he retire? What would he do? Isn't it as comfortable for him to read his newspaper over the fire in the office here as at home? Isn't it better for him to have his friends all around him, as he has here, than to sit up in his drawing-room in business hours with never a soul to speak to? Such men as Mr. Weatherley, Chetwode, or as Mr.

Weatherley's father was, don't retire. If they do, it means the end."

"Well, I'm sorry to hear what you tell me," Arnold said. "I haven't seen much of Mr. Weatherley, of course, but he seems devoted to his wife."

"Infatuated, sir! Infatuated is the word!" Mr. Jarvis declared.

"She is very charming," Arnold remarked, thoughtfully.

Mr. Jarvis looked as though there were many things which he could have said but refrained from saying.

"You will not suggest, Chetwode," he asked, "that she married Mr. Weatherley for any other reason than because he was a rich man?"

Arnold was silent for a moment. Somehow or other, he had accepted the fact of her being Mrs. Weatherley without thinking much as to its significance.

"I suppose," he admitted, "that Mr. Weatherley's money was an inducement."

"There is never anything but evil," Mr. Jarvis declared, "comes from a man or a woman marrying out of their own circle of friends. Now Mr. Weatherley might have married a dozen ladies from his own circle here. One I know of, a very handsome lady, too, whose father has been Lord Mayor. And then there's young Tidey's sisters, in the office there. Any one of them would have been most suitable. But no! Some unlucky chance seems to have sent Mr. Weatherley on that continental journey, and when you once get away from England, why, of course, anything may happen. I don't wish to say anything against Mrs. Weatherley, mind," Mr. Jarvis continued, "but she comes from the wrong class of people to make a city man a good wife, and I can't help associating her and her friends and her manner of living with the change that's come over Mr. Weatherley."

Arnold swung himself up on to the top of a barrel and sat looking down at his companion.

"Mr. Jarvis," he said, "you and I see this matter, naturally, from very different standpoints. You have known Mr. Weatherley for thirty-five years. I have known him for four months, and he never spoke a word to me until a few days ago. Practically, therefore, I have known Mr. and Mrs. Weatherley the same length of time. Under the circumstances, I must tell you frankly that my sympathies are with Mrs. Weatherley. Not only have I found her a very charming woman, but she has been most unnecessarily kind to me."

Mr. Jarvis was silent for a moment.

"I had forgotten," he admitted, "that that might be your point of view. It isn't, of course, possible to look for any feeling of loyalty for the chief from any one who has only been here a matter of a few months. Perhaps I was wrong to have spoken to you at all, Chetwode."

"If there is anything I can do," Arnold began, —

"It's in this way," Mr. Jarvis interrupted. "Owing, I dare say, to Mrs. Weatherley, you have certainly been put in a unique position here. You see more of Mr. Weatherley now than any one of us. For that reason I was anxious to make a confidant of you. I tell you that I am worried about Mr. Weatherley. He is a rich man and a prosperous man. There is no reason why he should sit in his office and gaze into the fire and look out of the window as though the place were full of shadows and he hated the sight of them. Yet that is what he does nowadays, Chetwode. What does it mean? I ask you frankly. Haven't you noticed yourself that his behavior is peculiar?"

"Now you mention it," Arnold replied, "I certainly have noticed that he was very strange in his manner this morning. He seemed very upset about that Rosario murder. Mr. Rosario was at his house the other night, you know. Were they great friends, do you think?"

Mr. Jarvis shook his head.

"Not at all," he said. "He was simply, I believe, one of Mrs. Weatherley's society acquaintances. But that there's something gone wrong with Mr. Weatherley, no one would deny who sees him as he is now and knows him as he was a year or so ago. There's Johnson, the foreman packer, who's been here as long as I have; and Elwick, the carter; and Hümmel, in the export department; — we've all been talking together about this."

"He doesn't speculate, I suppose?" Arnold enquired.

"Not a ha'penny," Mr. Jarvis replied, fervently. "He has spent large sums of money since his marriage, but he can afford it. It isn't money that's worrying him."

"Perhaps he doesn't hit it off with his wife," Arnold remarked.

Mr. Jarvis drew a little breath. For a moment he was speechless. To him it seemed something like profanity that this young man should make so casual a suggestion.

"Mrs. Weatherley, sir," he declared, "was, I believe, without any means whatever when Mr. Weatherley made her his wife. Mr. Weatherley, as you know, is at the head of this house, the house of Samuel Weatherley & Co., bankers Lloyds. It should be the business of the lady, sir, to see that she hits it off, as you put it, with a husband who has done her so much honor."

Arnold smiled.

"That is all very well, Mr. Jarvis," he said, "but you must remember that Mrs. Weatherley had compensations for her lack of wealth. She is very beautiful, and she is, too, of a different social rank."

Mr. Jarvis was frankly scornful.

"Why, she was a foreigner," he declared. "I should like to know of what account any foreign family is against our good city firms, such as I have been speaking of. No, Chetwode, my opinion is that she's brought a lot of her miserable, foreign hangers-on over here, and that somehow or other they are worrying Mr. Weatherley. I should like, if I could, to interest you in the chief. You can't be expected to feel as I do towards him. At the same time, he is the head of the firm, and you are bound, therefore, to feel a certain respect due to him, and I thought that if I talked to you and put these matters before you, which have occurred not only to me but to those others who have been with Mr. Weatherley for so many years, you might be able to help us by watching, and if you can find any clue as to what is bothering him, why, I'd be glad to hear of it, for there isn't one of us who wouldn't do anything that lay in his power to have the master back once more as he used to be a few years ago. Why, the business seems to have lost all its spring, nowadays," Mr. Jarvis went on, mournfully. "We do well, of course, because we couldn't help doing well, but we plod along more like a machine. It was different altogether in the days when Mr. Weatherley used to bring out the morning orders himself and chaff us about selling for no profit. You follow me, Chetwode?"

"I'll do what I can," Arnold agreed. "Of course, I see your point of view, and I must admit that the governor does seem depressed about something or other."

"If anything turns up," Mr. Jarvis asked eagerly, "anything tangible, I mean, you'll tell me of it, won't you, there's a good fellow? Of course, I suppose your future is outside my control now, but I engaged you first, you know, Chetwode. There aren't many things done here that I haven't a say in."

"You may rely upon me," Arnold promised, slipping down from the barrel. "He's really quite a decent old chap, and if I can find out what's worrying him, and can help, I'll do it."

Mr. Jarvis went back to his labors and Arnold made his way to Mr. Weatherley's room. His first knock remained unanswered. The "Come in!" which procured for him admittance at his second attempt sounded both flurried and startled. Mr. Weatherley had the air of one who has been engaged in some criminal task. He drew the blotting-paper over the letter which he had been writing as Arnold entered.

"Oh! it's you, is it, Chetwode?" he remarked, with an air of relief. "So you're back, eh? Pleasant luncheon?"

"Very pleasant indeed, thank you, sir," Arnold replied.

"Mrs. Weatherley send any message?" her husband asked, with ill-assumed indifference.

"None at all, sir."

Mr. Weatherley sighed. He seemed a little disappointed.

"Did you lunch at the Carlton?"

"We took our coffee there afterwards," Arnold said. "We lunched at a small foreign restaurant near Oxford Street."

"The Count Sabatini was there?"

"Yes, sir," Arnold told him. "Also Mr. Starling."

Mr. Weatherley nodded slowly.

"How do you get on with Count Sabatini?" he inquired. "Rather a gloomy person, eh?"

"I found him very pleasant, sir," Arnold said. "He was good enough to ask me to dine with him tonight."

Mr. Weatherley looked up, a little startled.

"Invited you to dine with him?" he repeated.

Arnold nodded.

"I thought it was very kind of him, sir."

Mr. Weatherley sat quite still in his chair. He had obviously forgotten his secretary's presence in the room, and Arnold, who had seated himself at his desk and was engaged in sorting out some papers, took the opportunity now and then to glance up and scrutinize with some attention his employer's features. There were certainly traces there of the change at which Mr. Jarvis had hinted. Mr. Weatherley had the appearance of a man who had once been florid and prosperous and comfortable-looking, but who had been visited by illness or some sort of anxiety. His cheeks were still fat, but they hung down toward the jaw, and his eyes were marked with crowsfeet. His color was unhealthy. He certainly had no longer the look of a prosperous and contented man.

"Chetwode," he said slowly, after a long pause, "I am not sure that I did you a kindness when I asked you to come to my house the other night."

"I thought so, at any rate, sir," Arnold replied. "It has been a great pleasure to me to make Mrs. Weatherley's acquaintance."

"I am glad that my wife has been kind to you," Mr. Weatherley continued, "but I hope you will not misunderstand me, Chetwode, when I say that I am not sure that such kindness is for your good. Mrs. Weatherley's antecedents are romantic, and she has many friends whose position in life is curiously different from my own, and whose ideas and methods of life are not such as I should like a son of my own to adopt. The Count Sabatini, for instance," Mr. Weatherley went on, "is a nobleman who has had, I believe, a brilliant career, in some respects, but who a great many people would tell you is a man without principles or morals, as we understand them down here. He is just the sort of man to attract youth because he is brave, and I believe him to be incapable of a really despicable action. But notwithstanding this, and although he is my wife's brother, if I were you I would not choose him for a companion."

"I am very much obliged to you, sir," Arnold answered, a little awkwardly. "I shall bear in mind all that you have said. You do not object, I presume, to my dining with him tonight?"

"I have no objection to anything you may do outside this building," Mr. Weatherley replied, "but as you are only a youngster, and you met the Count Sabatini at my house, I feel it only right to give you a word of warning. I may be wrong. One gets fancies sometimes, and there are some strange doings — not that they concern you, however," he added, hurriedly; "only you are a young man with your way to make in the world, and every chance of making it, I should think; but it won't do for you to get too many of Count Sabatini's ideas into your head if you are going to do any good at a wholesome, honest business like this."

"I quite understand, sir," Arnold assented. "I don't suppose that Count Sabatini will ask me to dine with him again. I think it was just kindness that made him think of it. In any case, I am not in a position to associate with these people regularly, at present, and that alone would preclude me from accepting invitations."

"You're young and strong," Mr. Weatherley said thoughtfully. "You must fight your own battle. You start, somehow, differently than I did. You see," he went on, with the air of one indulging in reminiscences, "my father was in this business and I was brought up to it. We lived only a stone's throw away then, in Bermondsey, and I went to the City of London School. At fourteen I was in the office here, and a partner at twenty-one. I never went out of England till I was over forty. I had plenty of friends, but they were all of one class. They wouldn't suit Mrs. Weatherley or the Count Sabatini. I have lost a good many of them. . . . You weren't brought up to business, Chetwode?" he asked suddenly.

"I was not, sir," Arnold admitted.

"What made you come into it?"

"Poverty, sir," Arnold answered. "I had only a few shillings in the world when I walked in and asked Mr. Jarvis for a situation."

Mr. Weatherley sighed.

"Your people are gentlefolk, I expect," he said. "You have the look of it."

Arnold did not reply. Mr. Weatherley shrugged his shoulders.

"Well," he concluded, "you must look after yourself, only remember what I have said. By the bye, Chetwode, I am going to repose a certain amount of confidence in you."

Arnold looked up from his desk.

"I think you may safely do so, sir," he declared.

Mr. Weatherley slowly opened a drawer at his right hand and produced two letters. He carefully folded up the sheet upon which he had been writing, and also addressed that.

"I cannot enter into explanations with you about this matter, Chetwode," he said, "but I require your promise that what I say to you now is not mentioned in the warehouse or to any one until the time comes which I am about to indicate. You are my confidential secretary and I have a right, I suppose, to demand your silence."

"Certainly, sir," Arnold assured him.

"There is just a possibility," Mr. Weatherley declared, speaking thoughtfully and looking out of the window, "that I may be compelled to take a sudden and quite unexpected journey. If this be so, I should have to leave without a word to any one — to any one, you understand."

Arnold was puzzled, but he murmured a word of assent.

"In case this should happen," Mr. Weatherley went on, "and I have not time to communicate with any of you, I am leaving in your possession these two letters. One is addressed jointly to you and Mr. Jarvis, and the other to Messrs. Turnbull & James, Solicitors, Bishopsgate Street Within. Now I give these letters into your charge. We shall lock them up together in this small safe which I told you you could have for your own papers," Mr. Weatherley continued, rising to his feet and crossing the room. "There you are, you see. The safe is empty at present, so you will not need to go to it. I am locking them up," he added, taking a key from his pocket, "and there is the key. Now you understand?"

"But surely, sir," Arnold began, —

"The matter is quite simple," Mr. Weatherley interrupted, sharply. "To put it plainly, if I am missing at any time, if anything should happen to me, or if I should disappear, go to that safe, take out the letters, open your own and deliver the other. That is all you have to do."

"Quite so, sir," Arnold replied. "I understand perfectly. I see that there is none for Mrs. Weatherley. Would you wish any message to be sent to her?"

Mr. Weatherley was silent for a moment. A boy passed along the pavement with a bundle of evening papers. Mr. Weatherley tapped at the window.

"Hurry out and get me a *Star*, Chetwode," he ordered.

Arnold obeyed him and returned a few moments later with a paper in his hand. Mr. Weatherley spread out the damp sheet under the electric light. He studied it for a few moments intently, and then folded it up.

"It will not be necessary for you, Chetwode," he said, "to communicate with my wife specially."

The accidental arrangement of his employer's coat and hat upon the rack suddenly struck Arnold.

"Why, I don't believe that you have been out to lunch, sir!" he exclaimed.

Mr. Weatherley looked as though the idea were a new one to him.

"To tell you the truth," he said, "I completely forgot. Help me on with my coat, Chetwode. There is nothing more to be done today. I will call and get some tea somewhere on my way home."

He rose to his feet, a little heavily.

"Tell them to get me a taxicab," he directed. "I don't feel much like walking today, and they are not sending for me."

Arnold sent the errand-boy off to London Bridge. Mr. Weatherley stood before the window looking out into the murky atmosphere.

"I hope, Chetwode," he said, "that I haven't said anything to make you believe that there is anything wrong with me, or to give you cause for uneasiness. This journey of which I spoke may never become necessary. In that case, after a certain time has elapsed, we will destroy those letters."

"I trust that it never may become necessary to open them, sir," Arnold remarked.

"As regards what I said to you about the Count," Mr. Weatherley continued, after a moment's hesitation, "remember who I am that give you the advice, and who you are that receive it. Your bringing-up, I should imagine, has been different. Still, a young man of your age has to make up his mind what sort of a life he means to lead. I suppose, to a good many people," he went on, reflectively, "my life would seem a common, dull, plodding affair. Somehow or other, I didn't seem to find it so until — until lately. Still, there it is. I suppose I have lived in a little corner of the world, and what seems strange and wild to me might, after all, seem not so much out of the way to a young man with different ideas like you. Only, this much I do believe, at any rate," he went on, buttoning up his coat and watching the taxicab which was coming along the street; "if you want a quiet, honest life, doing your duty to yourself and others, and living according to the old-fashioned standards of honesty and upright living, then when you have had that dinner with the Count Sabatini tonight, forget him, forget where he lives. Come back to your work here, and if the things of which the Count has been talking to you seem to have more glamor, forget them all the more zealously. The best sort of life is always the grayest. The life which attracts is generally the one to be avoided. We don't do our duty," Mr. Weatherley added, brushing his hat upon his sleeve reflectively, "by always looking out upon the pleasurable side of life. Good evening, Chetwode!"

He turned away so abruptly that Arnold had scarcely time to return his greeting. It seemed so strange to him to be talked to at such length by a man whom he had scarcely heard utter half a dozen words in his life, that he was left speechless. He was still standing before the window when Mr. Weatherley crossed the pavement to the waiting taxicab. In his walk and attitude the signs of the man's deterioration were obvious. The little swagger of his younger days was gone, the bumptiousness of his bearing forgotten. He cast no glance up and down the pavement to hail an acquaintance. He muttered an address to the driver and stepped heavily into the taxicab.

# CHAPTER XIII

## CASTLES IN SPAIN

Ruth welcomed him with her usual smile — once he had thought it the most beautiful thing in the world. In the twilight of the April evening her face gleamed almost marble white. He dragged a footstool up to her side.

"Little woman, you are looking pale," he declared. "Give me your hands to hold. Can't you see that I have come just at the right time? Even the coal barges look like phantom boats. See, there is the first light."

She shook her head slowly.

"Tonight," she murmured, "there will be no ships, Arnold. I have looked and looked and I am sure. Light the lamp, please."

"Why?" he asked, obeying her as a matter of course.

She turned in her chair.

"Do you think that I cannot tell?" she continued. "Didn't I see you turn the corner there, didn't I hear your step three flights down? Sometimes I have heard it come, and it sounds like something leaden beating time to the music of despair. And tonight you tripped up like a boy home for the holidays. You are going out tonight, Arnold."

He nodded.

"A man whom I met the other night has asked me to dine with him," he announced.

"A man! You are not going to see her, then?"

He laughed gayly and placed his hand upon the fingers which had drawn him towards her.

"Silly girl!" he declared. "No, I am going to dine alone with her brother, the Count Sabatini. You see, I am private secretary now to a merchant prince, no longer a clerk in a wholesale provision merchant's office. We climb, my dear Ruth. Soon I am going to ask for a holiday, and then we'll make Isaac leave his beastly lecturing and scurrilous articles, and come away with us somewhere for a day or two. You would like a few days in the country, Ruth?"

Her eyes met his gratefully.

"You know that I should love it, dear," she said, "but, Arnie, do you think that when the time for the holiday comes you will want to take us?"

He sat on the arm of her chair and held her hand.

"Foolish little woman!" he exclaimed. "Do you think that I am likely to forget? Why, I must have shared your supper nearly every night for a month, while I was walking about trying to find something to do. People don't forget who have lived through that sort of times, Ruth."

She sighed. Strangely enough, her tone had in it something of vague regret.

"For your sake, dear, I am glad that they are over."

"Things, too, will improve with you," he declared. "They shall improve. If only Isaac would turn sensible! He has brains and he is clever enough, if he weren't stuffed full with that foolish socialism."

She looked around the room and drew him a little closer to her.

"Arnold," she whispered, "now that you have spoken of it, let me tell you this. Sometimes I am afraid. Isaac is so mysterious. Do you know that he is away often for the whole day, and comes back white and exhausted, worn to a shadow, and sleeps for many hours? Sometimes he is in his room all right, but awake. I can hear him moving backwards and forwards, and hammering, tap, tap, tap, for hours."

"What does he do?" Arnold asked quickly.

"He has some sort of a little printing press in his room," she answered. "He prints some awful sheet there which the police have stopped. The night before last he had a message and everything was hidden. He spent hours with his face to the window, watching. I am so afraid that sometimes he goes outside the law. Arnold, I am afraid of what might happen to him. There are terrible things in his face if I ask him questions. And he moves about and mutters like a man in a dream — no, like a man in a nightmare!"

Arnold frowned, and looked up at the sky-signs upon the other side of the river.

"I, too, wish he were different, dear," he said. "He certainly is a dangerous protector for you."

"He is the only one I have," the girl replied, with a sigh, "and sometimes, when he remembers, he is so kind. But that is not often now."

"What do you do when he is away for all this time?" Arnold asked quickly. "Are you properly looked after? You ought to have some one here."

"Mrs. Sands comes twice a day, always," she declared. "It is not myself I trouble about, really. Isaac is good in that way. He pays Mrs. Sands always in advance. He tries even to buy wine for me, and he often brings me home fruit. When he has money, I am sure that he gives it to me. It isn't that so much, Arnold, but I get frightened of his getting into trouble. Now that room of his has got on my nerves. When I hear that tap, tap, in the night, I am terrified."

"Will you let me speak to him about it, Ruth?"

Her face was suddenly full of terror.

"Arnie, you mustn't think of it," she begged. "He would never forgive me — never. The first time I asked him what was going on there, I thought that he would have struck me."

"Would you like me to go in and see next time he is out?"

She shivered.

"Not for the world," she replied. "Besides, you couldn't. He has fixed on a Yale lock himself. No one could open the door."

"You have never seen what he prints?"

"Never," she replied. "He knows that I hate the sight of those pamphlets. He never shows them to me. He had a man to see him the other night — the strangest-looking man I ever saw — and they talked in whispers for hours. I saw the man's face when he went out. It was white and evil. And, Arnold, it was the face of a man steeped in sin to the lips. I wish I hadn't seen it," she went on, drearily. "It haunts me."

He did his best to reassure her.

"Little Ruth," he said, "you have been up here too long without a holiday. Wait till Saturday afternoon, when I draw my new salary for the first time. I shall hire a taxicab. We will have it open and drive out into the country."

Her face lit up for a moment. Her beautiful eyes were soft, although a few seconds later they were swimming with tears.

"Do you think you will want to go when Saturday afternoon comes?" she asked. "Don't you think, perhaps, that your new friends may invite you to go and see them? I am so jealous of your new friends, Arnold."

He drew her a little closer to him. There was something very pathetic in her complete dependence upon him, a few months ago a stranger. They had both been waifs, brought together by a wave of common adversity. Her intense weakness had made the same appeal to him as his youth and strength to her. There was almost a lump in his throat as he answered her.

"You aren't really feeling like that, Ruth?" he begged. "Don't! My new friends are part of the new life. You wouldn't have me cling to the old any longer than I can help? Why, you and I together have sat here hour after hour and prayed for a change, prayed for the mystic treasure that might come to us from those ships of chance. Dear, if mine comes first, it brings good for you, too. You can't believe that I should forget?"

For the first time in his life he bent over and kissed her upon the lips. She suffered his caress not only without resistance but for a single moment her arms clasped his neck passionately. Then she drew away abruptly.

"I don't know what I'm doing!" she panted. "You mustn't kiss me like that! You mustn't, Arnold!"

She began to cry, but before he could attempt to console her she dashed the tears away.

"Oh, we're impossible, both of us!" she declared. "But then, a poor creature like me must always be impossible. It isn't quite kind of fate, is it, to give any one a woman's heart and a woman's loneliness, and the poor frame of a hopeless invalid."

"You're not a hopeless invalid," he assured her, earnestly. "No one would ever know, to look at you as you sit there, that there was anything whatever the matter. Don't you remember our money-box for the doctor? Even that will come, Ruth. The day will come, I am sure, when we shall carry you off to Vienna, or one of those great cities, and the cure will be quite easy. I believe in it, really."

She sighed.

"I used to love to hear you talk about it," she said, "but, somehow, now it seems so far off. I don't even know that I want to be like other women. There is only one thing I do want and that is to keep you."

"That," he declared, fervently, "you are sure of. Remember, Ruth, that awful black month and what we suffered together. And you knew nothing about me. I just found you sitting on the stairs with your broken stick, waiting for some one to come and help you."

She nodded.

"And you picked me up and carried me into your room," she reminded him. "You didn't have to stop and take breath as Isaac has to."

"Why, no," he admitted, "I couldn't say you were heavy, dear. Some day or other, though," he added, "you will be. Don't lose your faith, Ruth. Don't let either of us leave off looking for the ships."

She smiled.

"Very well," she said, letting her hand fall once more softly into his, "I think that I am very foolish. I think that yours has come already, dear, and I am worse than foolish, I am selfish, because I once hoped that they might come together; that you and I might sit here, Arnold, hand in hand, and watch them with great red sails, and piles and piles of gold and beautiful things, with our names written on so big that we could read them even here from the window."

She burst into a peal of laughter.

"Oh, those children's days! What an escape they, were for us in the black times! Do you know that we once actually told one another fairy stories?"

"Not only that but we believed in them," he insisted. "I am perfectly certain that the night you found my star, and it seemed to us to keep on getting bigger and bigger while we looked at it, that from that night things have been getting better with me."

"At least," she declared, abruptly, "I am not going to spoil your dinner by keeping you here talking nonsense. Carry me back, please, Arnold. You must hurry up now and change your clothes. And, dear, you had better not come in and wish me good-night. Isaac went out this morning in one of his savage tempers, and he may be back at any moment. Carry me back now, and have a beautiful evening. Tomorrow you must tell me all about it."

He obeyed her. She was really only a trifle to lift, as light as air. She clung to him longingly, even to the last minute.

"And now, please, you are to kiss my forehead," she said, "and run away."

"Your forehead only?" he asked, bending over her.

"My forehead only, please," she begged gravely. "The other doesn't go with our fairy stories, dear. I want to go on believing in the fairy stories...."

Arnold had little enough time to dress, and he descended the stone steps towards the street at something like a run. Halfway down, however, he pulled up abruptly to avoid running into two men. One was Isaac. His worn, white face, with hooked nose and jet-black eyes, made him a noticeable figure even in the twilight. The other man was so muffled up as to be unrecognizable. Arnold stopped short.

"Glad you're home, Isaac," he said pleasantly. "I have just been talking to Ruth. I thought she seemed rather queer."

Isaac looked at him coldly from head to foot. Arnold was wearing his only and ordinary overcoat, but his varnished shoes and white tie betrayed him.

"So you're wearing your cursed livery again!" he sneered. "You're going to beg your bone from the rich man's plate."

Arnold laughed at him.

"Always the same, Isaac," he declared. "Never mind about me. You look after your niece and take her out, if you can, somewhere. I am going to give her a drive on Saturday."

"Are you?" Isaac said calmly. "I doubt it. Drives and carriages are not for the like of us poor scum."

His companion nudged him impatiently. Isaac moved away. Arnold turned after him.

"You won't deny the right of a man to spend what he earns in the way he likes best?" he asked. "I've had a rise in my salary, and I am going to spend a part of it taking Ruth out."

Isaac laughed scornfully.

"A rise in your salary!" he muttered. "You poor slave! Did you go and kiss your master's foot when he gave it to you?"

"I didn't," Arnold declared. "To tell you the truth, I believe it would have annoyed him. He hasn't any sense of humor, you see. Good night, Isaac. If you're writing one of those shattering articles tonight, remember that Ruth can hear you, and don't keep her awake too late."

Arnold walked on. Suddenly his attention was arrested. Isaac was leaning over the banister of the landing above.

"Stop!"

Arnold paused for a moment.

"What is it?" he asked.

Isaac came swiftly down. He brushed his cloth hat further back on his head as though it obscured his vision. With both hands he gripped Arnold's arm.

"Tell me," he said, "what do you mean by that?"

"What I said," Arnold answered; "but, for Heaven's sake, don't visit it on poor Ruth. She told me that you had some printing-press in your room to set up your pamphlets, and that the tap, tap at night had kept her awake. It's no concern of mine. I don't care what you do or what rubbish you print, but I can't bear to see the little woman getting frailer and frailer, Isaac."

"She told you that?" Isaac muttered.

"She told me that," Arnold assented. "What is there in it?"

Isaac looked at him for a moment with an intentness which was indescribable. His black eyes seemed on fire with suspicion, with searchfulness. At last he let go the arm which he was clutching, and turned away.

"All right," he said. "Ruth shouldn't talk, that's all. I don't want every one to know that I am reduced to printing my little sheet in my bedroom. Good night!"

Arnold looked after him in surprise. It was very seldom that Isaac vouchsafed any form of greeting or farewell. And then the shock came. Isaac's companion, who had been leaning over the banisters, waiting for him, had loosened the muffler about his neck and opened his overcoat. His features were now recognizable — a pale face with deep-set eyes and prominent forehead, a narrow chin, and a mouth which seemed set in a perpetual snarl. Arnold stood gazing up at him in rapt amazement. He had seen that face but once before, yet there was no possibility of any mistake. It seemed, indeed, as though the recognition were mutual, for the man above, with an angry cry, turned suddenly away, buttoning up his overcoat with feverish fingers. He called out to Isaac — a hurried sentence, in a language which was strange to Arnold. There was a brief exchange of breathless words. Arnold moved slowly away, but before he had reached the street Isaac's hand was upon his shoulder.

"One moment!" Isaac panted. "My friend would like to know why you looked at him like that?"

Arnold did not hesitate.

"Isaac," he said, gravely, "no doubt I seemed surprised. I have seen that man before, only a night or two ago."

"Where? When?" Isaac demanded.

"I saw him hanging around the house of my employer," Arnold said firmly, "under very suspicious circumstances. He was inquiring then for Mr. Rosario. It was the night before Rosario was murdered."

"What do you mean by that?" Isaac asked, hoarsely.

"You had better ask yourself what it means," Arnold replied. "For Ruth's sake, Isaac, don't have anything to do with that man. I don't know anything about him — I don't want to know anything about him. I simply beg you, for Ruth's sake, to keep out of trouble."

Isaac laughed harshly.

"You talk like a young fool!" he declared, turning on his heel.

# CHAPTER XIV

## SABATINI'S DOCTRINES

The apartments of Count Sabatini were situated in the somewhat unfamiliar quarter of Queen Anne's Gate. Arnold found his way there on foot, crossing Parliament Square in a slight drizzling rain, through which the figures of the passers-by assumed a somewhat phantasmal appearance. Around him was a glowing arc of lights, and, dimly visible beyond, shadowy glimpses of the river. He rang the bell with some hesitation at the house indicated by his directions — a large gray stone building, old-fashioned, and without any external signs of habitation. His summons, however, was answered almost immediately by a man-servant who took his hat and coat.

"If you will step into the library for a moment, sir," he said, with a slight foreign accent, "His Excellency will be there."

Arnold was immensely impressed by the room into which he was shown. He stood looking around him for several minutes. The whole atmosphere seemed to indicate a cultivated and luxurious taste, kept in bounds by a certain not unpleasing masculine severity. The coloring of the room was dark green, and the walls were everywhere covered with prints and etchings, and trophies of the chase and war. A huge easychair was drawn up to the fire, and by its side was a table covered with books and illustrated papers. A black oak writing desk stood open, and a huge bowl of violets set upon it was guarded by an ivory statuette of the Venus of Milo. The furniture was comfortably worn. There was a faint atmosphere of cigarette smoke, — the whole apartment was impregnated by an intensely liveable atmosphere. The glowing face of a celebrated Parisian *danseuse* laughed at him from over the mantelpiece. Arnold was engaged in examining it when Sabatini entered.

"A thousand apologies, my dear Mr. Chetwode," he said softly. "I see you pass your time pleasantly. You admire the divine Fatime?"

"The face is beautiful," Arnold admitted. "I am afraid I was a few minutes early. It began to rain and I walked fast."

Sabatini smiled. A butler had followed him into the room, bearing on a tray two wine-glasses full of clear yellow liquid.

"Vermouth and one tiny cigarette," Sabatini suggested, — "the best *apéritif* in the world. Permit me, Mr. Chetwode — to our better acquaintance!"

"I never need an *apéritif*," Arnold answered, raising the wine-glass to his lips, "but I will drink to your toast, with pleasure."

Sabatini lit his cigarette, and, leaning slightly against the back of a chair, stood with folded arms looking at the picture over the fireplace.

"Your remark about Fatime suggested reservations," he remarked. "I wonder why? I have a good many curios in the room, and some rather wonderful prints, but it was Fatime who held you while you waited. Yet you are not one of those, I should imagine," he added, blowing out a cloud of cigarette smoke, "to whom the call of sex is irresistible."

Arnold shook his head.

"No, I don't think so," he admitted simply. "To tell you the truth, I think that it was the actual presence of the picture here, rather than its suggestions, which interested me most. Your room is so masculine," Arnold added, glancing around. "It breathes of war and sport and the collector. And then, in the middle of it all, this girl, with her barely veiled limbs and lascivious eyes. There is something a little brutal about the treatment, don't you think?"

Sabatini shrugged his shoulders.

"The lady is too well known," remarked Sabatini, shrugging his shoulders. "A single touch of the ideal and the greatness of that picture would be lost. Grève was too great an artist to try for it."

"Nevertheless," Arnold persisted, "she disturbs the serenity of your room."

Sabatini threw away his cigarette and passed his arm through his companion's.

"It is as well always to be reminded that life is many-sided," he murmured. "You will not mind a *tête-à-tête* dinner?"

Some curtains of dark green brocaded material had been silently drawn aside, and they passed into a smaller apartment, of which the coloring and style of decoration was the same. A round table, before which stood two high-backed, black oak chairs, and which was lit with softly-shaded candles, stood in the middle of the room. It was very simply set out, but the two wine-glasses were richly cut in quaint fashion, and the bowl of violets was of old yellow Sèvres. Arnold sat opposite his host and realized how completely the man seemed to fit in with his surroundings. In Mrs. Weatherley's drawing-room there had been a note of incongruity. Here he seemed so thoroughly in accord with the air of masculine and cultivated refinement which dominated the atmosphere. He carried himself with the ease and dignity to which his race entitled him, but, apart from that, his manner had qualities which Arnold found particularly attractive. His manicured nails, his spotless linen, his links and waistcoat buttons, — cut from some quaint stone, — the slight affectations of his dress, the unusual manner of brushing back his hair and arranging his tie, gave him only a note of individuality. Every word he spoke — and he talked softly but continually during the service of the meal — confirmed Arnold's first impressions of him. He was a man, at least, who had lived a man's life without fear or weakness, and, whatever his standards might be, he would adhere to them.

Dinner was noiselessly and perfectly served by the butler who had first appeared, and a slighter and smaller edition of himself who brought him the dishes. There was no champagne, but other wines were served in their due order, the quality of which Arnold appreciated, although more than one was strange to him. With the removal of the last course, fruit was placed upon the table, with a decanter of *Chateau Yquem*. On a small table near was a brass pot of coffee and a flask of green liqueur. Sabatini pushed the cigarettes towards his companion.

"I have a fancy to talk to you seriously," he said, without any preamble.

Arnold looked at him in some surprise.

"I am not a philanthropist," continued Sabatini. "When I move out of my regular course of life it is usually for my own advantage. I warn you of that before we start."

Arnold nodded and lit his cigarette fearlessly. There was no safety in life, he reflected, thinking for the moment of the warning which he had received, like the safety of poverty.

"I am a man of forty-one," Sabatini said. "You, I believe, are twenty-four. There can, therefore, be no impertinences in the truth from me to you."

"There could be none in any case," Arnold assured him.

Sabatini gazed thoughtfully across the table into his guest's face.

"I do not know your history or your parentage," he went on. "Such knowledge is unnecessary. It is obvious that your position at the present moment is the result of an accident."

"It is the outcome of actual poverty," Arnold told him softly.

Sabatini assented.

"Ah! well," he said, "it is a poverty, then, which you have accepted. Tell me, then, of your ambition! You are young, and the world lies before you. You have the gifts which belong to those who are born. Are you doing what is right to yourself in working at a degrading employment for a pittance?"

"I must live," Arnold protested simply.

"Precisely," replied Sabatini. "We all must live. We all, however, are too apt to accept the rulings of circumstance. I maintain that we all have a right to live in the manner to which we are born."

"And how," asked Arnold, "does one enforce that right?"

Sabatini leaned over and helped himself to the liqueur.

"You possess the gift," he remarked, "which I admire most — the gift of directness. Now I would speak to you of myself. When I was young, I was penniless, with no inheritance save a grim castle, a barren island, and a great name. The titular head of my family was a Cardinal of Rome, my father's own brother. I went to him, and I demanded the means of support. He answered me with an epigram which I will not repeat, besides which it is untranslatable. I will only tell you that he gave me a sum equivalent to a few hundred pounds, and bade me seek my fortune."

Arnold was intensely interested.

"Tell me how you started!" he begged.

"A few hundred pounds were insufficient," Sabatini answered coolly, "and my uncle was a coward. I waited my opportunity, and although three times I was denied an audience, on the fourth I found him alone. He would have driven me out but I used the means which I have never known to fail. I left him with a small but sufficient fortune."

Arnold looked at him with glowing eyes.

"You forced him to give it you!" he exclaimed.

"Without a doubt," Sabatini answered, coolly. "He was wealthy and he was my uncle. I was strong and he was weak. It was as necessary for me to live as for him. So I took him by the throat and gave him thirty seconds to reflect. He decided that the life of a Cardinal of Rome was far too pleasant to be abandoned precipitately."

There was a short silence. Sabatini glanced twice at his companion and smiled.

"I will read your thoughts, my young friend," he continued. "Your brain is a little confused. You are wondering whether indeed I have robbed my elderly relative. Expunge that word and all that it means to you from your vocabulary, if you can. I took that to which I had a right by means of the weapons which have been given to me — strength and opportunity. These are the weapons which I have used through life."

"Supposing the Cardinal had refused?" Arnold asked.

"One need not suppose," Sabatini replied. "It is not worth while. I should probably have done what the impulse of the moment demanded. So far, however, I have found most people reasonable."

"There have been others, then?" Arnold demanded.

"There have been others," Sabatini agreed calmly; "always people, however, upon whom I have had a certain claim. Life to different people means different things. Life to a person of my tastes and descent meant this — it meant playing a part in the affairs of the country which gave me my birthright; it meant the carrying forward of a great enmity which has burned within the family of Sabatini for the house which now rules my country, for hundreds of years. If I were a person who sought for excuses, I might say that I have robbed my relatives for the cause of the patriot. Life to a sawer of wood means bread. The two states themselves are identical. The man who is denied bread breaks into riot and gains his ends. I, when I have been denied what amounts to me as bread, have also helped myself."

"I am not sure," Arnold protested, frankly, "whether you are not amusing yourself with me."

"Then let me put that doubt to rest, once and for all," Sabatini replied. "It does not amuse me to trifle with the truth."

"Why do you make me your confidant?" Arnold asked.

"Because it is my intention to make a convert of you," Sabatini said calmly.

Arnold shook his head.

"I am afraid that that is quite hopeless," he answered. "I have not the excuse of a country which needs my help, although I have more than one relative," he added, with a smile, "whom I should not mind taking by the throat."

"One needs no excuse," Sabatini murmured.

"When one —"

He hesitated.

"I have no scruples," Sabatini interrupted, "in using the word which seems to trouble you. Perhaps I am a robber. What, however, you do not appreciate is that nine-tenths of the people in the world are in the same position."

"I cannot admit that either," Arnold protested.

"It is, then, because you have not considered the matter," Sabatini declared. "You live in a very small corner of the world and you have accepted a moral code as ridiculously out of date as Calvinism in religion. The whole of life is a system of robbery. The strong help themselves, the weak go down. Did you call your splendid seamen of Queen Elizabeth's time robbers, because they nailed the English flag to their mast and swept the seas for plunder? 'We are strong,' they cried to the country they robbed, 'and you are weak. Stand and deliver!' I spare you a hundred instances. Take your commercial life of today. The capitalist stretches out his hand and swallows up the weaker man. He does it ten or fifty times a day and there is no one to stop him. It is the strong taking from the weak. You cannot walk from here to Charing Cross without seeing it. Some forms of plunder come under the law, some do not. Your idea as to which are right and which are wrong is simply the law's idea. The man who is strong enough is the law."

"Your doctrines are far-reaching," Arnold said. "What about the man who sweeps the crossings, the beggars who ask for alms?"

"They sweep crossings and they beg for alms," Sabatini replied, "because they are weak or foolish and because I am strong. You work for twenty-eight shillings a week because you are foolish. You can do it if you like, if it affords you any satisfaction to make a martyr of yourself for the sake of bolstering up a conventional system. Either that or you have not the spirit for adventure."

"The spirit for adventure," Arnold repeated quietly. "Well, there have been times when I thought I had that, but it certainly never occurred to me to go out and rob."

"That," Sabatini declared, "is because you are an Englishman and extraordinarily susceptible to conventions. Now I speak with many experiences behind me. I had ancestors who enriched themselves with fire and sword. I would much prefer to do the same thing. As a matter of fact, when the conditions admit of it, I do. I have fought in whatever war has raged since the days when I was eighteen. If another war should break out tomorrow, I should weigh the causes, choose the side I preferred, and fight for it. But when there is no war, I must yet live. I cannot drill troops all day, or sit in the cafés. I must use my courage and my brains in whatever way seems most beneficial to the cause which lies nearest to my heart."

"I cannot imagine," Arnold said frankly, "what that cause is."

"Some day, and before long," Sabatini replied, "you may know. At any rate, we have talked enough of this for the present. Think over what I have said. If at any time I should have an enterprise to propose to you, you will at least recognize my point of view."

He touched the bell. A servant entered almost at once, carrying his overcoat and silk hat.

"I have taken a box at a music-hall," he announced. "I believe that my sister may join us there. I hope it will amuse you?"

Arnold rose eagerly to his feet. His eyes were bright already with anticipation.

"And as for our conversation," Sabatini continued, as they stepped into his little electric brougham, "dismiss it, for the present, from your memory. Try and look out upon life with larger eyes, from a broader point of view. Forget the laws that have been made by other men. Try and frame for yourself a more rational code of living. And judge not with the ready-made judgment of laws, but from your own consciousness of right and wrong. You are at an impressionable age, and the effort should help to make a man of you."

They glided softly along the crowded streets and up into Leicester Square, where the blaze of lights seemed somehow comforting after the cold darkness of the night. They stopped outside the *Empire* and Arnold followed his guide with beating heart as they were shown to their box. The door was thrown open. Fenella was there alone. She was sitting a little way back in the box so as to escape observation from the house. At the sound of their entrance she turned eagerly toward them. Arnold, who was in advance, stopped short in the act of greeting her. She was looking past him at her brother. She was absolutely colorless, her lips were parted, her eyes distended as though with terror. She had all the appearance of a woman who has looked upon some terrible thing.

# CHAPTER XV

## THE RED SIGNET RING

The few minutes which followed inspired Arnold with an admiration for his companion which he never wholly lost. Sabatini recognized in a moment his sister's state, but he did no more than shrug his shoulders.

"My dear Fenella!" he said, in a tone of gentle reproof.

"You haven't heard?" she gasped.

Sabatini drew out a chair and seated himself. He glanced around at the house and then began slowly to unbutton his white kid gloves.

"I did not buy an evening paper," he remarked. "Your face tells me the news, of course. I gather that Starling has been arrested."

"He was arrested at five o'clock!" she exclaimed. "He will be charged before the magistrates tomorrow."

"Then tomorrow," Sabatini continued calmly, "will be quite time enough for you to begin to worry."

She looked at him for a moment steadfastly. She had ceased to tremble now and her own appearance was becoming more natural.

"If one had but a man's nerve!" she murmured. "Dear Andrea, you make me very much ashamed. Yet this is serious — surely it is very serious?"

Arnold had withdrawn as far as possible out of hearing, but Sabatini beckoned him forward.

"You are missing the ballet," he said. "You must take the front chair there. You, too, will be interested in this news which my sister has been telling me. Our friend Starling has been arrested, after all. I was afraid he was giving himself away."

"For the murder of Mr. Rosario?" Arnold asked.

"Precisely," Sabatini replied. "A very unfortunate circumstance. Let us hope that he will be able to prove his innocence."

"I don't see how he could have done it," Arnold said slowly. "We saw him only about ten minutes or a quarter of an hour later coming up from the restaurant on the other side of the hotel."

"Oh! he will come very near proving an alibi, without a doubt," Sabatini declared. "He is quite clever when it comes to the point. I wonder what sort of evidence they have against him."

"Is there any reason," Arnold asked, "why he should kill Mr. Rosario?"

Sabatini studied his program earnestly.

"Well," he admitted, "that is rather a difficult question to answer. Mr. Rosario was a very obstinate man, and he was certainly persisting in a course of action against which I and many others had warned him, a course of action which was certain to make him exceedingly unpopular with a good many of us. I am not sure, however, whether the facts were sufficiently well known —"

Fenella interrupted. She rose hurriedly to her feet.

"I am afraid, after all, that you will have to excuse me," she declared, moving to a seat at the back of the box. "I do not think that I can stay here."

Sabatini nodded gravely.

"Perhaps you are right," he said. "For my own part, I, too, wish I had more faith in Starling. As a matter of fact, I have none. When they caught Crampton, one could sleep in one's bed; one knew. But this man Starling is a nervous wreck. Who knows what story he may tell — consciously or unconsciously — in his desperate attempts to clear himself? You see," he continued, looking at Arnold, "there are a great many of us to whom Mr. Rosario was personally, just at this moment, obnoxious."

Fenella swayed in her chair.

"I am going home," she murmured.

"As you will," Sabatini agreed. "Perhaps Mr. Chetwode will be so kind as to take you back? I have asked a friend to call here this evening."

She turned to Arnold.

"Do!" she pleaded. "I am fit for nothing else. You will come with me?"

Arnold was already standing with his coat upon his arm.

"Of course," he replied.

Her brother helped her on with her cloak.

"For myself," he declared, "I shall remain. I should not like to miss my friend, if he comes, and they tell me that the second ballet is excellent."

She took his hands.

"You have courage, dear one," she murmured.

He smiled.

"It is not courage," he replied, "it is philosophy. If tomorrow were to be the end, would you not enjoy today? The true reasonableness of life is to live as though every day might be one's last. We shall meet again very soon, Mr. Chetwode."

Arnold held out his hands. The whole affair was intensely mysterious, and there were many things which he did not understand in the least, but he knew that he was in the presence of a brave man.

"Good night, Count Sabatini," he said. "Thank you very much for our dinner. I am afraid I am an unconverted Philistine, and doomed to the narrow ways, but, nevertheless, I have enjoyed my evening very much."

Sabatini smiled charmingly.

"You are very British," he declared, "but never mind. Even a Briton has been known to see the truth by gazing long enough. Take care of my little sister, and au revoir!"

Her fingers clutched his arm as they passed along the promenade and down the corridor into the street. The car was waiting, and in a moment or two they were on their way to Hampstead. She was beginning to look a little more natural, but she still clung to him. Arnold felt his head dizzy as though with strong wine.

"Fenella," he said, using her name boldly, "your brother has been talking to me tonight. All that he said I can understand, from his point of view, but what may be well for him is not well for others who are weaker. If you have been foolish, if the love of adventure has led you into any folly, think now and ask yourself whether it is worth while. Give it up before it is too late."

"It is because I have so little courage," she murmured, looking at him with swimming eyes, "and one must do something. I must live or the tugging of the chain is there all the time."

"There are many things in life which are worth while," he declared. "You are young and rich, and you have a husband who would do anything in the world for you. It isn't worth while to get mixed up in these dangerous schemes."

"What do you know of them?" she asked, curiously.

"Not much," he admitted. "Your brother was talking tonight a little recklessly. One gathered —"

"Andrea sometimes talks wildly because it amuses him to deceive people, to make them think that he is worse than he really is," she interrupted. "He loves danger, but it is because he is a brave man."

"I am sure of it," Arnold replied, "but it does not follow that he is a wise one."

She shrugged her shoulders.

"Tell me one of those many ways of living which are worth while!" she whispered. "Point out one of them only. Remember that I, too, have the spirit of restlessness in my veins. I must have excitement at any cost."

He sighed. She was, indeed, in a strange place.

"It seems so hopeless," he said, "to try and interest you in the ordinary things of life."

"No one could do it," she admitted. "I was not made for domesticity. Sometimes I think that I was not made to be wife to any man. I am a gambler at heart. I love the fierce draughts of life. Without them I should die."

"Yet you married Samuel Weatherley!" Arnold exclaimed.

She laughed bitterly.

"Yes, I was in a prison house," she answered, "and I should have welcomed any jailer who had come to set me free. I married him, and sometimes I try to do my duty. Then the other longings come, and Hampstead and my house, and my husband and my parties and my silly friends, seem like part of a dream. Mr. Chetwode — Arnold!"

"Fenella!"

"We were to be friends, we were to help one another. Tonight I am afraid and I think that I am a little remorseful. It was my doing that you dined tonight with Andrea. I have wanted to bring you, too, into the life that my brother lives, into the life where I also make sometimes excursions. It is not a wicked life, but I do not know that it is a wise one. I was foolish. It was wrong of me to disturb you. After all, you are good and solid and British, you were meant for the other ways. Forget everything. It is less than a week since you came first to dine with us. Blot out those few days. Can you?"

"Not while I live," Arnold replied. "You forget that it was during those few days that I met you."

"But you are foolish," she declared, laying her hand upon his and smiling into his face, so that the madness came back and burned in his blood. "There is no need for you to be a gambler, there is no need for you to stake everything upon these single coups. You haven't felt the call. Don't listen for it."

"Fenella," he whispered hoarsely, "what was I doing when Samuel Weatherley was shipwrecked on your island!"

She laughed.

"Oh, you foolish boy!" she cried. "What difference would it have made?"

"You can't tell," he answered. "Has no one ever moved you, Fenella? Have you never known what it is to care for any one?"

"Never," she replied. "I only hope that I never shall."

"Why not?"

"Because I am a gambler," she declared; "because to me it would mean risking everything. And I have seen no man in the whole world strong enough and big enough for that. You are my very dear friend, Arnold, and you are feeling very sentimental, and your head is turned just a little, but after all you are only a boy. The taste of life is not yet between your teeth."

He leaned closer towards her. She put his arm gently away, shaking her head all the time.

"Do not think that I am a prude," she said. "You can kiss me if you like, and yet I would very much rather that you did not. I do not know why. I like you well enough, and certainly it is not from any sense of right or wrong. I am like Andrea in that way. I make my own laws. Tonight I do not wish you to kiss me."

She was looking up at him, her eyes filled with a curious light, her lips slightly parted. She was so close that the perfume in which her clothes had lain, faint though it was, almost maddened him.

"I don't think that you have a heart at all!" he exclaimed, hoarsely.

"It is the old selfish cry, that," she answered. "Please do not be foolish, Arnold. Do not be like those silly boys who only plague one. With you and me, things are more serious."

The car came to a standstill before the portals of Pelham Lodge. Arnold held her fingers for a moment or two after he had rung the bell. Then he turned away. She called him back.

"Come in with me for a moment," she murmured. "Tonight I am afraid. Mr. Weatherley will be in bed. Come in and sit with me for a little time until my courage returns."

He followed her into the house. There seemed to Arnold to be a curious silence everywhere. She looked in at several rooms and nodded.

"Mr. Weatherley has gone to bed," she announced. "Come into my sitting-room. We will stay there for five minutes, at least."

She led the way across the hall towards the little room into which she had taken Arnold on his first visit. She tried the door and came to a sudden standstill, shook the handle, and looked up at Arnold in amazement.

"It seems as though it were locked," she remarked. "It's my own sitting-room. No one else is allowed to enter it. Groves!"

She turned round. The butler had hastened to her side.

"What is the meaning of this?" she asked. "My sitting-room is locked on the inside."

The man tried the handle incredulously. He, too, was dumbfounded.

"Where is your master?" Mrs. Weatherley asked.

"He retired an hour ago, madam," the man replied. "It is most extraordinary, this."

She began to shiver. Groves leaned down and tried to peer through the keyhole. He rose to his feet hastily.

"The lights are burning in the room, madam," he exclaimed, "and the key is not in the door on the other side! It looks very much as though burglars were at work there. If you will allow me, I will go round to the window outside. There is no one else up."

"I will go with you," Arnold said.

"If you please, sir," the man replied.

They hurried out of the front door and around to the side of the house. The lights were certainly burning in the room and the blind was half drawn up. Arnold reached the windowsill with a spring and peered in.

"I can see nothing," he said to Groves. "There doesn't seem to be any one in the room."

"Can you get in, sir?" the man asked from below. "The sash seems to be unfastened."

Arnold tried it and found it yielded to his touch. He pushed it up and vaulted lightly into the room. Then he saw that a table was overturned and a key was lying on the floor. He picked it up and fitted it into the door. Fenella was waiting outside.

"I can see nothing here," he announced, "but a table has been upset."

She pointed to the sofa and gripped his arm.

"Look!" she cried. "What is that?"

Arnold felt a thrill of horror, and for a moment the room swam before his eyes. Then he saw clearly again. From underneath the upholstery of the sofa, a man's hand was visible stretching into the room almost as far as his elbow. They both stared, Arnold stupefied with horror. On the little finger of the hand was a ring with a blood-red seal!

# CHAPTER XVI

## AN ADVENTURE

Arnold, for a moment or two, felt himself incapable of speech or movement. Fenella was hanging, a dead weight, upon his arm. The eyes of both of them were riveted upon the hand which stretched into the room.

"There is some one under the couch!" Fenella faltered at last.

He took a step forward.

"Wait," he begged, " — or perhaps you had better go away. I will see who it is."

He moved toward the couch. She strove to hold him back.

"Arnold," she cried, hoarsely, "this is no business of yours! You had better leave me! Groves is here, and the servants. Slip away now, while you have the chance."

He looked at her in amazement.

"Why, Fenella," he exclaimed, "how can you suggest such a thing! Besides," he added, "Groves saw me climb in at the window. He was with me outside."

She wrung her hands.

"I forgot!" she moaned. "Don't move the sofa while I am looking!"

There was a knock at the door. They both turned round. It was Groves' voice speaking. He had returned to the house and was waiting outside.

"Can I come in, madam?"

Fenella moved slowly towards the door and admitted him. Then Arnold, setting his teeth, rolled back the couch. A man was lying there, stretched at full length. His face was colorless except for a great blue bruise near his temple. Arnold stared at him for a moment with horrified eyes.

"My God!" he muttered.

There was a brief silence. Fenella looked across at Arnold.

"You know him!"

Arnold's first attempt at speech failed. When the words came they sounded choked. There was a horrible dry feeling in his throat.

"It is the man who looked in at the window that night," he whispered. "I saw him — only a few hours ago. It is the same man."

Fenella came slowly to his side. She leaned over his shoulder.

"Is he dead?" she asked.

Her tone was cold and unnatural. Her paroxysm of fear seemed to have passed.

"I don't know," Arnold answered. "Let Groves telephone for a doctor."

The man half turned away, yet hesitated. Fenella fell on her knees and bent over the prostrate body.

"He is not dead," she declared. "Groves, tell me exactly who is in the house?"

"There is no one here at all, madam," the man answered, "except the servants, and they are all in the other wing. We have had no callers whatever this evening."

"And Mr. Weatherley?"

"Mr. Weatherley arrived home about seven o'clock," Groves replied, "dined early, and went to bed immediately afterwards. He complained of a headache and looked very unwell."

Fenella rose slowly to her feet. She looked from Arnold to the prostrate figure upon the carpet.

"Who has done this?" she asked, pointing downwards.

"It may have been an accident," Arnold suggested.

"An accident!" she repeated. "What was he doing in my sitting-room? Besides, he could not have crept underneath the couch of his own accord."

"Do you know who it is?" Arnold asked.

"Why should I know?" she demanded.

He hesitated.

"You remember the night of my first visit here — the face at the window?"

She nodded. He pointed downward to the outstretched hand.

"That is the man," he declared. "He is wearing the same ring — the red signet ring. I saw it upon his hand the night you and I were in this room alone together, and he was watching the house. I saw it again through the window of the swing-doors on the hand of the man who killed Rosario. What does it mean, Fenella?"

"I do not know," she faltered.

"You must have some idea," he persisted, "as to who he is. You seemed to expect his coming that night. You would not let me give an alarm or send for the police. It was the same man who killed Rosario."

She shook her head.

"I do not believe that," she declared.

"If it were not the same man," Arnold continued, "it was at least some one who was wearing the same ring. Tell me the truth, Fenella!"

She turned her head. Groves had come once more within hearing.

"I know nothing," she replied, hardly. "Groves, go and knock at the door of your master's room," she added. "Ask him to put on his dressing-gown and come down at once. Mr. Chetwode, come with me into the library while I telephone for the doctor."

Arnold hesitated for a moment.

"Don't you think that I had better stay by him?" he suggested.

She shook her head.

"I will not be left alone," she replied. "I told you on the way here that I was afraid. All the evening I knew that something would happen."

They made their way to the front of the house and into the library. She turned up the electric lights and fetched a telephone book. Arnold rang up the number she showed him.

"What about the police station?" he asked, turning towards her with the receiver still in his hand. "Oughtn't I to send for some one?"

"Not yet," she replied. "We are not supposed to know. The man may have come upon some business. Let us wait and see what the doctor says."

He laid down the receiver. She had thrown herself into an easychair and with a little impulsive gesture she held out one hand towards him.

"Poor Arnold!" she murmured. "I am afraid that this is all very bewildering to you, and your life was so peaceful until a week ago."

He held her fingers tightly. Notwithstanding the shadows under her eyes, and the gleam of terror which still lingered there, she was beautiful.

"I don't care about that," he answered, fervently. "I don't care about anything except that I should like to understand a little more clearly what it all means. I hate mysteries. I don't see why you can't tell me. I am your friend. If it is necessary for me to say nothing, I shall say nothing, but I hate the thoughts that come to me sometimes. Tell me, why should that man have been haunting your house the other evening? What did he want? And tonight — what made him break into your room?"

She sighed.

"If it were only so simple as all that," she answered, "oh! I would tell you so willingly. But it is not. There is so much which I do not understand myself."

He leaned a little closer towards her. The silence of the room and the house was unbroken.

"The man will die!" he said. "Who do you believe could have struck him that blow in your room?"

"I do not know," she answered; "indeed I do not."

"You heard what Groves said," Arnold continued. "There is no one in the house except the servants."

"That man was here," she answered. "Why not others? Listen."

There was the sound of shuffling footsteps in the hall. She held up her finger cautiously.

"Be very careful before Mr. Weatherley," she begged. "It is an ordinary burglary, this — no more."

The door was opened. Mr. Weatherley, in hasty and most unbecoming deshabille, bustled in. His scanty gray hair was sticking out in patches all over his head. He seemed, as yet, scarcely awake. With one hand he clutched at the dressing-gown, the girdle of which was trailing behind him.

"What is the meaning of this, Fenella?" he demanded. "Why am I fetched from my room in this manner? You, Chetwode? What are you doing here?"

"I have brought Mrs. Weatherley home, sir," Arnold answered. "We noticed a light in her room and we made a discovery there. It looks as though there has been an attempted burglary within the last hour or so."

"Which room?" Mr. Weatherley asked. "Which room? Is anything missing?"

"Nothing, fortunately," Arnold replied. "The man, by some means or other, seems to have been hurt."

"Where is he?" Mr. Weatherley demanded.

"In my boudoir," Fenella replied. "We will all go. I have telephoned for a doctor."

"A doctor? What for?" Mr. Weatherley inquired. "Who needs a doctor?"

"The burglar, if he is a burglar," she explained, gently. "Don't you understand that all we found was a man, lying in the centre of the room? He has had a fall of some sort."

"God bless my soul!" Mr. Weatherley said. "Well, come along, let's have a look at him."

They trooped down the passage. Groves, waiting outside for them, opened the door. Mr. Weatherley, who was first, looked all around the apartment.

"Where is this man?" he demanded. "Where is he?"

Arnold, who followed, was stricken speechless. Fenella gave a little cry. The couch had been wheeled back to its place. The body of the man had disappeared!

"Where is the burglar?" Mr. Weatherley repeated, irritably. "Was there ever any one here? Who in the name of mischief left that window open?"

The window through which Arnold had entered the room was now wide open. They hurried towards it. Outside, all was darkness. There was no sound of footsteps, no sign of any person about. Mr. Weatherley was distinctly annoyed.

"I should have thought you would have had more sense, Chetwode," he said, testily. "You found a burglar here, and, instead of securing him properly, you send up to me and go ringing up for doctors, and in the meantime the man calmly slips off through the window."

Arnold made no reply. Mr. Weatherley's words seemed to come from a long way off. He was looking at Fenella.

"The man was dead!" he muttered.

She, too, was white, but she shook her head.

"We thought so," she answered. "We were wrong."

Mr. Weatherley led the way to the front door.

"As the dead man seems to have cleared out," he said, "without taking very much with him, I suggest that we go to bed. Groves had better ring up the doctor and stop him, if he can; if not, he must explain that he was sent for in error. Good night, Chetwode!" he added, pointedly.

Arnold scarcely remembered his farewells. He passed out into the street and stood for several moments upon the pavement. He looked back at the house.

"The man was dead or dying!" he muttered to himself. "What does it all mean?"

He walked slowly away. There was a policeman on the other side of the road, taxicabs and carriages coming and going. He passed the gate of Pelham Lodge and looked back toward the window of the sitting-room. Within five minutes the man must have left that room by the window. That he could have left it unaided, even if alive, was impossible. Yet there was not anything in the avenue, or thereabouts, to denote that anything unusual had occurred. He was on the point of turning away when a sudden thought struck him. He re-entered the gate softly and walked up the drive. Arrived at within a few feet of the window, he paused and turned to the right. A narrow path led him into a shrubbery. A few more yards and he reached a wire fence. Stepping across it, he found himself in the next garden. Here he paused for a moment and listened. The house before which he stood was smaller than Pelham Lodge, and woefully out of repair. The grass on the lawn was long and dank — even the board containing the notice "To Let" had fallen flat, and lay among it as in a jungle. The paths were choked with weeds, the windows were black and curtainless. He made his way to the back of the house and suddenly stopped short. This was a night of adventures, indeed! On a level with the ground, the windows of one of the back rooms were boarded up. Through the chinks he could distinctly see gleams of light. Standing there, holding his breath, he could even hear the murmur of voices. There were men there — several of them, to judge by the sound. He drew nearer and nearer until he found a chink through which he could see. Then, for the first time, he hesitated. It was not his affair, this. There were mysteries connected with Pelham Lodge and its occupants which were surely no concern of his. Why interfere? Danger might come of it — danger and other troubles. Fenella would have told him if she had wished him to know. She herself must have some idea as to the reason of this attempt upon her house. Why not slip away quietly and forget it? It was at least the most prudent course. Then, as he hesitated, the memory of Sabatini's words, so recently spoken, came into his mind. Almost he could see him leaning back in his chair with the faint smile upon his lips. "You have not the spirit for adventure!" Then Arnold hesitated no longer. Choosing every footstep carefully, he crept to the window until he could press his face close to the chink through which the light gleamed out into the garden.

# CHAPTER XVII

## THE END OF AN EVENING

To see into the room at all, Arnold had been compelled to step down from the grass on to a narrow, tiled path about half a yard wide, which led to the back door. Standing on this and peering through the chink in the boards, he gained at last a view of the interior of the house. From the first, he had entered upon this search with a certain presentiment. He looked into the room and shivered. It was apparently the kitchen, and was unfurnished save for half a dozen rickety chairs, and a deal table in the middle of the room. Upon this was stretched the body of a motionless man. There were three others in the room. One, who appeared to have some knowledge of medicine, had taken off his coat and was listening with his ear against the senseless man's heart. A brandy bottle stood upon the table. They had evidently been doing what they could to restore him to consciousness. Terrible though the sight was, Arnold found something else in that little room to kindle his emotion. Two of the men were unknown to him — dark-complexioned, ordinary middle-class people; but the third he recognized with a start. It was Isaac who stood there, a little aloof, waiting somberly for what his companion's verdict might be.

Apparently, after a time, they gave up all hope of the still motionless man. They talked together, glancing now and then towards his body. The window was open at the top and Arnold could sometimes hear a word. With great difficulty, he gathered that they were proposing to remove him, and that they were taking the back way. Presently he saw them lift the body down and wrap it in an overcoat. Then Arnold stole away across the lawn toward a gate in the wall. It was locked, but it was easy for him to climb over. He had barely done so when he saw the three men come out of the back of the house, carrying their wounded comrade. He waited till he was sure they were coming, and then looked around for a hiding-place. He was now in a sort of lane, ending in a *cul de sac* at the back of Mr. Weatherley's house. There were gardens on one side, parallel with the one through which he had just passed, and opposite were stables, motor sheds and tool houses. He slipped a little way down the lane and concealed himself behind a load of wood. About forty yards away was a street, for which he imagined that they would probably make. He held his breath and waited.

In a few minutes he saw the door in the wall open. One of the men slipped out and looked up and down. He apparently signaled that the coast was clear, and soon the others followed him. They came down the lane, walking very slowly — a weird and uncanny little procession. Arnold caught a glimpse of them as they passed. The two larger men were supporting their fallen companion between them, each with an arm under his armpits, so that the fact that he was really being carried was barely noticeable. Isaac came behind, his hands thrust deep into his overcoat pocket, a cloth cap drawn over his features. So they went on to the end of the lane. As soon as they had reached it, Arnold followed them swiftly. When he gained the street, they were about twenty yards to the right, looking around them. It was a fairly populous neighborhood, with a row of villas on the other side of the road, and a few shops lower down. They stood there, having carefully chosen a place remote from the gas lamps, until at last a taxicab came crawling by. They hailed it, and Isaac engaged the driver's attention apparently with some complicated direction, while the others lifted their burden into the taxicab. One man got in with him. Isaac and the other, with ordinary good-nights, strode away. The taxicab turned around and headed westward. Arnold, with a long breath, watched them all disappear. Then he, too, turned homewards.

It was almost midnight when Arnold was shown once more into the presence of Sabatini. Sabatini, in a black velvet smoking jacket, was lying upon a sofa in his library, with a recently published edition *de luxe* of Alfred de Musset's poems upon his knee. He looked up with some surprise at Arnold's entrance.

"Why, it is my strenuous young friend again!" he declared. "Have you brought me a message from Fenella?"

Arnold shook his head.

"She does not know that I have come."

"You have brought me some news on your own account, then?"

"I have brought you some news," Arnold admitted.

Sabatini looked at him critically.

"You look terrified," he remarked. "What have you been doing? Help yourself to a drink. You'll find everything on the sideboard there."

Arnold laid down his hat and mixed himself a whiskey and soda. He drank it off before he spoke.

"Count Sabatini," he said, turning round, "I suppose you are used to all this excitement. A man's life or death is little to you. I have never seen a dead man before tonight. It has upset me."

"Naturally, naturally," Sabatini said, tolerantly. "I remember the first man I killed — it was in a fair fight, too, but it sickened me. But what have you been doing, my young friend, to see dead men? Have you, too, been joining the army of plunderers?"

Arnold shook his head.

"I took your sister home," he announced. "We found a light in her sitting-room and the door locked. I got in through the window."

"This is most interesting," Sabatini declared, carefully marking the place in his book and laying it aside. "What did you find there?"

"A dead man," Arnold answered, "a murdered man!"

"You are joking!" Sabatini protested.

"He had been struck on the forehead," Arnold continued, "and dragged half under the couch. Only his arm was visible at first. We had to move the couch to discover him."

"Do you know who he was?" Sabatini asked.

"No one had any idea," Arnold answered. "I think that I was the only one who had ever seen him before. The night I dined at Mr. Weatherley's for the first time and met you, I was with Mrs. Weatherley in her room, and I saw that man steal up to the window as though he were going to break in."

"This is most interesting," Sabatini declared. "Evidently a dangerous customer. But you say that you found him dead. Who killed him?"

"There was no one there who could say," Arnold declared. "There were no servants in that part of the house, there had been no visitors, and Mr. Weatherley had been in bed since half-past nine. We telephoned for a doctor, and we fetched Mr. Weatherley out of bed. Then a strange thing happened. We took Mr. Weatherley to the room, which we had left for less than five minutes, and there was no one there. The man had been carried away."

"Really," Sabatini protested, "your story gets more interesting every moment. Don't tell me that this is the end!"

"It is not," Arnold replied. "It seemed then as though there were nothing more to be done. Evidently he had either been only stunned and had got up and left the room by the window, or he had accomplices who had fetched him away. Mr. Weatherley was very much annoyed with us and we had to make excuses to the doctor. Then I left."

"Well?" Sabatini said. "You left. You didn't come straight here?"

Arnold shook his head.

"When I got into the road, I could see that there was a policeman on duty on the other side of the way, and quite a number of people moving backwards and forwards all the time. It seemed impossible that they could have brought him out there if he had been fetched away. Something made me remember what I had noticed on the evening I had dined there — that there was a small empty house next door. I walked back up the drive of Pelham Lodge, turned into the shrubbery, and there I found that there was an easy way into the next garden. I made my way to the back of the house. I saw lights in the kitchen. There were three of his companions there, and the dead man. They were trying to see if they could revive him. I looked through a chink in the boarded window and I saw everything."

"Trying to revive him," Sabatini remarked. "Evidently there was some doubt as to his being dead, then."

"I think they had come to the conclusion that he was dead," Arnold replied; "for after a time they put on his overcoat and dragged him out by the back entrance, down some mews, into another street. I followed them at a distance. They hailed a taxi. One man got in with him and drove away, the others disappeared. I came here."

Sabatini reached out his hand for a cigarette.

"I have seldom," he declared, "listened to a more interesting episode. You didn't happen to hear the direction given to the driver of the taxicab?"

"I did not."

"You have no idea, I suppose," Sabatini asked, with a sudden keen glance, "as to the identity of the man whom you believe to be dead?"

"None whatever," Arnold replied, "except that it was the same man who was watching the house on the night when I dined there. He told me then that he wanted Rosario. There was something evil in his face when he mentioned the name. I saw his hand grasping the windowsill. He was wearing a ring — a signet ring with a blood-red stone."

"This is most engrossing," Sabatini murmured. "A signet ring with a blood-red stone! Wasn't there a ring answering to that description upon the finger of the man who stabbed Rosario?"

"There was," Arnold answered.

Sabatini knocked the ash from his cigarette.

"The coincidence," he remarked, "if it is a coincidence, is a little extraordinary. By the bye, though, you have as yet given me no explanation as to your visit here. Why do you connect me with this adventure of yours?"

"I do not connect you with it at all," Arnold answered; "yet, for some reason or other, I am sure that your sister knew more about this man and his presence in her sitting-room than she cared to confess. When I left there, everything was in confusion. I have come to tell you the final result, so far as I know it. You will tell her what you choose. What she knows, I suppose you know. I don't ask for your confidence. I have had enough of these horrors. Tooley Street is bad enough, but I think I would rather sit in my office and add up figures all day long, than go through another such night."

Sabatini smiled.

"You are young, as yet," he said. "Life and death seem such terrible things to you, such tragedies, such enormous happenings. In youth, one loses one's sense of proportion. Life seems so vital, the universe so empty, without one's own personality. Take a pocketful of cigarettes, my dear Mr. Chetwode, and make your way homeward. We shall meet again in a day or two, I dare say, and by that time your little nightmare will not seem so terrible."

"You will let your sister know?" Arnold begged.

"She shall know all that you have told me," Sabatini promised. "I do not say that it will interest her — it may or it may not. In any case, I thank you for coming."

Arnold was dismissed with a pleasant nod, and passed out into the streets, now emptying fast. He walked slowly back to his rooms. Already the sense of unwonted excitement was passing. Sabatini's strong, calm personality was like a wonderful antidote. After all, it was not his affair. It was possible, after all, that the man was an ordinary burglar. And yet, if so, what was Isaac doing with him? He glanced in front of him to where the lights of the two great hotels flared up to the sky. Somewhere just short of them, before the window of her room, Ruth would be sitting watching. He quickened his steps. Perhaps he should find her before he went to bed. Perhaps he might even see Isaac come in!

Big Ben was striking the half-hour past midnight as Arnold stood on the top landing of the house at the corner of Adam Street, and listened. To the right was his own bare apartment; on the left, the rooms where Isaac and Ruth lived together. He struck a match and looked into his own apartment. There was a note twisted up for him on his table, scribbled in pencil on a half sheet of paper. He opened it and read:

If you are not too late, will you knock at the door and wish me good night? Isaac will be late. Perhaps he will not be home at all.

He stepped back and knocked softly at the opposite door. In a moment or two he heard the sound of her stick. She opened the door and came out. Her eyes shone through the darkness at him but her face was white and strained. He shook his head.

"Ruth," he said, "you heard the time? And you promised to go to bed at ten o'clock!"

She smiled. He passed his arm around her, holding her up.

"Tonight I was afraid," she whispered. "I do not know what it was but there seemed to be strange voices about everywhere. I was afraid for Isaac and afraid for you."

"My dear girl," he laughed, "what was there to fear for me? I had a very good dinner with a very charming man. Afterwards, we went to a music-hall for a short time, I went back to his rooms, and here I am, just in time to wish you good night. What could the voices have to tell you about that?"

She shook her head.

"Sometimes," she said, "there is danger in the simplest things one does. I don't understand what it is," she went on, a little wearily, "but I feel that I am losing you, you are slipping away, and day by day Isaac gets more mysterious, and when he comes home sometimes his face is like the face of a wolf. There is a new desire born in him, and I am afraid. I think that if I am left alone here many more nights like this, I shall go mad. I tried to undress, Arnie, but I couldn't. I threw myself down on the bed and I had to bite my handkerchief. I have been trembling. Oh, if you could hear those voices! If you could understand the fears that are nameless, how terrible they are!"

She was shaking all over. He passed his other arm around her and lifted her up.

"Come and sit with me in my room for a little time," he said. "I will carry you back presently."

She kissed him on the forehead.

"Dear Arnold!" she whispered. "For a few minutes, then — not too long. Tonight I am afraid. Always I feel that something will happen. Tell me this?"

"What is it, dear?"

"Why should Isaac press me so hard to tell him where you were going tonight? You passed him on the stairs, didn't you?"

Arnold nodded.

"He was with another man," he said, with a little shiver. "Did that man come up to his rooms?"

"They both came in together," Ruth said. "They talked in a corner for some time. The man who was with Isaac seemed terrified about something. Then Isaac came over to me and asked about you."

"What did you tell him?" Arnold asked.

"I thought it best to know nothing at all," she replied. "I simply said that you were going to have dinner with some of your new friends."

"Does he know who they are?"

Ruth nodded.

"Yes, we have spoken of that together," she admitted. "I had to tell him of your good fortune. He knows how well you have been getting on with Mr. and Mrs. Weatherley. Listen! — is that some one coming?"

He turned around with her still in his arms, and started so violently that if her fingers had not been locked behind his neck he must have dropped her. Within a few feet of them was Isaac. He had come up those five flights of stone steps without making a sound. Even in that first second or two of amazement, Arnold noticed that he was wearing canvas shoes with rubber soles. He stood with his long fingers gripping the worn balustrade, only two steps below them, and his face was like the face of some snarling animal.

"Ruth," he demanded, hoarsely, "what are you doing out here at this time of night — with him?"

She slipped from Arnold's arms and leaned on her stick. To all appearance, she was the least discomposed of the three.

"Isaac," she answered, "Uncle Isaac, I was lonely — lonely and terrified. You left me so strangely, and it is so silent up here. I left a little note and asked Arnold, when he came home, to bid me good night. He knocked at my door two minutes ago."

Isaac threw open the door of their apartments.

"Get in," he ordered. "I'll have an end put to it, Ruth. Look at him!" he cried, mockingly, pointing to Arnold's evening clothes. "What sort of a friend is that, do you think, for us? He wears the fetters of his class. He is a hanger-on at the tables of our enemies."

"You can abuse me as much as you like," Arnold replied, calmly, "and I shall still believe that I am an honest man. Are you, Isaac?"

Isaac's eyes flashed venom.

"Honesty! What is honesty?" he snarled. "What is it, I ask you? Is the millionaire honest who keeps the laws because he has no call to break them? Is that honesty? Is he a better man than the father who steals to feed his hungry children? Is the one honest and the other a thief? You smug hypocrite!"

Arnold was silent for a moment. It flashed into his mind that here, from the other side, came very nearly the same doctrine as Sabatini had preached to him across his rose-shaded dining table.

"It is too late to argue with you, Isaac," he said, pleasantly. "Besides, I think that you and I are too far apart. But you must leave me Ruth for my little friend. She would be lonely without me, and I can do her no harm."

Isaac opened his lips, — lips that were set in an ugly sneer — but he met the steady fire of Arnold's eyes, and the words he would have spoken remained unsaid.

"Get to your room, then," he ordered.

He passed on as though to enter his own apartments. Then suddenly he stopped and listened. There was the sound of a footstep, a heavy, marching footstep, coming along the Terrace below. With another look now upon his face, he slunk to the window and peered down. The footsteps came nearer and nearer, and Arnold could hear him breathing like a hunted animal. Then they passed, and he stood up, wiping the sweat from his forehead.

"I have been hurrying," he muttered, half apologetically. "We had a crowded meeting. Good night!"

He turned into his rooms and closed the door. Arnold looked after him for a moment and then up the street below. When he turned into his own rooms, he was little enough inclined for sleep. He drew up his battered chair to the window, threw it open, and sat looking out. The bridge and the river were alike silent now. The sky signs had gone, the murky darkness blotted out the whole scene, against which the curving arc of lights shone with a fitful, ghostly light. For a moment his fancy served him an evil trick. He saw the barge with the blood-red sails. A cargo of evil beings thronged its side. He saw their faces leering at him. Sabatini was there, standing at the helm, calm and scornful. There was the dead man and Isaac, Groves the butler, Fenella herself — pale as death, her hands clasping at her bosom as though in pain. Arnold turned, shivering, away; his head sank into his hands. It seemed to him that poison had crept into those dreams.

# CHAPTER XVIII

## DISCUSSING THE MYSTERY

At precisely half-past nine the next morning, Mr. Weatherley entered his office in Tooley Street. His appearance, as he passed through the outer office, gave rise to some comment.

"The governor looks quite himself again," young Tidey remarked, turning round on his stool.

Mr. Jarvis, who was collecting the letters, nodded.

"It's many months since I've heard him come in whistling," he declared.

Arnold, in the outer office, received his chief's morning salutation with some surprise. Mr. Weatherley was certainly, to all appearance, in excellent spirits.

"Glad to see your late hours don't make any difference in the morning, Chetwode," he said, pleasantly. "You seem to be seeing quite a good deal of the wife, eh?"

Arnold was almost dumbfounded. Any reference to the events of the preceding evening was, for the moment, beyond him. Mr. Weatherley calmly hung up his silk hat, took out the violets from the button-hole of his overcoat and carried them to his desk.

"Come along, Jarvis," he invited, as the latter entered with a rustling heap of correspondence. "We'll sort the letters as quickly as possible this morning. You come on the other side, Chetwode, and catch hold of those which we keep to deal with together. Those Mr. Jarvis can handle, I'll just initial. Let me see — you're sure those bills of lading are in order, Jarvis?"

Mr. Jarvis plunged into a few particulars, to which his chief listened with keen attention. For half an hour or so they worked without a pause. Mr. Weatherley was quite at his best. His instructions were sage, and his grasp of every detail referred to in the various letters was lucid and complete. When at last Mr. Jarvis left with his pile, he did not hesitate to spread the good news. Mr. Weatherley had got over his fit of depression, from whatever cause it had arisen; a misunderstanding with his wife, perhaps, or a certain amount of weariness entailed by his new manner of living. At all events, something had happened to set matters right. Mr. Jarvis was quite fluent upon the subject, and every one started his day's work with renewed energy.

Mr. Weatherley's energy did not evaporate with the departure of his confidential clerk. He motioned Arnold to a chair, and for another three-quarters of an hour he dictated replies to the letters which he had sorted out for personal supervision. When at last this was done, he leaned back in his seat, fetched out a box of cigars, carefully selected one and lit it.

"Now you had better get over to your corner and grind that lot out, Chetwode," he said pleasantly. "How are you getting on with the typing, eh?"

"I am getting quicker," Arnold replied, still wondering whether the whole events of last week had not been a dream. "I think, with a little more practice, I shall be able to go quite fast enough."

"Just so," his employer assented. "By the bye, is it my fancy, or weren't you reading the newspaper when I came in? No time for newspapers, you know, after nine o'clock."

Arnold rose to his feet. This was more than he could bear!

"I am sorry if I seemed inattentive, sir," he said. "Under the circumstances, I could not help dwelling a little over this paragraph. Perhaps you will look at it yourself, sir?"

He brought it over to the desk. Mr. Weatherley put on his spectacles with great care and drew the paper towards him.

"Hm!" he ejaculated. "My eyesight isn't so good as it was, Chetwode, and your beastly ha'penny papers have such small print. Read it out to me — read it out to me while I smoke."

He leaned back in his padded chair, his hands folded in front of him, his cigar in the corner of his mouth. Arnold smoothed the paper out and read:

### TERRIBLE DEATH OF AN UNKNOWN MAN.
### FOUND DEAD IN A TAXICAB.

Early this morning, a taxicab driver entered the police station at Finchley Road North, and alleged that a passenger whom he had picked up some short time before, was dead. Inspector Challis, who was on duty at the time, hastened out to the vehicle and found that the driver's statement was apparently true. The deceased was carried into the police station and a doctor was sent for. The chauffeur's statement was that about midnight he was hailed in the Grove End Road, Hampstead, by four men, one of whom, evidently the deceased, he imagined to be the worse for drink. Two of them entered the taxicab, and one of the others directed him to drive to Finchley. After some distance, however, the driver happened to glance inside, and saw that only one of his passengers was there. He at once stopped the vehicle, looked in at the window, and, finding that the man was unconscious, drove on to the police station.

Later information seems to point to foul play, and there is no doubt whatever that an outrage has been committed. There was a wound upon the deceased's forehead, which the doctor pronounces as the cause of death, and which had evidently been dealt within the last hour or so with some blunt instrument. The taxicab driver has been detained, and a full description of the murdered man's companions has been issued to the police. It is understood that nothing was found upon the deceased likely to help towards his identification.

Arnold looked up as he finished. Mr. Weatherley was still smoking. He seemed, indeed, very little disturbed.

"A sensational story, that, Chetwode," he remarked. "You're not supposing, are you, that it was the same man who broke into my house last night?"

"I know that it was, sir," Arnold replied.

"You know that it was," Mr. Weatherley repeated, slowly. "Come, what do you mean by that?"

"I mean that after I left your house last night, sir," Arnold explained, "I realized the impossibility of that man having been carried down your drive and out into the road, with a policeman on duty directly opposite, and a cabstand within a few yards. I happened to remember that there was an empty house next door, and it struck me that it might be worth while examining the premises."

Mr. Weatherley withdrew the cigar from his mouth.

"You did that, eh?"

"I did," Arnold admitted. "I made my way to the back, and I found a light in the room which presumably had been the kitchen. From a chink in the boarded-up window I saw several men in the room, including the man whom we discovered in your wife's boudoir, and who had been spirited away. He was lying motionless upon the table, and one of the others was apparently trying to restore him. When they found that it was useless, they took him off with them by the back way into Grove Lane. I saw two of them enter a taxicab and the other two make off."

"And what did you do then?" Mr. Weatherley asked.

"I went and told Count Sabatini what I had seen," Arnold replied.

"And after that?"

"I went home."

"You told no one else but Count Sabatini?" Mr. Weatherley persisted.

"No one," Arnold answered. "I bought a paper on my way to business this morning, and read what I have just read to you."

"You haven't been rushing about ringing up to give information, or anything of that sort?"

"I have done nothing," Arnold asserted. "I waited to lay the matter before you."

Mr. Weatherley knocked the ash from his cigar, and, discovering that it was out, carefully relit it.

"Chetwode," he said, "I have advanced you from something a little better than an office-boy, very rapidly, because it seemed to me that you had qualities. The time has arrived to test them. The secret of success in life is minding your own business. I am going to ask you to mind your own business in this matter."

"You mean," Arnold asked, "that you do not wish me to give any information, to say anything about last night?"

"I do not wish my name, or the name of my wife, or the name of my house, to be associated with this affair at all," Mr. Weatherley replied. "Mrs. Weatherley would be very much upset and it is, besides, entirely unnecessary."

Arnold hesitated for a moment.

"It is a serious matter, sir, if you will permit me to say so," he said slowly. "The man was murdered — that seems to be clear — and, from what you and I know, it certainly seems that he was murdered in your house."

Mr. Weatherley shook his head.

"That is not my impression," he declared. "The man was found dead in Mrs. Weatherley's boudoir, but there was no one in the house or apparently within reach who was either likely to have committed such a crime, or who even could possibly have done so. On the other hand, there are this man's companions, desperate fellows, no doubt, within fifty yards all the time. My own impression is that he was killed first and then placed in the spot where he was found. However that may be, I don't want my house made the rendezvous of all the interviewers and sightseers in the neighborhood. You and I will keep our counsel, Arnold Chetwode."

"Might I ask," Arnold said, "if you knew this man — if you had ever come into contact with him or seen him before?"

"Certainly not," Mr. Weatherley replied. "What business could I possibly have with a person of that description? He seems to have been, if not an habitual criminal himself, at least an associate of criminals, and he was without doubt a foreigner. Between you and me, Chetwode, I haven't the least doubt that the fellow was one of a gang of the worst class of burglars. Wherever he got that blow from, it was probably no more than he deserved."

"But, Mr. Weatherley," Arnold protested, "don't you think that you ought to have an investigation among your household?"

"My dear young fellow," Mr. Weatherley answered, testily, "I keep no men-servants at all except old Groves, who's as meek-spirited as a baby, and a footman whom my wife has just engaged, and who was out for the evening. A blow such as the paper describes was certainly never struck by a woman, and there was just as certainly no other man in my house. There is nothing to inquire about. As a matter of fact, I am not curious. The man is dead and there's an end of it."

"You will bear in mind, sir," Arnold said, "that if it comes to light afterwards, as it very probably may, that the man was first discovered in Mrs. Weatherley's boudoir, the scandal and gossip will be a great deal worse than if you came forward and told the whole truth now."

"I take my risk of that," Mr. Weatherley replied, coolly. "There isn't a soul except Groves who saw him, and Groves is my man. Now be so good as to get on with those letters, Chetwode, and consider the incident closed."

Arnold withdrew to his typewriter and commenced his task. The day had commenced with a new surprise to him. The nervous, shattered Mr. Weatherley of yesterday was gone. After a happening in his house which might well have had a serious effect upon him, he seemed not only unmoved but absolutely restored to cheerfulness. He was reading the paper for himself now, and the room was rapidly becoming full of tobacco smoke. Arnold spelled out his letters one by one until the last was finished. Then he took them over to his employer to sign. One by one Mr. Weatherley read them through, made an alteration here and there, then signed them with his large, sprawling hand. Just as he had finished the last, the telephone by his side rang. He took the receiver and placed it to his ear. Arnold waited until he had finished. Mr. Weatherley himself said little. He seemed to be listening. Towards the end, he nodded slightly.

"Yes, I quite understand," he said, "quite. That was entirely my own opinion. No case at all, you say? Good!"

He replaced the receiver and leaned back in his chair. For the first time, when he spoke his voice was a little hoarse.

"Chetwode," he said, "ring up my house – 16, Post Office, Hampstead. Ask Groves to tell his mistress that I thought she might be interested to hear that Mr. Starling will be discharged this morning. The police are abandoning the case against him, at present, for lack of evidence."

Arnold stood for a moment quite still. Then he took up the receiver and obeyed his orders. Groves' voice was as quiet and respectful as ever. He departed with the message and Arnold rang off. Then he turned to Mr. Weatherley.

"Have you any objection to my ringing up some one else and telling him, too?" he asked.

Mr. Weatherley looked at him.

"You are like all of them," he remarked. "I suppose you think he's a sort of demigod. I never knew a young man yet that he couldn't twist round his little finger. You want to ring up Count Sabatini, I suppose?"

"I should like to," Arnold admitted.

"Very well, go on," Mr. Weatherley grumbled. "Let him know. Perhaps it will be as well."

Arnold took from his pocket the note which Sabatini had written to him, and which contained his telephone number. Then he rang up. The call was answered by his valet.

"In one moment, sir," he said. "The telephone rings into His Excellency's bedchamber. He shall speak to you himself."

A minute or two passed. Then the slow, musical voice of Sabatini intervened.

"Who is that speaking?"

"It is I — Arnold Chetwode," Arnold answered. "I am speaking from the office in the city. I heard some news a few minutes ago which I thought might interest you."

"Good!" Sabatini replied, stifling what seemed to be a yawn. "You have awakened me from a long sleep, so let your news be good, my young friend."

"Mr. Weatherley hears from a solicitor at Bow Street that the police have abandoned the charge against Mr. Starling," Arnold announced. "He will be set at liberty as soon as the court opens."

There was a moment's silence. It was as though the person at the other end had gone away.

"Did you hear?" Arnold asked.

"Yes, I heard," Sabatini answered. "I am very much obliged to you for ringing me up, my young friend. I quite expected to hear your news during the day. No one would really suppose that a respectable man like Starling would be guilty of such a ridiculous action. However, it is pleasant to know. I thank you. I take my coffee and rolls this morning with more appetite."

Arnold set down the telephone. Mr. Weatherley, had risen to his feet and walked as far as the window. On his way back to his place, he looked at the little safe which he had made over to his secretary.

"You've got my papers there all right, Chetwode?" he asked.

"Certainly, sir," Arnold answered. "I hope, however, we may never need to use them."

Mr. Weatherley smiled. He was busy choosing another cigar.

# CHAPTER XIX

## IN THE COUNTRY

They sat on the edge of the wood, and a west wind made music for them overhead among the fir trees. From their feet a clover field sloped steeply to a honeysuckle-wreathed hedge. Beyond that, meadow-land, riven by the curving stream which stretched like a thread of silver to the blue, hazy distance. Arnold laughed softly with the pleasure of it, but the wonder kept Ruth tongue-tied.

"I feel," she murmured, "as though I were in a theatre for the first time. Everything is strange."

"It is the theatre of nature," Arnold replied. "If you close your eyes and listen, you can hear the orchestra. There is a lark singing above my head, and a thrush somewhere back in the wood there."

"And see, in the distance there are houses," Ruth continued softly. "Just fancy, Arnold, people, if they had no work to do, could live here, could live always out of sight of the hideous, smoky city, out of hearing of its thousand discords."

He smiled.

"There are a great many who feel like that," he said, his eyes fixed upon the horizon, "and then, as the days go by, they find that there is something missing. The city of a thousand discords generally has one clear cry, Ruth."

"For you, perhaps," she answered, "because you are young and because you are ambitious. But for me who lie on my back all day long, think of the glory of this!"

Arnold slowly sat up.

"Upon my word!" he exclaimed. "Why not. Why shouldn't you stay in the country for the summer? I hate London, too. There are cheap tickets, and bicycles, and all sorts of things. I wonder whether we couldn't manage it."

She said nothing. His thoughts were busy with the practical side of it. There was an opportunity here, too, to prepare her for what he felt sure was inevitable.

"You know, Ruth," he said, "I don't wish to say anything against Isaac, and I don't want to make you uneasy, but you know as well as I do that he has a strange maggot in his brain. When I first heard him talk, I thought of him as a sort of fanatic. It seems to me that he has changed. I am not sure that such changes as have taken place in him lately have not been for the worse."

"Tell me what you mean?" she begged.

"I mean," he continued, "that Isaac, who perhaps in himself may be incapable of harm, might be an easy prey to those who worked upon his wild ideas. Hasn't it struck you that for the last few days —"

She clutched at his hand and stopped him.

"Don't!" she implored. "These last few days have been horrible. Isaac has not left his room except to creep out sometimes into mine. He keeps his door locked. What he does I don't know, but if he hears a step on the stairs he slinks away, and his face is like the face of a hunted wolf. Arnold, do you think that he has been getting into trouble?"

"I am afraid," Arnold said, regretfully, "that it is not impossible. Tell me, Ruth, you are very fond of him?"

"He was my mother's brother — the only relative I have in the world," she answered. "What could I do without him?"

"He doesn't seem to want you particularly, just now, at any rate," Arnold said. "I don't see why we shouldn't take rooms out at one of these little villages. I could go back and forth quite easily. You'd like it, wouldn't you, Ruth? Fancy lying in a low, comfortable chair, and looking up at the blue sky, and listening to the birds and the humming of bees. The hours would slip by."

"I should love it," she murmured.

"Then why not?" he cried. "I'll stop the car at the next village we come to, and make inquiries."

She laid her hand softly upon his.

"Arnold, dear," she begged, "it sounds very delightful, and yet, can't you see it is impossible? I am not quite like other women, perhaps, but, after all, I am a woman. It is for your sake — for your sake, mind — that I think of this."

He turned and looked at her — looked at her, perhaps, with new eyes. She was stretched almost at full length upon the grass, her head, which had been supported by her clasped hands, now turned towards him. As she lay there, with her stick out of sight, her lips a little parted, her eyes soft with the sunlight, a faint touch of color in her cheeks, he suddenly realized the significance of her words. Her bosom was rising and falling quickly. Her plain black dress, simply made though it was, showed no defect of figure. Her throat was soft and white. The curve of her body was even graceful. The revelation of these things came as a shock to Arnold, yet it was curious that he found a certain pleasure in it.

"I had forgotten, Ruth," he said slowly, "but does it matter? You have no one in the world but Isaac, and I have no one in the world at all. Don't you think we can afford to do what seems sensible?"

Her eyes never left his face. She made no sign either of assent or dissent.

"Arnold," she declared, "it is true that I am an outcast. I have scarcely a relative in the world. But what you say about yourself is hard to believe. I have never asked you questions because it is not my business, but there are many little things by which one tells. I think that somewhere you have a family belonging to you with a name, even if, for any reason, you do not choose just now to claim them."

He made no direct reply. He watched for some moments a white-sailed boat come tacking down the narrow strip of river.

"I am my own master, Ruth," he said; "I have no one else to please or to consider. I understand what you have just told me, but if I gave you my word that I would try and be to you what Isaac might have been if he had not been led away by these strange ideas, wouldn't you trust me, Ruth?"

"It isn't that!" she exclaimed. "Trust you? Why, you know that I would! It isn't that I mind for myself either what people would say — or anything, but I am thinking of your new friends, of your future. If they knew that you were living down in the country with a girl, even though she were an invalid, who was no relation at all, don't you think that it might make a difference?"

"Of course not," he replied, "and, in any case, what should I care? It would be the making of you, Ruth. You would be able to pick up your strength, so that when our money-box is full you would be able to have that operation and never dare to call yourself an invalid again."

She half closed her eyes. The spell of summer was in the air, the spell of life was stirring slowly in her frozen blood.

"Ah! Arnold," she murmured, "I do not think that you must talk like that. It makes me feel so much like yielding. Somehow, the dreams out here seem even more wonderful than the visions which come floating up the river. There's more life here. Don't you feel it? Something seems to creep into your heart, into your pulses, and tell you what life is."

He made no answer. The world of the last few throbbing weeks seemed far enough away with him, too. He picked a handful of clover and thrust it into the bosom of her gown. Then he rose reluctantly to his feet and held out his hands.

"I think," he said, "that the great gates of freedom must be somewhere out here, but just now one is forced to remember that we are slaves."

He drew her to her feet, placed the stick in her hand, and supported her other arm. They walked for a step or two down the narrow path which led through the clover field to the lane below. Then, with a little laugh, he caught her up in his arms.

"It will be quicker if I carry you, Ruth," he proposed. "The weeds twine their way all the time around your stick."

She linked her arms around his neck; her cheek touched his for a moment, and he was surprised to find it as hot as fire. He stepped out bravely enough, but with every step it seemed to him that she was growing heavier. Her hands were still tightly linked around his neck, but her limbs were inert. She seemed to be falling away. He held her tighter, his breath began to grow shorter. The perfume of the clover, fragrant and delicate, grew stronger with every step they took. Somehow he felt that that walk along the narrow path was carving its way into his life. The fingers at the back of his neck were cold, yet she, too, was breathing as though she had been running. Her eyes were half closed. He looked once into her face, bent over her until his lips nearly touched hers. He set his teeth hard. Some instinct warned him of the dangers of the moment. Her stick slipped and a lump arose in his throat. The moment had passed. He kissed her softly upon the forehead.

"Dear Ruth!" he whispered.

She turned very pale and very soon afterward she insisted upon being set down. They walked slowly to where the motor car was waiting at the corner of the lane. Ruth began to talk nervously.

"It was charming of Mrs. Weatherley," she declared, "to lend you this car. Tell me how it happened, Arnie?"

"I simply told her," he replied, "that I was going to take a friend, who needed a little fresh air, out into the country, and she insisted upon sending this car instead of letting me hire a taxicab. It was over the telephone and I couldn't refuse. Besides, Mr. Weatherley was in the office, and he insisted upon it, too. They only use this one in London, and I know that they are away somewhere for the week-end."

"It has been so delightful," Ruth murmured. "Now I am going to lie back among these beautiful cushions, and just watch and think."

The car glided on along the country lane, passing through leafy hamlets, across a great breezy moorland, from the top of which they could see the Thames winding its way into Oxfordshire, a sinuous belt of silver. Then they sped down into the lower country, and Arnold looked at the milestones in some surprise.

"We don't seem to be getting any nearer to London," he remarked.

Ruth only shook her head.

"It will come soon enough," she said, with a little shiver. "It will pass, this, like everything else."

They had dropped to the level now, and suddenly, without warning, the car swung through a low white gate up along an avenue of shrubs. Arnold leaned forward.

"Where are you taking us?" he asked the driver. "There is some mistake."

But there was no mistake. A turn of the wheel and the car was slowing down before the front of a long, ivy-covered house, with a lawn as smooth as velvet, and beyond, the soft murmur of the river. Ruth clutched at his arm.

"Arnold!" she exclaimed. "What does this mean? Who lives here?"

"I have no idea," he answered, "unless —"

The windows in front of the house were all of them open and all of them level with the drive. Through the nearest of them at that moment stepped Fenella. She stood, for a moment, framed in the long French window, hung with clematis, — a wonderful picture even for Arnold, a revelation to Ruth, — in her cool muslin frock, open at the throat, and held together by a brooch with a great green stone. She wore no hat, and her wonderful hair seemed to have caught the sunlight in its meshes. Her eyebrows were a little raised; her expression was a little supercilious, faintly inquisitive. Already she had looked past Arnold. Her eyes were fixed upon the girl by his side.

"I began to think that you were lost," she said gayly. "Won't you present me to your friend, Arnold?"

# CHAPTER XX

## WOMAN'S WILES

Arnold sprang to his feet. It was significant that, after his first surprise, he spoke to Fenella with his head half turned towards his companion, and an encouraging smile upon his lips.

"I had no idea that we were coming here," he said. "We should not have thought of intruding. It was your chauffeur who would not even allow us to ask a question."

"He obeyed my orders," Fenella replied. "I meant it for a little surprise for you. I thought that it would be pleasant after your drive to have you call here and rest for a short time. You must present me to your friend."

Arnold murmured a word of introduction. Ruth moved a little in her seat. She lifted herself with her left hand, leaning upon her stick. Fenella's expression changed as though by magic. Her cool, good-humored, but almost impertinent scrutiny suddenly vanished. She moved to the side of the motor car and held out both her hands.

"I am so glad to see you here," she declared. "I hope that you will like some tea after your long ride. Perhaps you would prefer Mr. Chetwode to help you out?"

"You are very kind," Ruth murmured. "I am sorry to be such a trouble to everybody."

Arnold lifted her bodily out of the car and placed her on the edge of the lawn. Fenella, a long parasol in her hand, was looking pleasantly down at her guest.

"You will find it quite picturesque here, I think," she said. "It is not really the river itself which comes to the end of the lawn, but a little stream. It is so pretty, though, and so quiet. I thought you would like to have tea down there. But, my poor child," she exclaimed, "your hair is full of dust! You must come to my room. It is on the ground floor here. Mr. Chetwode and I together can help you so far."

They turned back toward the house and passed into the cool white hall, the air of which was fragrant with the perfume of geraniums and clematis. On the threshold of Fenella's room they were alone for a moment. Fenella was summoning her maid. Ruth clung nervously to Arnold. The room into which they looked was like a fairy chamber, full of laces and perfume and fine linen.

"Arnold," she whispered, "you are sure that you did not know about coming here?"

"I swear that I had no idea," he answered. "I would not have thought of bringing you without telling you first."

Then Fenella returned and he was banished into the garden. At the end of the lawn he found Mr. Weatherley, half asleep in a wicker chair. The latter was apparently maintaining his good spirits.

"Glad to see you, Chetwode," he said. "Sort of plot of my wife's, I think. Your young lady friend in the house?"

"Mrs. Weatherley was kind enough to take her to her room," Arnold replied. "We have had a most delightful ride, and I suppose it was dusty, although we never noticed it."

Mr. Weatherley relit his cigar, which had gone out while he dozed.

"Thought we'd like a little country air ourselves for the week-end," he remarked. "Will you smoke?"

Arnold shook his head.

"Not just now, thank you, sir. Is that the river through the trees there?"

Mr. Weatherley nodded.

"It's about a hundred yards down the stream," he replied. "Bourne End is the nearest station. The cottage belongs to my brother-in-law — Sabatini. I believe he's coming down later on. Any news at the office yesterday morning?"

"There was nothing whatever requiring your attention, sir," Arnold said. "There are a few letters which we have kept over for tomorrow, but nothing of importance."

Mr. Weatherley pursed his lips and nodded. He asked a further question or two concerning the business and then turned his head at the sound of approaching footsteps. Ruth, looking very pale and fragile, was leaning on the arm of a man-servant. Fenella walked on the other side, her lace parasol drooping over her shoulder, her head turned towards Ruth's, whose shyness she was doing her best to melt. Mr. Weatherley rose hastily from his chair.

"God bless my soul!" he declared. "I didn't know — you didn't tell me —"

"Miss Lalonde has been a great sufferer," Arnold said. "She has been obliged to spend a good deal of her time lying down. For that reason, today has been such a pleasure to her."

He hurried forward and took the butler's place. Together they installed her in the most comfortable chair. Mr. Weatherley came over and shook hands with her.

"Pretty place, this, Miss Lalonde, isn't it?" he remarked. "It's a real nice change for business men like Mr. Chetwode and myself to get down here for an hour or two's quiet."

"It is wonderfully beautiful," she answered. "It is so long since I was out of London that perhaps I appreciate it more, even, than either of you."

"What part of London do you live in?" Fenella asked her.

"My uncle and I have rooms in the same house as Mr. Chetwode," she replied. "It is in Adam Street, off the Strand."

"Not much air there this hot weather, I don't suppose," Mr. Weatherley remarked.

"We are on the top floor," she replied, "and it is the end house, nearest to the river. Still, one feels the change here."

Tea was brought out by the butler, assisted by a trim parlor-maid. Fenella presided. The note of domesticity which her action involved seemed to Arnold, for some reason or other, quaintly incongruous. Arnold waited upon them, and Fenella talked all the time to the pale, silent girl at her side. Gradually Ruth overcame her shyness; it was impossible not to feel grateful to this beautiful, gracious woman who tried so hard to make her feel at her ease. The time slipped by pleasantly enough. Then Fenella rose to her feet.

"You must carry Miss Lalonde and her chair down to the very edge of the lawn, where she can see the river," she told Arnold. "Afterwards, I am going to take you to see my little rose garden. I say mine, but it is really my brother's, only it was my idea when he first took the place. Mr. Weatherley is going down to the boat-builder's to see some motor-launches — horrible things they are, but necessary if we stay here for the summer. Would you like some books or magazines, Miss Lalonde, or do you think you would care to come with us if we helped you very carefully?"

Ruth shook her head.

"I should like to sit quite close to the river," she said shyly, "just where you said, and close my eyes. You don't know how beautiful it is to get the roar of London out of one's ears, and be able to hear nothing except these soft, summer sounds. It is like a wonderful rest."

They arranged her comfortably. Mr. Weatherley returned to the house. Fenella led the way through a little iron gate to a queer miniature garden, a lawn brilliant with flower-beds, ending in a pergola of roses. They passed underneath it and all around them the soft, drooping blossoms filled the whole air with fragrance. At the end was the river and a wooden seat. She motioned to him to sit by her side.

"You are not angry with me?" she asked, a little timidly.

"Angry? Why should I be?" he answered. "The afternoon has been delightful. I can't tell you how grateful I feel."

"All the same," she said, "I think you know that I laid a plot to bring you here because I was curious about this companion of yours, for whose sake you refused my invitation. However, you see I am penitent. Poor girl, how can one help feeling sorry for her! You forgive me?"

"I forgive you," he answered.

She closed her parasol and leaned back in her corner of the seat. She seemed to be studying his expression.

"There is something different about you this afternoon," she said. "I miss a look from your face, something in your tone when you are talking to me."

He shook his head.

"I am not conscious of any difference."

She laughed softly, but she seemed, even then, a little annoyed.

"You are not appreciating me," she declared. "Do you know that here, in the wilderness, I have put on a Paquin muslin gown, white shoes from Paris, white silk stockings — of which you can see at least two inches," she added, glancing downwards. "I have risked my complexion by wearing no hat, so that you can see my hair really at its best. I looked in the glass before you came and even my vanity was satisfied. Now I bring you away with me and find you a seat in a bower of roses, and you look up into that elm tree as though you were more anxious to find out where the thrush was singing than to look at me."

He laughed. Through the raillery of her words he could detect a certain half-girlish earnestness which seemed to him delightful.

"Try and remember," he said, "how wonderful a day like this must seem to any one like myself, who has spent day after day for many months in Tooley Street. I have been sitting up on the hills, listening to the wind in the trees. You can't imagine the difference when you've been used to hearing nothing but the rumble of drays on their way to Bermondsey."

She looked up at him.

"You know," she declared, "you are rather a mysterious person. I cannot make up my mind that you are forced to live the life you do."

"You do not suppose," he replied, "that any sane person would choose it? It is well enough now, thanks to you," he added, dropping his voice a little. "A week ago, I was earning twenty-eight shillings a week, checking invoices and copying letters — an errand boy's work; pure, unadulterated drudgery, working in a wretched atmosphere, without much hope of advancement or anything else."

"But even then you leave part of my question unanswered," she insisted. "You were not born to this sort of thing?"

"I was not," he admitted; "but what does it matter?"

"You don't care to tell me your history?" she asked lazily. "Sometimes I am curious about it."

"If I refuse," he answered, "it may give you a false impression. I will tell you a little, if I may. A few sentences will be enough."

"I should really like to hear," she told him.

"Very well, then," he replied. "My father was a clergyman, his family was good. He and I lived almost alone. He had an income and his stipend, but he was ambitious for me, and, by some means or other, while I was away he was led to invest all his money with one of these wretched bucket-shop companies. A telegram fetched me home unexpectedly just as I was entering for my degree. I found my father seriously ill and almost broken-hearted. I stayed with him, and in a fortnight he died. There was just enough — barely enough — to pay what he owed, and nothing left of his small fortune. His brother, my uncle, came down to the funeral, and I regret to say that even then I quarreled with him. He made use of language concerning my father and his folly which I could not tolerate. My father was very simple and very credulous and very honorable. He was just the sort of man who becomes the prey of these wretched circular-mongering sharks. What he did, he did for my sake. My uncle spoke of him with contempt, spoke as though he were charged with the care of me through my father's foolishness. I am afraid I made no allowance for my uncle's peculiar temperament. The moment the funeral was over, I turned him out of the house. I have no other relatives. I came to London sooner than remain down in the country and be found a position out of charity, which is, I suppose, what would have happened. I took a room and looked for work. Naturally, I was glad to get anything. I used to make about forty calls a day, till I called at your husband's office in Tooley Street and got a situation."

She nodded.

"I thought it was something like that," she remarked. "Supposing I had not happened to discover you, I wonder how long you would have gone on?"

"Not much longer," he admitted. "To tell you the truth, I should have enlisted but for that poor little girl whom I brought down with me this afternoon."

His tone had softened. There was the slightest trace of a frown upon her face as she looked along the riverside.

"But tell me," she asked, "what is your connection with her?"

"One of sympathy and friendliness only," he answered. "I never saw her till I took the cheapest room I could find at the top of a gaunt house near the Strand. The rest of the top floor is occupied by this girl and her uncle. He is a socialist agitator, engaged on one of the trades' union papers, — a nervous, unbalanced creature, on fire with strange ideas, — the worst companion in the world for any one. Sometimes he is away for days together. Sometimes, when he is at home, he talks like a prophet, half mad, half inspired, as though he were tugging at the pillars which support the world. The girl and he are alone as I am alone, and there is something which brings people very close together when they are in that state. I found her fallen upon the landing one day and unable to reach her rooms, and I carried her in and talked. Since then she looks for me every evening, and we spend some part of the time together."

"Is she educated?"

"Excellently," he answered. "She was brought up in a convent after her parents' death. She has read a marvellous collection of books, and she is very quick-witted and appreciative."

"But you," she said, "are no longer a waif. These things are passing for you. You cannot carry with you to the new world the things which belong to the old."

"No prosperity should ever come to me," he declared, firmly, "in which that child would not share to some extent. With the first two hundred pounds I possess, if ever I do possess such a sum," he added, with a little laugh, "I am going to send her to Vienna, to the great hospital there."

She shrugged her shoulders.

"Two hundred pounds is not a large sum," she remarked. "Would you like me to lend it to you?"

He shook his head.

"She would not hear of it," he said. "In her way, she is very proud."

"It may come of its own accord," she whispered, softly. "You may even have an opportunity of earning it."

"I am doing well enough just now," he remarked, "thanks to Mr. Weatherley, but sums of money like that do not fall from the clouds."

They were both silent. She seemed to be listening to the murmur of the stream. His head was lifted to the elm tree, from somewhere among whose leafy recesses a bird was singing.

"One never knows," she said softly. "You yourself have seen and heard of strange things happening within the last few days."

He came back to earth with a little start.

"It is true," he confessed.

"There is life still," she continued, "throbbing sometimes in the dull places, adventures which need only the strong arm and the man's courage. One might come to you, and adventures do not go unrewarded."

"You talk like your brother," he remarked.

"Why not?" she replied. "Andrea and I have much in common. Do you know that sometimes you provoke me a little?"

"I?"

She nodded.

"You have so much the air of a conqueror," she said. "You look as though you had courage and determination. One could see that by your mouth. And yet you are so much like the men of your nation, so stolid, so certain to move along the narrow lines which convention has drawn for you. Oh! if I could," she went on, leaning towards him and looking intently into his face, "I would borrow the magic from somewhere and mix a little in your wine, so that you should drink and feel the desire for new things; so that the world of Tooley Street should seem to you as though it belonged to a place inhabited only by inferior beings; so that you should feel new blood in your veins, hot blood crying for adventures, a new heart beating to a new music. I would like, if I could, Arnold, to bring those things into your life."

He turned and looked at her. Her face was within a few inches of his. She was in earnest. The gleam in her eyes was half-provocative, half a challenge. Arnold rose uneasily to his feet.

"I must go back," he said, a little thickly. "I forgot that Ruth is so shy. She will be frightened alone."

He walked away down the pergola without even waiting for her. It was very rude, but she only leaned back in her chair and laughed. In a way, it was a triumph!

# CHAPTER XXI

## ARNOLD SPEAKS OUT

Ruth was still alone, and her welcome was almost pathetic. She stretched out her arms – long, thin arms they seemed in the tight black sleeves of her worn gown. She had discarded her carefully mended gloves and her hands were bare.

"Arnold," she murmured, "how long you have been away!"

He threw himself on the grass by her side.

"Silly little woman!" he answered. "Don't tell me that you are not enjoying it?"

"It is all wonderful," she whispered, "but can't you see that I am out of place? When could we go, Arnie?"

"Are you so anxious to get away?" he asked, lazily.

"In a way, I should be content to stay here for ever," she answered. "If you and I only could be here – why, Arnold, it is like Heaven! Just close your eyes as I have been doing – like that. Now listen. There isn't any undernote, none of that ceaseless, awful monotony of sound that seems like the falling of weary men's feet upon the eternal pavement. Listen – there is a bird singing somewhere in that tree, and the water goes lapping and lapping and lapping, as though it had something pleasant to say but were too lazy to say it. And every now and then, if you listen very intently, you can hear laughing voices through the trees there from the river, laughter from people who are happy, who are sailing on somewhere to find their city of pleasure. And the perfumes, Arnold! I don't know what the rose garden is like, but even from here I can smell it. It is wonderful."

"Yet you ask me when we are going," he reminded her.

She shivered for a moment.

"It is not my world," she declared. "I am squeezed for a moment into a little corner of it, but it is not mine and I have nothing to do with it. She is so beautiful, that woman, and so gracious. She talks to me out of pity, but when I first came she looked at me and there was a challenge in her eyes. What did it mean, Arnold? Is she fond of you? Is she going to be fond of you?"

He laughed, a little impatiently.

"My dear Ruth," he said, "she is my employer's wife. She has been kind to me because I think that she is naturally kind, and because lately she has not found among her friends many people of her own age. Beyond that, there is nothing; there is never likely to be anything. She mixes in a world where she can have all the admiration she desires, and all the friends."

"Yet she looks at you," Ruth persisted, in a troubled tone, "as though she had some claim; as though I, even poor I, were an interloper for the tiny share I might have of your thoughts or sympathy. I do not understand it."

He touched her hand lightly with his.

"You are too sensitive, dear," he said, "and a little too imaginative. You must remember that she is half a foreigner. Her moods change every moment, and her expression with them. She was curious to see you. I have tried to explain to her what friends we are. I am sure that her interest is a friendly one."

A motor horn immediately behind startled them both. They turned their heads. A very handsome car, driven by a man in white livery, had swept up the little drive and had come to a standstill in front of the hall door. From the side nearest to them Count Sabatini descended, and stood for a moment looking around him. The car moved on towards the stables. Sabatini came slowly across the lawn.

"Who is it?" she whispered. "How handsome he is!"

"He is Mrs. Weatherley's brother — Count Sabatini," Arnold replied.

He came very slowly and, recognizing Arnold, waved his gray Homburg hat with a graceful salute. He was wearing cool summer clothes of light gray, with a black tie, boots with white linen gaiters, and a flower in his coat. Even after his ride from London he looked immaculate and spotless. He greeted Arnold kindly and without any appearance of surprise.

"I heard that you were to be here," he said. "My sister told me of her little plot. I hope that you approve of my bungalow?"

"I think that it is wonderful," Arnold answered. "I have never seen anything of the river before — this part of it, at any rate."

Sabatini turned slightly towards Ruth, as though expecting an introduction. His lips were half parted; he had the air of one about to make a remark. Then suddenly a curious change seemed to come over his manner. His natural ease seemed to have entirely departed. He stood stiff and rigid, and there was something forbidding in his face as he looked down at the girl who had glanced timidly towards him. A word — it was inaudible but it sounded like part of a woman's name — escaped him. He had the appearance, during those few seconds, of a man who looks through the present into a past world. It was all over before even they could appreciate the situation. With a little smile he had leaned down towards Ruth.

"You will do me the honor," he murmured, "of presenting me to your companion?"

Arnold spoke a word or two of introduction. Sabatini pulled up a chair and sat down at once by the girl's side. He had seen the stick and seemed to have taken in the whole situation in a moment.

"Please be very good-natured," he begged, turning to Arnold, "and go and find my sister. She will like to know that I am here. I am going to talk to Miss Lalonde for a time, if she will let me. You don't mind my being personal?" he went on, his voice soft with sympathy. "I had a very dear cousin once who was unable to walk for many years, and since then it has always interested me to find any one suffering in the same way."

There was a simple directness about his speech which seemed to open the subject so naturally that Ruth found herself talking without effort of her accident, and the trouble it had brought. They drifted so easily into conversation that Arnold left them almost at once. He had only a little distance to go before he found Fenella returning. She was carrying a great handful of roses which she had just gathered, and to his relief there was no expression of displeasure in her face. Perhaps, though, he reflected with a sinking heart, she had understood!

"Your brother has just arrived," he announced. "I think that he has motored down from London. He wished me to let you know that he was here."

"Where is he?" she asked.

"He is on the lawn, talking to Miss Lalonde," Arnold replied.

"I will go to them presently," she said. "In the meantime, you are to make yourself useful, if you please," she added, holding out the roses. "Take these into the house, will you, and give them to one of the women."

He took them from her.

"With pleasure! And then, if you will excuse us, —"

"I excuse no word which is spoken concerning your departure," she declared. "Tonight I give a little fête. We change our dinner into what you call supper, and we will have the dining table moved out under the trees there. You and your little friend must stop, and afterwards my brother will take you back to London in his car, or I will send you up in my own."

"You are too kind," Arnold answered. "I am afraid —"

"You are to be afraid of nothing," she interrupted, mockingly. "Is that not just what I have been preaching to you? You have too many fears for your height, my friend."

"We will put it another way, then. I was thinking of Miss Lalonde. She is not strong, and I think it is time we were leaving. If you could send us so far as the railway station —"

"There are no trains that leave here," she asserted; "at least, I never heard of them. I shall go and talk to her myself. We shall see. No, on second thoughts, she is too interested. You and I will walk to the house together. That is one thing," she continued, "which I envy my brother, which makes me admire him so much. I think he is the most charmingly sympathetic person I ever met. Illness of any sort, or sickness, seems to make a woman of him. I never knew a child or a woman whose interest or sympathy he could not win quickly."

"It is a wonderful thing to say of any man, that," Arnold remarked.

"Wonderful?" she repeated. "Why, yes! So far as regards children, at any rate. You know they say — one of the writers in my mother's country said — that men are attracted by beauty, children by goodness; and women by evil. It is of some such saying that you are thinking. Now I shall leave these flowers in the hall and ring the bell. Tell me, would you like me to show you my books?"

She laid her fingers upon the white door of her little drawing-room and looked at him.

"If you do not mind," he replied, "I should like to hear what Ruth says about going."

This time she frowned. She stood looking at him for a moment. Arnold's face was very square and determined, but there were still things there which she appreciated.

"You are very formal, today," she declared. "You give too many of your thoughts to your little friend. I do not think that you are treating me kindly. I should like to sit with you in my room and to talk to you of my books. Look, is it not pretty?"

She threw open the door. It was a tiny little apartment, in which all the appointments and the walls were white, except for here and there a little French gilded furniture of the best period. A great bowl of scarlet geraniums stood in one corner. Though the windows were open, the blinds were closely drawn, so that it was almost like twilight.

"You won't come for five minutes?" she begged.

"Yes!" he answered, almost savagely. "Come in and shut the door. I want to talk to you — not about your books. Yes, let us sit down — where you will. That couch is big enough for both of us."

The sudden change in his manner was puzzling. The two had changed places. The struggle was at an end, but it was scarcely as a victim that Arnold leaned towards her.

"Give me your hands," he said.

"Arnold!" she whispered.

He took them both and drew her towards him.

"What is it you want?" he asked. "Not me — I know that. You are beautiful, you know that I admire you, you know that a day like this is like a day out of some wonderful fairy story for me. I am young and foolish, I suppose, just as easily led away as most young men are. Do you want to make me believe impossible things? You look at me from the corners of your eyes and you laugh. Do you want to make use of me in any way? You're not a flirt. You are a wife, and a good wife. Do you know that men less impressionable than I have been made slaves for life by women less beautiful than you, without any effort on their part, even? No, I won't be laughed at! This is reality! What is it you want?" He leaned towards her. "Do you want me to kiss you? Do you want me to hold you in my arms? I could do it. I should like to do it. I will, if you tell me to. Only afterwards —"

"Afterwards, what?"

"I shall do what I should have done if your husband hadn't taken me into his office — I should enlist," he said. "I mayn't be particularly ambitious, but I've no idea of hanging about, a penniless adventurer, dancing at a woman's heels. Be honest with me. At heart I do believe in you, Fenella. What is it you want?"

She leaned back on the couch and laughed. It was no longer the subtle, provoking laugh of the woman of the world. She laughed frankly and easily, with all the lack of restraint to which her twenty-four years entitled her.

"My dear boy," she declared, "you have conquered. I give in. You have seen through me. I am a fraud. I have been trying the old tricks upon you because I am very much a woman, because I want you to be my slave and to do the things I want you to do and live in the world I want you to live in, and I was jealous of this companion for whose sake you would not accept my invitation. Now I am sane again. I see that you are not to be treated like other and more foolish young men. My brother wants you. He wants you for a companion, he wants you to help him in many ways. He has been used to rely upon me in such cases. I have my orders to place you there." She pointed to her feet. "Alas, that I have failed!" she added, laughing once more. "But, Arnold, we shall be friends?"

"Willingly," he answered, with an immense sense of relief. "Only remember this. I may have wisdom enough to see the lure, but I may not always have strength enough not to take it. I have spoken to you in a moment of sanity, but — well, you are the most compellingly beautiful person I ever saw, and compellingly beautiful women have never made a habit of being kind to me, so please —"

"Don't do it any more," she interrupted. "Is that it?"

"As you like."

"Now I am going to put a piece of scarlet geranium in your buttonhole, and I am going to take you out into the garden and hand you over to my brother, and tell him that my task is done, that you are my slave, and that he has only to speak and you will go out into the world with a revolver in one hand and a sword in the other, and wear any uniform or fight in any cause he chooses. Come!"

"You know," Arnold said, as they left the room, "I don't know any man I admire so much as your brother, but I am almost as frightened of him as I am of you."

"One who talks of fear so glibly," she answered, "seldom knows anything about it."

"There are as many different sorts of fear as there are different sorts of courage," he remarked.

"How we are improving!" she murmured. "We shall begin moralizing soon. Presently I really think we shall compare notes about the books we have read and the theatres we have been to, and before we are gray-headed I think one of us will allude to the weather. Now isn't my brother a wonderful man? Look at that flush upon Miss Lalonde's cheeks. Aren't you jealous?"

"Miserably!"

Sabatini rose to his feet and greeted his sister after his own fashion, holding both her hands and kissing her on both cheeks.

"If only," he sighed, "our family had possessed morals equal to their looks, what a race we should have been! But, my dear sister, — a question of taste only, — you should leave Doucet and Paquin at home when you come to my bungalow."

"You men never altogether understand," she replied. "Nothing requires a little artificial aid so much as nature. It is the piquancy of the contrast, you see. That is why the decorations of Watteau are the most wonderful in the world. He knew how to combine the purely, exquisitely artificial with the entirely simple. Now to break the news to Miss Lalonde!"

Ruth turned a smiling face towards her.

"It is to say that our fête day is at an end," she said, looking for her stick.

"Fête days do not end at six o'clock in the afternoon," Fenella replied. "I want you to be very kind and give us all a great deal of pleasure. We want to make a little party — you and Mr. Chetwode, my brother, myself and Mr. Weatherley — and dine under that cedar tree, just as we are. We are going to call it supper. Then, afterwards, you will have a ride back to London in the cool air. Either my brother will take you, or we will send a car from here."

"It is a charming idea," Sabatini said. "Miss Lalonde, you will not be unkind?"

She hesitated only for a moment. They saw her glance at her frock, the little feminine struggle, and the woman's conquest.

"If you really mean it," she said, "why, of course, I should love it. It is no good my pretending that if I had known I should have been better prepared," she continued, "because it really wouldn't have made any difference. If you don't mind —"

"Then it is settled!" Sabatini exclaimed. "My young friend Arnold is now going to take me out upon the river. I trust myself without a tremor to those shoulders."

Arnold rose to his feet with alacrity.

"You get into the boat-house down that path," Sabatini continued. "There is a comfortable punt in which I think I could rest delightfully, or, if you prefer to scull, I should be less comfortable, but resigned."

"It shall be the punt," Arnold decided, with a glance at the river. "Won't any one else come with us?"

Fenella shook her head.

"I am going to talk to Miss Lalonde," she said. "After we have had an opportunity of witnessing your skill, Mr. Chetwode, we may trust ourselves another time. Au revoir!"

They watched the punt glide down the stream, a moment or two later, Sabatini stretched between the red cushions with a cigarette in his mouth, Arnold handling his pole like a skilled waterman.

"You like my brother?" Fenella asked.

The girl looked at her gratefully.

"I think that he is the most charming person I ever knew in my life," she declared.

# CHAPTER XXII

## THE REFUGEE'S RETURN

Sabatini's attitude of indolence lasted only until they had turned from the waterway into the main river. Then he sat up and pointed a little way down the stream.

"Can you cross over somewhere there?" he asked.

Arnold nodded and punted across towards the opposite bank.

"Get in among the rushes," Sabatini directed. "Now listen to me."

Arnold came and sat down.

"You don't mean to tire me," he remarked.

Sabatini smiled.

"Do you seriously think that I asked you to bring me on the river for the pleasure of watching your prowess with that pole, my friend?" he asked. "Not at all. I am going to ask you to do me a service."

Arnold was suddenly conscious that Sabatini, for the first time since he had known him, was in earnest. The lines of his marble-white face seemed to have grown tenser and firmer, his manner was the manner of a man who meets a crisis.

"Turn your head and look inland," he said. "You follow the lane there?"

Arnold nodded.

"Quite well," he admitted.

"At the corner," Sabatini continued, "just out of sight behind that tall hedge, is my motor car. I want you to land and make your way there. My chauffeur has his instructions. He will take you to a village some eight miles up the river, a village called Heslop Wood. There is a boat-builder's yard at the end of the main street. You will hire a boat and row up the river. About three hundred yards up, on the left hand side, is an old, dismantled-looking house-boat. I want you to board it and search it thoroughly."

Sabatini paused, and Arnold looked at him, perplexed.

"Search it!" he exclaimed. "But for whom? For what?"

"It is my belief," Sabatini went on, "that Starling is hiding there. If he is, I want you to bring him to me by any means which occur to you. I had sooner he were dead, but that is too much to ask of you. I want him brought in the motor car to that point in the lane there. Then, if you succeed, you will bring him down here and your mission is ended. Will you undertake it?"

Arnold never hesitated for a moment. He was only too thankful to be able to reply in the affirmative. He put on his coat and propelled the punt a little further into the rushes.

"I'll do my best," he asserted.

Sabatini said never a word, but his silence seemed somehow eloquent. Arnold sprang onto the bank and turned once around.

"If he is there, I'll bring him," he promised.

Sabatini waved his hand and Arnold sped across the meadow. He found the motor car waiting behind the hedge, and he had scarcely stepped in before they were off. They swung at a great speed along the narrow lanes, through two villages, and finally came to a standstill at the end of a long, narrow street. Arnold alighted and found the boat-builder's yard, with rows of boats for hire, a short distance along the front. He chose one and paddled off, glancing at his watch as he did so. It was barely a quarter of an hour since he had left Sabatini.

The river at this spot was broad, but it narrowed suddenly on rounding a bend about a hundred yards away. The house-boat was in sight now, moored close to a tiny island. Arnold pulled up alongside and paused to reconnoiter. To all appearance, it was a derelict. There were no awnings, no carpets, no baskets of flowers. The outside was grievously in need of paint. It had an entirely uninhabited and desolate appearance. Arnold beached his boat upon the little island and swung himself up onto the deck. There was still no sign of any human occupancy. He descended into the saloon. The furniture there was mildewed and musty. Rain had come in through an open window, and the appearance of the little apartment was depressing in the extreme. Stooping low, he next examined the four sleeping apartments. There was no bedding in any one of them, nor any sign of their having been recently occupied. He passed on into the kitchen, with the same result. It seemed as though his journey had been in vain. He made his way back again on deck, and descended the stairs leading to the fore part of the boat. Here were a couple of servant's rooms, and, though there was no bedding, one of the bunks gave him the idea that some one had been lying there recently. He looked around him and sniffed — there was a distinct smell of tobacco smoke. He stepped lightly back into the passageway. There was nothing to be heard, and no material indication of any one's presence, yet he had the uncomfortable feeling that some one was watching him — some one only a few feet away. He waited for almost a minute. Nothing happened, yet his sense of apprehension grew deeper. For the first time, he associated the idea of danger with his enterprise.

"Is any one about here?" he asked.

There was no reply. He tried another door, which led into a sort of pantry, without result. The last one was fastened on the inside.

"Is Mr. Starling in there?" Arnold demanded.

There was still no reply, yet it was certain now that the end of his search was at hand. Distinctly he could hear the sound of a man breathing.

"Will you tell me if you are there, Mr. Starling?" Arnold again demanded. "I have a message for you."

Starling, if indeed he were there, seemed now to be even holding his breath. Arnold took one step back and charged the door. It went crashing in, and almost at once there was a loud report. The closet — it was little more — was filled with smoke, and Arnold heard distinctly the hiss of a bullet buried in the woodwork over his shoulder. He caught the revolver from the shaking fingers of the man who was crouching upon the ground, and slipped it into his pocket. With his other hand, he held his prisoner powerless.

"What the devil do you mean by that?" he cried, fiercely.

Starling — for it was Starling — seemed to have no words. Arnold dragged him out into the light and for a moment found it hard to recognize the man. He had lost over a stone in weight. His cheeks were hollow, and his eyes had the hunted look in them of some wild animal.

"What do you want with me?" he muttered. "Can't you see I am hiding here? What business is it of yours to interfere?"

Arnold looked at him from head to foot. The man was shaking all over; the coward's fear was upon him.

"What on earth are you in this state for?" he exclaimed. "Whom are you hiding from? You have been set free. Is it the Rosario business still? You have been set free once."

Starling moistened his lips rapidly.

"They set me free," he muttered, "because one of their witnesses failed. They had no case; they wouldn't bring me up. But I am still under surveillance. The sergeant as good as told me that they'd have me before long."

"Well, at present, I've got you," Arnold said coolly. "Have you any luggage?"

"No! Why?"

"Because you are coming along with me."

"Where?"

"I am taking you to Count Sabatini," Arnold informed him. "He is at his villa about ten miles down the river."

Starling flopped upon his knees.

"For the love of God, don't take me to him!" he begged.

"Why not?"

"He is a devil, that man," Starling whispered, confidentially. "He would blow out my brains or yours or his own, without a second's hesitation, if it suited him. He hasn't any nerves nor any fear nor any pity. He will laugh at me — he won't understand, he is so reckless!"

"Well, we're going to him, anyhow," Arnold said. "I don't see how you can be any worse off than hiding in this beastly place. Upstairs and into the boat, please."

Starling struggled weakly to get away but he was like a child in Arnold's hands.

"You had much better come quietly," the latter advised. "You'll have to come, anyway, and if you're really afraid of being arrested again, I should think Count Sabatini would be the best man to aid your escape."

"But he won't let me escape," Starling protested. "He doesn't understand danger. I am not made like him. My nerve has gone. I came into this too late in life."

"Jump!" Arnold ordered, linking his arm into his companion's.

They landed, somehow, upon the island. Arnold pointed to the boat.

"Please be sensible," he begged, "now, at any rate. There may be people passing at any moment."

"I was safe in there," Starling mumbled. "Why the devil couldn't you have left me alone?"

Arnold bent over his oars.

"Safe!" he repeated, contemptuously. "You were doing the one thing which a guilty man would do. People would have known before long that you were there, obviously hiding. I think that Count Sabatini will propose something very much better."

"Perhaps so," Starling muttered. "Perhaps he will help me to get away."

They reached the village and Arnold paid for the hire of his boat. Then he hurried Starling into the car, and a moment or two later they were off.

"Is it far away?" Starling asked, nervously.

"Ten minutes' ride. Sabatini has arranged it all very well. We get out, cross a meadow, and find him waiting for us in the punt."

"You won't leave me alone with him on the river?" Starling begged.

"No, I shall be there," Arnold promised.

"There's nothing would suit him so well," Starling continued, "as to see me down at the bottom of the Thames, with a stone around my neck. I tell you I'm frightened of him. If I can get out of this mess," he went on, "I'm off back to New York. Any job there is better than this. What are we stopping for? Say, what's wrong now?"

"It's all right," Arnold answered. "Step out. We cross this meadow on foot. When we reach the other end, we shall find Sabatini. Come along."

They turned toward the river, Starling muttering, now and then, to himself. In a few minutes they came in sight of the punt. Sabatini was still there, with his head reclining among the cushions. He looked up and waved his hand.

"A record, my young friend!" he exclaimed. "I congratulate you, indeed. You have been gone exactly fifty-five minutes, and I gave you an hour and a half at the least. Our friend Starling was glad to see you, I hope?"

"He showed his pleasure," Arnold remarked dryly, "in a most original manner. However, here he is. Shall I take you across now?"

"If you please," Sabatini agreed.

He sat up and looked at Starling. The latter hung his head and shook like a guilty schoolboy.

"It was so foolish of you," Sabatini murmured, "but we'll talk of that presently. They were civil to you at the police court, eh?"

"I was never charged," Starling replied. "They couldn't get their evidence together."

"Still, they asked you questions, no doubt?" Sabatini continued.

"I told them nothing," Starling replied. "On my soul and honor, I told them nothing!"

"It was very wise of you," Sabatini said. "It might have led to disappointments — to trouble of many sorts. So you told them nothing, eh? That is excellent. After we have landed, I must hand you over to my valet. Then we will have a little talk."

They were in the backwater now, drifting on toward the lawn. Starling shrank back at the sight of the two women.

"I can't face it," he muttered. "I tell you I have lost my nerve."

"You have nothing to fear," Sabatini said quietly. "There is no one here likely to do you or wish you any harm."

Fenella came down to the steps to meet them.

"So our prodigal has returned," she remarked, smiling at Starling.

"We have rescued Mr. Starling from a solitary picnic upon his houseboat," Sabatini explained, suavely. "We cannot have our friends cultivating misanthropy."

Mr. Weatherley, who had returned from the boat-builder's, half rose from his chair and sat down again, frowning. He watched the two men cross the lawn towards the house. Then he turned to Ruth and shook his head.

"I have a great regard for Count Sabatini," he declared, "a great regard, but there are some of his friends — very many of them, in fact — whose presence here I could dispense with. That man is one of them. Do you know where he was a few nights ago, Miss Lalonde?"

She shook her head.

"In prison," Mr. Weatherley said, impressively; "arrested on a serious charge."

Her eyes asked him a question. He stooped towards her and lowered his voice.

"Murder," he whispered; "the murder of Mr. Rosario!"

# CHAPTER XXIII

## TROUBLE BREWING

Through the winding lanes, between the tall hedges, honeysuckle wreathed and starred with wild roses, out onto the broad main road, Sabatini's great car sped noiselessly on its way back to London. They seemed to pass in a few moments from the cool, perfumed air of the country into the hot, dry atmosphere of the London suburbs. Almost before they realized that they were on their homeward way, the fiery glow of the city was staining the clouds above their heads. Arnold leaned a little forward, watching, as the car raced on to its goal. This ride through the darkness seemed to supply the last thrill of excitement to their wonderful day. He glanced towards Ruth, who lay back among the cushions, as though sleeping, by his side.

"You are tired?"

"Yes," she answered simply.

They were in the region now of electric cars — wonderful vehicles ablaze with light, flashing towards them every few minutes, laden with Sunday evening pleasure seekers. Their automobile, however, perfectly controlled by Sabatini's Italian chauffeur, swung from one side of the road to the other and held on its way with scarcely abated speed.

"You have enjoyed the day?" he asked.

She opened her eyes and looked at him. He saw the shadows, and wondered.

"Of course," she whispered.

His momentary wonder at her reticence passed. Again he was leaning a little forward, looking up the broad thoroughfare with its double row of lights, its interminable rows of houses growing in importance as they rushed on.

"It is we ourselves who pass now along the lighted way!" he exclaimed, holding her arm for, a moment. "It is an enchanted journey, ours, Ruth."

She laughed bitterly.

"An enchanted journey which leads to two very dreary attic rooms on the sixth floor of a poverty-stricken house," she reminded him. "It leads back to the smoke-stained city, to the four walls within which one dreams empty dreams."

"It isn't so bad as that," he protested.

Her lips trembled for a moment; she half closed her eyes. An impulse of pain passed like a spasm across her tired features.

"It is different for you," she murmured. "Every day you escape. For me there is no escape."

He felt a momentary twinge of selfishness. Yet, after all, the great truths were incontrovertible. He could lighten her lot but little. There was very little of himself that he could give her — of his youth, his strength, his vigorous hold upon life. Through all the tangle of his expanding interests in existence, the medley of strange happenings in which he found himself involved, one thing alone was clear. He was passing on into a life making larger demands upon, him, a life in which their companionship must naturally become a slighter thing. Nevertheless, he spoke to her reassuringly.

"You cannot believe, Ruth," he said, "that I shall ever forget? We have been through too much together, too many dark days."

She sighed.

"There wasn't much for either of us to look forward to, was there, when we first looked down on the river together and you began to tell me fairy stories."

"They kept our courage alive," he declared. "I am not sure that they are not coming true."

She half closed her eyes.

"For you, Arnold," she murmured. "Not all the fancies that were ever spun in the brain of any living person could alter life very much for me."

He took her hand and held it tightly. Yet it was hard to know what to say to her. It was the inevitable tragedy, this, of their sexes and her infirmity. He realized in those few minutes something of how she was feeling, — the one who is left upon the lonely island while the other is borne homeward into the sunshine and tumult of life. There was little, indeed, which he could say. It was not the hour, this, for protestation.

They passed along Piccadilly, across Leicester Square, and into the Strand. The wayfarers in the streets, of whom there were still plenty, seemed to be lingering about in sheer joy of the cooler night after the unexpected heat of the day, the women in light clothes, the men with their coats thrown open and carrying their hats. They passed down the Strand and into Adam Street, coming at last to a standstill before the tall, gloomy house at the corner of the Terrace. Arnold stepped out onto the pavement and helped his companion to alight. The chauffeur lifted his hat and the car glided away. As they stood there, for a moment, upon the pavement, and Arnold pushed open the heavy, shabby door, it seemed, indeed, as though the whole day might have been a dream.

Ruth moved wearily along the broken, tesselated pavement, and paused for a moment before the first flight of stairs. Arnold, taking her stick from her, caught her up in his arms. Her fingers closed around his neck and she gave a little sigh of relief.

"Will you really carry me up all the way, Arnie?" she whispered. "I am so tired tonight. You are sure that you can manage it?"

He laughed gayly.

"I have done it many times before," he reminded her. "Tonight I feel as strong as a dozen men."

One by one they climbed the flight of stone steps. Curiously enough, notwithstanding the strength of which he had justly boasted, as they neared the top of the house he felt his breath coming short and his heart beating faster, as though some unusual strain were upon him. She had tightened her grasp upon his neck. She seemed, somehow, to have come closer to him, yet to hang like a dead weight in his arms. Her cheek was touching his. Once, toward the end, he looked into her face, and the fire of her eyes startled him.

"You are not really tired," he muttered.

"I am resting like this," she whispered.

He stood at last upon the top landing. He set her down with a little thrill, assailed by a medley of sensations, the significance of which confused him. She seemed still to cling to him, and she pointed to his door.

"For five minutes," she begged, "let us sit in our chairs and look down at the river. Tonight it is too hot to sleep."

Even while he opened his door, he hesitated.

"What about Isaac?" he asked.

She shivered and looked over her shoulder. They were in his room now and she closed the door. On the threshold she stood quite still for a moment, as though listening. There was something in her face which alarmed him.

"Do you know, I believe that I am afraid to go back," she said. "Isaac has been stranger than ever these last few days. All the time he is locked up in his room, and he shows himself only at night."

Arnold dragged her chair up to the window and installed her comfortably. He himself was thinking of Isaac's face under the gaslight, as he had seen him stepping away from the taxicab.

"Isaac was always queer," he reminded her, reassuringly.

She drew him down to her side.

"There has been a difference these last few days," she whispered. "I am afraid — I am terribly afraid that he has done something really wrong."

Arnold felt a little shiver of fear himself.

"You must remember," he said quietly, "that after all Isaac is, in a measure, outside your life. No one can influence him for either good or evil. He is not like other men. He must go his own way, and I, too, am afraid that it may be a troublous one. He chose it for himself and neither you nor I can help. I wouldn't think about him at all, dear, if you can avoid it. And for yourself, remember always that you have another protector."

The faintest of smiles parted her lips. In the moonlight, which was already stealing into the room through the bare, uncurtained window, her face seemed like a piece of beautiful marble statuary, ghostly, yet in a single moment exquisitely human.

"I have no claim upon you, Arnold," she reminded him, "and I think that soon you will pass out of my life. It is only natural. You must go on, I must remain. And that is the end of it," she added, with a little quiver of the lips. "Now let us finish talking about ourselves. I want to talk about your new friends."

"Tell me what you really think of them?" he begged. "Count Sabatini has been so kind to me that if I try to think about him at all I am already prejudiced."

"I think," she replied slowly, "that Count Sabatini is the strangest man whom I ever met. Do you remember when he stood and looked down upon us? I felt — but it was so foolish!"

"You felt what?" he persisted.

She shook her head.

"I cannot tell. As though we were not strangers at all. I suppose it is what they call mesmerism. He had that soft, delightful way of speaking, and gentle mannerism. There was nothing abrupt or new about him. He seemed, somehow, to become part of the life of any one in whom he chose to interest himself in the slightest. And he talked so delightfully, Arnold. I cannot tell you how kind he was to me."

Arnold laughed.

"It's a clear case of hero worship," he declared. "You're going to be as bad as I have been."

"And yet," she said slowly, "it is his sister of whom I think all the time. Fenella she calls herself, doesn't she?"

"You like her, too?" Arnold asked eagerly.

"I hate her," was the low, fierce reply.

Arnold drew a little away.

"You can't mean it!" he exclaimed. "You can't really mean that you don't like her!"

Ruth clutched at his arm as though jealous of his instinctive disappointment.

"I know that it's brutally ungracious," she declared. "It's a sort of madness, even. But I hate her because she is the most beautiful thing I have ever seen here in life. I hate her for that, and I hate her for her strength. Did you see her come across the lawn to us tonight, Arnold?"

He nodded enthusiastically.

"You mean in that smoke-colored muslin dress?"

"She has no right to wear clothes like that!" Ruth cried. "She does it so that men may see how beautiful she is. I — well, I hate her!"

There was a silence. Then Ruth rose slowly to her feet. Her tone was suddenly altered, her eyes pleaded with his.

"Don't take any notice of me tonight, Arnold," she implored. "It has been such a wonderful day, and I am not used to so much excitement. I am afraid that I am a little hysterical. Do be kind and help me across to my room."

"Is there any hurry?" he asked. "It hasn't struck twelve yet."

"I want to go, please," she begged. "I shall say foolish things if I stay here much longer, and I don't want to. Let me go."

He obeyed her without further question. Once more he supported her with his arms, but she kept her face turned away. When he had reached her door he would have left her, but she still clutched his arm.

"I am foolish," she whispered, "foolish and wicked tonight. And besides, I am afraid. It is all because I am overtired. Come in with me for one moment, please, and let me be sure that Isaac is all right. Feel how I am trembling."

"Of course I will come," he answered. "Isaac can't be angry with me tonight, anyhow, for my clothes are old and dusty enough."

He opened the door and they passed across the threshold. Then they both stopped short and Ruth gave a little start. The room was lit with several candles. There was no sign of Isaac, but a middle-aged man, with black beard and moustache, had risen to his feet at their entrance. He glanced at Ruth with keen interest, at Arnold with a momentary curiosity.

"What are you doing here?" Ruth demanded. "What right have you in this room?"

The man did not answer her question.

"I shall be glad," he said, "if you will come in and shut the door. If you are Miss Ruth Lalonde, I have a few questions to ask you."

# CHAPTER XXIV

## ISAAC AT BAY

Arnold had a swift premonition of what had happened. He led Ruth to a chair and stood by her side. Ruth gazed around the room in bewilderment. The curtained screen which divided it had been torn down, and the door of the inner apartment, which Isaac kept so zealously locked, stood open. Not only that, but the figure of a second man was dimly seen moving about inside, and, from the light shining out, it was obviously in some way illuminated.

"I don't understand who you are or what you are doing here," Ruth declared, trembling in every limb.

"My name is Inspector Grant," the man replied. "My business is with Isaac Lalonde, who I understand is your uncle."

"What do you want with him?" she asked.

The inspector made no direct reply.

"There are a few questions," he said, "which it is my duty to put to you."

"Questions?" she repeated.

"Do you know where your uncle is?"

Ruth shook her head.

"I left him here this morning," she replied. "He has not been out for several days. I expected to find him here when I returned."

"We have been here since four o'clock," the man said. "There was no one here when we arrived, nor has any one been since. Your uncle has no regular hours, I suppose?"

"He is very uncertain," Ruth answered. "He does newspaper reporting, and he sometimes has to work late."

"Can you tell me what newspaper he is engaged upon?"

"The *Signal*, for one," Ruth replied.

Inspector Grant was silent for a moment.

"The *Signal* newspaper offices were seized by the police some days ago," he remarked. "Do you know of any other journal on which your uncle worked?"

She shook her head.

"He tells me very little of his affairs," she faltered.

The inspector pointed backwards into the further corner of the apartment.

"Do you often go into his room there?" he asked.

"I have not been for months," Ruth assured him. "My uncle keeps it locked up. He told me that there had been some trouble at the office and he was printing something there."

The inspector rose slowly to his feet. On the table by his side was a pile of articles covered over with a tablecloth. Very deliberately he removed the latter and looked keenly at Ruth. She shrank back with a little scream. There were half a dozen murderous-looking pistols there, a Mannerlicher rifle, and a quantity of ammunition.

"What does your uncle need with these?" the inspector asked dryly.

"How can I tell?" Ruth replied. "I have never seen one of them before. I never knew that they were in the place."

"Nor I," Arnold echoed. "I have been a constant visitor here, too, and I have never seen firearms of any sort before."

The inspector turned towards him.

"Are you a friend of Isaac Lalonde?" he asked.

"I am not," Arnold answered. "I am a friend of his niece here, Miss Ruth Lalonde. I know very little of Isaac, although I see him here sometimes."

"I should like to know your name, if you have no objection," the inspector remarked.

"My name is Chetwode," Arnold told him. "I occupy a room on the other side of the passage."

"When did you last see Isaac Lalonde?"

Arnold did not hesitate for a moment. What he had seen at Hampstead belonged to himself. He deliberately wiped out the memory of it from his thoughts.

"On Thursday evening here."

The inspector made a note in his pocket-book. Then he turned again to Ruth.

"You can give me no explanation, then, as to your uncle's absence tonight?"

"None at all. I can only say what I told you before — that I expected to find him here on my return."

"Was he here when you left this morning?"

"I believe so," Ruth assured him. "He very seldom comes out of his room until the middle of the day, and he does not like my going to him there. As we started very early, I did not disturb him."

"Have you any objection," the inspector asked, "to telling me where you have spent the whole of today?"

"Not the slightest," Arnold interposed. "We have been to Bourne End, and to a village in the neighborhood."

The inspector nodded thoughtfully. Ruth leaned a little forward in her chair. Her voice trembled with anxiety.

"Please tell me," she begged, "what is the charge against my uncle?"

The inspector glanced over his shoulder at that inner room, from which fitful gleams of light still came. He looked down at the heap of pistols and ammunition by his side.

"The charge," he said slowly, "is of a somewhat serious nature."

Ruth was twisting up her glove in her hand.

"I do not believe," she declared, "that Isaac has ever done anything really wrong. He is a terrible socialist, and he is always railing at the rich, but I do not believe that he would hurt any one."

The inspector looked grimly at the little pile of firearms.

"A pretty sort of armory, this," he remarked, "for a peace-loving man. What do you suppose he keeps them here for, in his room? What do you suppose —"

They all three heard it at the same time. The inspector broke off in the middle of his sentence. Ruth, shrinking in her chair, turned her head fearfully towards the door, which still stood half open. Arnold was looking breathlessly in the same direction. Faintly, but very distinctly, they heard the patter of footsteps climbing the stone stairs. It sounded as though a man were walking upon tiptoe, yet dragging his feet wearily. The inspector held up his hand, and his subordinate, who had been searching the inner room, came stealthily out. Ruth, obeying her first impulse, opened her lips to shriek. The inspector leaned forward and his hand suddenly closed over her mouth. He looked towards Arnold, who was suffering from a moment's indecision.

"If you utter a sound," he whispered, "you will be answerable to the law."

Nobody spoke or moved. It was an odd little tableau, grouped together in the dimly lit room. The footsteps had reached the last flight of stairs now. They came slowly across the landing, then paused, as though the person who approached could see the light shining through the partly open door. They heard a voice, a voice almost unrecognizable, a voice hoarse and tremulous with fear, the voice of a hunted man.

"Are you there, Ruth?"

Ruth struggled to reply, but ineffectually. Slowly, and as though with some foreboding of danger, the footsteps came nearer and nearer. An unseen hand cautiously pushed the door open. Isaac stood upon the threshold, peering anxiously into the room. The inspector turned and faced him.

"Isaac Lalonde," he said, "I have a warrant for your arrest. I shall want you to come with me to Bow Street."

With the certainty of danger, Isaac's fear seemed to vanish into thin air. He saw the open door of his ransacked inner room and the piled-up heap of weapons upon the table. Face to face with actual danger, the, courage of a wild animal at bay seemed suddenly vouchsafed to him.

"Come with you to Hell!" he cried. "I think not, Mr. Inspector. Are these the witnesses against me?"

He pointed to Ruth and Arnold. Ruth clutched her stick and staggered tremblingly to her feet.

"How can you say that, Isaac!" she exclaimed. "Arnold and I have only been home from the country a few minutes. We walked into the room and found these men here. Isaac, I am terrified. Tell me that you have not done anything really wrong!"

Isaac made no reply. All the time he watched the inspector stealthily. The latter moved forward now, as though to make the arrest. Then Isaac's hand shot out from his pocket and a long stream of yellow fire flashed through the room. The inspector sprang back. Isaac's hand, with the smoke still curling from the muzzle of his pistol, remained extended.

"That was only a warning," Isaac declared, calmly. "I aimed at the wall there. Next time it may be different."

There was a breathless silence. The inspector stood his ground but he did not advance.

"Let me caution you, Isaac Lalonde," he said, "that the use of firearms by any one in your position is fatal. You can shoot me, if you like, and my assistant, but if you do you will certainly be hanged. It is my duty to arrest you and I am going to do it."

Isaac's hand was still extended. This time he had lowered the muzzle of his pistol. The inspector was only human and he paused, for he was looking straight into the mouth of it. Isaac slowly backed toward the door.

"Remember, you are warned!" he cried. "If any one pursues me, I shoot!"

His departure was so sudden and so speedy that he was down the first flight of stairs before the inspector started. Arnold, who was nearest the door, made a movement as though to follow, but Ruth threw her arms around him. The policeman who had been examining the other room rushed past them both.

"You shall not go!" Ruth sobbed. "It is no affair of yours. It is between the police and Isaac."

"I want to stop his shooting," Arnold replied. "He must be mad to use firearms against the police. Let me go, Ruth."

"You can't!" she shrieked. "You can't catch him now!"

Then she suddenly held her ears. Three times quickly they heard the report of the pistol. There was a moment's silence, then more shots. Arnold picked Ruth up in his arms and, running with her across the landing, laid her in his own easychair.

"I must see what has happened!" he exclaimed, breathlessly. "Wait here."

She was powerless to resist him. He tore himself free from the clutch of her fingers and rushed down the stairs, expecting every moment to come across the body of one of the policemen. To his immense relief, he reached the street without discovering any signs of the tragedy he feared. Adam Street was deserted, but in the gardens below the Terrace he could hear the sound of voices, and a torn piece of clothing hung from the spike of one of the railings. Isaac had evidently made for the gardens and the river. The sound of the chase grew fainter and fainter, and there were no more shots. Arnold, after a few minutes' hesitation, turned round and reclimbed the stairs. The place smelt of gunpowder, and little puffs of smoke were curling upwards.

Arrived on the top landing, he closed the door of Isaac's room and entered his own apartment. Ruth had dragged herself to the window and was leaning out.

"He has gone across the gardens," she cried breathlessly. "I saw him running. Perhaps he will get away, after all. I saw one of the policemen fall down, and he was quite a long way ahead then."

"At any rate, no harm was done by the firing," Arnold declared. "I don't think he really shot at them at all."

They knelt side by side before the windowsill. The gardens were still faintly visible in the dim moonlight, but all signs of disturbance had passed away. She clung nervously to his arm.

"Arnold," she whispered, "tell me, what do you think he has done?"

"I don't suppose he has done anything very much," Arnold replied, cheerfully. "What I really think is that he has got mixed up with some of these anarchists, writing for this wretched paper, and they have probably let him in for some of their troubles."

They stayed there for a measure of time they were neither of them able to compute. At last, with a little sigh, he rose to his feet. For the first time they began to realize what had happened.

"Isaac will not come back," he said.

She clung to him hysterically.

"Arnold," she cried, "I am nervous. I could not sleep in that room. I never want to see it again as long as I live."

For a moment he was perplexed. Then he smiled. "It's rather an awkward situation for us attic dwellers," he remarked. "I'll bring your couch in here, if you like, and you can lie before the window, where it's cool."

"You don't mind?" she begged. "I couldn't even think of going to sleep. I should sit up all night, anyhow."

"Not a bit," he assured her. "I don't think it would be much use thinking about bed."

He made his way back into Isaac's apartments, brought out her couch and arranged it by the window. She lay down with a little sigh of relief. Then he dragged up his own easy chair to her side and held her hand. They heard Big Ben strike two o'clock, and soon afterwards Arnold began to doze. When he awoke, with a sudden start, her hand was still in his. Eastward, over the city, a faint red glow hung in the heavens. The world was still silent, but in the delicate, pearly twilight the trees in the gardens, the bridge, and the buildings in the distance — everything seemed to stand out with a peculiar and unfamiliar distinctness. She, too, was sitting up, and they looked out of the window together. Five o'clock was striking now.

"I've been asleep!" Arnold exclaimed. "Something woke me up."

She nodded.

"There is some one knocking at the door outside," she whispered. "That is what woke you. I heard it several minutes ago."

He jumped up at once.

"I will go and see what it is," he declared.

He opened the door and looked out onto the landing. The knocking was at the door of Isaac's apartment. Two policemen and a man in plain clothes were standing there.

"There is no one in those rooms," Arnold said. "The door shuts with a spring lock, but I have a key here, if you wish to enter."

The sergeant looked at Arnold and approved of him.

"I have an order to remove some firearms and other articles," he announced. "Also, can you tell me where the young woman — Ruth Lalonde — is?"

"She is in my room," Arnold replied. "She was too terrified to remain alone over there. You don't want her, do you?" he asked, anxiously.

The man shook his head.

"I have no definite instructions concerning her," he said, "but we should like to know that she has no intention of going away."

Arnold threw open the door before them.

"I am sure that she has not," he declared. "She is quite an invalid, and besides, she has nowhere else to go."

The sergeant gave a few orders respecting the movement of a pile of articles covered over by a tablecloth, which had been dragged out of Isaac's room. Before he had finished, Arnold ventured upon the question which had been all the time trembling upon his lips.

"This man Isaac Lalonde — was he arrested?"

The sergeant made no immediate reply.

"Tell me, at least, was any one hurt?" Arnold begged.

"No one was shot, if you mean that," the sergeant admitted.

"Is Isaac in custody?"

"He very likely is by this time," the sergeant said. "As a matter of fact, he got away. A friend of yours, is he?"

"Certainly not," Arnold answered. "I have an attic on the other side of the landing there, and I have made friends with the girl. My interest in Isaac Lalonde is simply because she is his niece. Can you tell me what the charge is against him?"

"We believe him to be one of a very dangerous gang of criminals," the sergeant replied. "I can't tell you more than that. If you take my advice, sir," he continued, civilly, "you will have as little as possible to do with either the man or the girl. There's no doubt about the man's character, and birds of a feather generally flock together."

"I am perfectly certain," Arnold declared, vigorously, "that if there has been anything irregular in her uncle's life, Miss Lalonde knew nothing of it. We both knew that he talked wildly, but, for the rest, his doings have been as much a mystery to her as to me."

The sergeant was summoned by one of his subordinates. The two men stood whispering together for a few moments. He turned finally toward Arnold.

"I shall have to ask you to leave us now, sir," he said civilly.

"There's nothing more you can tell me about this affair, I suppose?" Arnold asked.

The sergeant shook his head.

"You will hear all about it later on, sir."

Arnold turned reluctantly back to his own room, where Ruth, was anxiously waiting. He closed the door carefully behind him.

"Isaac has escaped," he announced, "and no one was hurt."

She drew a little sigh of immense relief.

"Did they tell you what the charge was?"

"Not definitely," he replied. "So far as I could make out from what the sergeant said, it was keeping bad company as much as anything."

"The police are in the rooms now?" she asked.

"Three more of them," he assented. "I don't know what they want but evidently you'll have to stay here. Now I'm going to light this spirit-lamp and make some coffee."

He moved cheerfully about the room, and she watched him all the time with almost pathetic earnestness. Presently he brought the breakfast things over to her side and sat at the foot of her couch while the water boiled. He took her hand and held it caressingly.

"I shouldn't worry about Isaac," he said. "I don't suppose he is really very much mixed up with these fellows. He'll have to keep out of the way for a time, that's all."

"There were the pistols," she faltered, doubtfully.

"I expect they saddled him with them because he was the least likely to be suspected," Arnold suggested. "There's the water boiling already. Now for it."

He cut some bread and butter and made the coffee. They ate and drank almost in silence. Through the open window now the roar of traffic was growing every minute in volume. Across the bridge the daily stream of men and vehicles had commenced to flow. Presently he glanced at the clock and, putting down his coffee cup, rose to his feet.

"In a few minutes, dear, I must be off," he announced. "You won't mind being left, will you?"

Her lips trembled.

"Why should I?" she murmured. "Of course you must go to work."

He went behind his little screen, where he plunged his head into a basin of cold water. When he reappeared, a few minutes later, he was ready to start.

"I expect those fellows will have cleared out from your rooms by now," he said, throwing open the door. "Hullo, what's this?"

A trunk and hatbox had been dragged out onto the landing. A policeman was sitting on a chair in front of the closed door, reading a newspaper.

"We have collected the young lady's belongings, so far as possible, sir," he remarked. "If there is anything else belonging to her, she may be able to get it later on."

"Do you mean to say that she can't go back to her own rooms?" Arnold demanded.

"I am sorry, sir," the man replied, "but I am here to see that no one enters them under any pretext."

Arnold looked at him blankly.

"But what is the young lady to do?" he protested. "She has no other home."

The policeman remained unmoved.

"Sorry, sir," he said, "but her friends will have to find her one for the time being. She certainly can't come in here."

Arnold felt a sudden weight upon his arm. Ruth had been standing by his side and had heard everything. He led her gently back. She was trembling violently.

"Don't worry about me, Arnold," she begged. "You go away. By the time you come back, I — I shall have found a home somewhere."

He passed his arm around her. A wild flash in her eyes had suddenly revealed her thought.

"Unless you promise me," he said firmly, "that I shall find you on that couch when I return this evening, I shall not leave this room."

"But, Arnold, —"

"The business of Samuel Weatherley & Company," he interrupted, glancing at the clock, "will be entirely disorganized unless you promise."

"I promise," she murmured faintly.

# CHAPTER XXV

## MR. WEATHERLEY'S DISAPPEARANCE

Arnold arrived at Tooley Street only a few minutes after his usual time. He made his way at once into the private office and commenced his work. At ten o'clock Mr. Jarvis came in. The pile of letters upon Mr. Weatherley's desk was as yet untouched.

"Any idea where the governor is?" the cashier asked. "He's nearly half an hour late."

Arnold glanced at the clock.

"Mr. Weatherley is spending the week-end down the river," he said. "I dare say the trains up are a little awkward."

Mr. Jarvis looked at him curiously.

"How do you happen to know that?"

"I was there yesterday for a short time," Arnold told him.

Mr. Jarvis whistled softly.

"Seems to me you're getting pretty chummy with the governor," he remarked; "or is it Mrs. Weatherley, eh?"

Arnold lifted his head and looked fixedly at Mr. Jarvis. The latter suddenly remembered that he had come in to search among the letters for some invoices. He busied himself for a moment or two, sorting them out.

"Well, well," he said, "I hope the governor will soon be here, anyway. There are a lot of things I want to ask him about this morning."

A telephone bell at Arnold's desk began to ring. Arnold lifted the receiver to his ear.

"Is that Mr. Weatherley's office?" a familiar voice inquired.

"Good morning, Mrs. Weatherley," he replied. "This is the office, and I am Arnold Chetwode. We were just wondering what had become of Mr. Weatherley."

"What had become of him?" the voice repeated. "But is he not there?"

"No sign of him at present," Arnold answered.

There was a short silence. Then Mrs. Weatherley spoke again.

"He left here," she said, "absurdly early — soon after seven, I think it was — to motor up."

"Has the car returned?" Arnold asked.

"More than an hour ago," was the prompt reply.

"I can assure you that he has not been here," Arnold declared. "You're speaking from Bourne End, I suppose?"

"Yes!"

"Will you please ask the chauffeur," Arnold suggested, "where he left Mr. Weatherley?"

"Of course I will," she replied. "That is very sensible. You must hold the line until I come back."

Arnold withdrew the receiver for a few minutes from his ear. Mr. Jarvis had been listening to the conversation, his mouth open with curiosity.

"Is that about the governor?" he asked.

Arnold nodded.

"It was Mrs. Weatherley speaking," he said. "It seems Mr. Weatherley left Bourne End soon after seven o'clock this morning."

"Soon after seven o'clock?" Mr. Jarvis repeated.

"The car has been back there quite a long time," Arnold continued. "Mrs. Weatherley has gone to make inquiries of the chauffeur."

"Most extraordinary thing," Mr. Jarvis muttered. "I can't say that I've ever known the governor as late as this, unless he was ill."

Arnold put the receiver once more to his ear. In a moment or two Mrs. Weatherley returned. Her voice was a little graver.

"I have spoken to the chauffeur," she announced. "He says that they called first up in Hampstead to see if there were any letters, and that afterwards he drove Mr. Weatherley over London Bridge and put him down at the usual spot, just opposite to the London & Westminster Bank. For some reason or other, as I dare say you know," she went on, "Mr. Weatherley never likes to bring the car into Tooley Street. It was ten minutes past nine when he set him down and left him there."

Arnold glanced at the clock.

"It is now," he said, "a quarter to eleven. The spot you speak of is only two hundred yards away, but I can assure you that Mr. Weatherley has not yet arrived."

Mrs. Weatherley began to laugh softly. Even down the wires, that laugh seemed to bring with it some flavor of her own wonderful personality.

"Will there be a paragraph in the evening papers?" she asked, mockingly. "I think I can see it now upon all the placards: 'Mysterious disappearance of a city merchant.' Poor Samuel!"

Arnold found it quite impossible to answer her lightly. The fingers, indeed, which held the receiver to his ear, were shaking a little.

"Mrs. Weatherley," he said, "can I see you today — as soon as possible?"

"Why, of course you can, you silly boy," she laughed back. "I am here all alone and I weary myself. Come by the next train or take a taxicab. You can leave word for Mr, Weatherley, when he arrives, that you have come by my special wish. He will not mind then."

"There is no sign of Mr. Weatherley at present," Arnold replied, "and I could not leave here until I had seen him. I thought that perhaps you might be coming up to town for something."

He could almost hear her yawn.

"Really," she declared, after a slight pause, "it is not a bad idea. The sun will not shine today; there is a gray mist everywhere and it depresses me. You will lunch with me if I come up?"

"If you please."

"I do please," she declared. "I think we will go to our own little place — the Café André, and I will be there at half-past twelve. You will be waiting for me?"

"Without a doubt," Arnold promised.

She began to laugh again.

"Without a doubt!" she mocked him. "You are a very stolid young man, Arnold."

"To tell you the truth," he admitted, "I am a little bothered just now. We want Mr. Weatherley badly, and I don't understand his having been within a few hundred yards of the office nearly two hours ago and not having turned up here."

"He will arrive," she replied confidently. "Have no fear of that. There are others to whom accidents and adventures might happen, but not, I think, to Mr. Samuel Weatherley. I am sorry that you are bothered, though, Mr. Chetwode. I think that to console you I shall wear one of my two new muslin gowns which have just arrived from Paris."

"What is she talking about all this time?" Mr. Jarvis, who was itching with curiosity, broke in.

"I am called away now," Arnold declared down the telephone. "I shall be quite punctual. Good-bye!"

He heard her laugh again as he hung up the receiver.

"Well, well," Mr. Jarvis demanded, "what is it all about? Have you heard anything?"

"Nothing of any importance, I am afraid," Arnold admitted. "Mrs. Weatherley laughs at the idea of anything having happened to her husband."

"If nothing has happened to him," Mr. Jarvis protested, "where is he?"

"Is there any call he could have paid on the way?" Arnold suggested.

"I have never known him to do such a thing in his life," Mr. Jarvis replied. "Besides, there is no business call which could take two hours at this time of the morning."

They rang up the few business friends whom Mr. Weatherley had in the vicinity, Guy's Hospital, the bank, and the police station. The reply was the same in all cases. Nobody had seen or heard anything of Mr. Weatherley. Arnold even took down his hat and walked aimlessly up the street to the spot where Mr. Weatherley had left the motor car. The policeman on duty had heard nothing of any accident. The shoe-black, at the top of the steps leading down to the wharves, remembered distinctly Mr. Weatherley's alighting at the usual hour. Arnold returned to the office and sat down facing the little safe which Mr. Weatherley had made over to him. After all, it might be true, then, this thing which he had sometimes dimly suspected. Beneath his very commonplace exterior, Mr. Weatherley had carried with him a secret....

At half-past twelve precisely, Arnold stood upon the threshold of the passage leading into André's Café. Already the people were beginning to crowd into the lower room, a curious, cosmopolitan mixture, mostly foreigners, and nearly all arriving in twos and threes from the neighboring business houses. At twenty minutes to one, Mr. Weatherley's beautiful car turned slowly into the narrow street and drove up to the entrance. Arnold hurried forward to open the door and Fenella descended. She came to him with radiant face, a wonderful vision in her spotless white gown and French hat with its drooping veil. Arnold, notwithstanding his anxieties, found it impossible not to be carried away for the moment by a wave of admiration. She laughed with pleasure as she looked into his eyes.

"There!" she exclaimed. "I told you that for a moment I would make you forget everything."

"There is a good deal to forget, too," he answered.

She shrugged her shoulders.

"You are always so gloomy, my young friend," she said. "We will have luncheon together, you and I, and I will try and teach you how to be gay. Tell me, then," she went on, as they reached the landing and she waited for Arnold to open the door leading into the private room, "how is the little invalid girl this morning?"

"The little invalid girl is well," Arnold replied.

"She was not too tired yesterday, I hope?" Fenella asked.

"Not in the least," Arnold assured her. "We both of us felt that we did not thank you half enough for our wonderful day."

"Oh, la, la!" Fenella exclaimed. "It was a whim of mine, that is all. I liked having you both there. Some day you must come again, and, if you are very good, I may let you bring the young lady, though I'm not so sure of that. Do you know that my brother was asking me questions about her until I thought my head would swim last night?" she continued, curiously.

"Count Sabatini was very kind to her," Arnold remarked. "Poor little girl, I am afraid she is going to have rather a rough time. She had quite an alarming experience last night after our return."

"You must tell me all about it presently," Fenella declared. "Shall we take this little round table near the window? It will be delightful, that, for when we are tired with one another we can watch the people in the street. Have you ever sat and watched the people in the street, Arnold?"

"Not often," he answered, giving his hat to a waiter and following her across the little room. "You see, there are not many people to watch from the windows of where I live, but there is always the river."

"A terribly dreary place," Fenella declared.

Arnold shook his head.

"Don't believe it," he replied. "Only a short time ago, the days were very dark indeed. Ruth and I together did little else except watch the barges come up, and the slowly moving vessels, and the lights, and the swarms of people on Blackfriars Bridge. Life was all watching then."

"One would weary soon," she murmured, "of being a spectator. You are scarcely that now."

"There has been a great change," he answered simply. "In those days I was very near starvation. I had no idea how I was going to find work. Yet even then I found myself longing for adventures of any sort, — anything to quicken the blood, to feel the earth swell beneath my feet."

She was watching him with that curious look in her eyes which he never wholly understood — half mocking, half tender.

"And after all," she murmured, "you found your way to Tooley Street and the office of Mr. Samuel Weatherley."

She threw herself back in her chair and laughed so irresistibly that Arnold, in a moment or two, found himself sharing her merriment.

"It is all very well," he said presently, "but I am not at all sure that adventures do not sometimes come even to Tooley Street."

She shook her head.

"I shall never believe it. Tell me now about Mr. Weatherley? Was he very sorry when he arrived for having caused you so much anxiety?"

"I have not yet seen Mr. Weatherley," Arnold replied. "Up till the time when I left the office, he had not arrived."

She set down the glass which she had been in the act of raising to her lips. For the first time she seemed to take this matter seriously.

"What time was that?" she asked.

"Ten minutes past twelve."

She frowned.

"It certainly does begin to look a little queer," she admitted. "Do you think that he has met with an accident?"

"We have already tried the hospitals and the police station," he told her.

She looked at him steadfastly.

"You have an idea — you have some idea of what has happened," she said.

"Nothing definite," Arnold replied, gravely. "I cannot imagine what it all means, but I believe that Mr. Weatherley has disappeared."

# CHAPTER XXVI

## ARNOLD BECOMES INQUISITIVE

For several moments Fenella sat quite still. She was suddenly an altered woman. All the natural gayety and vivacity seemed to have faded from her features. There were suggestions of another self, zealously kept concealed. It was a curious revelation. Even her tone, when she spoke, was altered. The words seemed to be dragged from her lips.

"You have some reason for saying this," she murmured.

"I have," Arnold admitted.

Just then the waiter entered the room, bringing in a portion of the lunch which they had ordered. Fenella rose and walked to a mirror at the other end of the apartment. She stood there powdering her cheeks for a moment, with her back turned to Arnold. When the waiter had gone, she returned, humming a tune. Her effort at self-rehabilitation was obvious.

"You gave me a shock, my friend," she declared, sitting down. "Please do not do it again. I am not accustomed to having things put to me quite so plainly."

"I am sorry," Arnold said. "It was hideously clumsy of me."

"It is of no consequence now," she continued. "Please to give me some of that red wine and go on with your story. Tell me exactly what you mean!"

"It is simply this," Arnold explained. "A few days ago, I noticed that Mr. Weatherley was busy writing for several hours. It was evidently some private matter and nothing whatever to do with the business. When he had finished, he put some documents into a small safe, locked them up, and, very much to my surprise, gave me the key."

"This was long ago?"

"It was almost immediately after Mr. Rosario's murder," he replied. "When he gave me the key, he told me that if anything unexpected should happen to him, I was to open the safe and inspect the documents. He particularly used the words 'If anything unexpected should happen to me, or if I should disappear.'"

"You really believe, then," she asked, "that he had some idea in his mind that something was likely to happen to him, or that he intended to disappear?"

"His action proves it," Arnold reminded her. "So far as we know, there is no earthly reason for his not having turned up at the office this morning.

This afternoon I shall open the safe."

"You mean that you will open it if you do not find him in the office when you return?"

"He will not be there," Arnold said, decidedly.

Her eyes were filled with fear. He went on hastily.

"Perhaps I ought not to say that. I have nothing in the world to go on. It is only just an idea of mine. It isn't that I am afraid anything has happened to him, but I feel convinced, somehow, that we shall not hear anything more of Mr. Weatherley for some time."

"You will open the safe, then, this afternoon?"

"I must," Arnold replied.

For several minutes neither of them spoke a word. Fenella made a pretense at eating her luncheon. Arnold ate mechanically, his thoughts striving in vain to focus themselves upon the immediate question. It was she who ended the silence.

"What do you think you will find in those documents?"

"I have no idea," Arnold answered. "To tell you the truth," he went on earnestly, "I was going to ask you whether you knew of anything in his life or affairs which could explain this?"

"I am not sure that I understand you," she said.

"It seems a strange question," Arnold continued, "and yet it presents itself. I was going to ask you whether you knew of any reason whatsoever why Mr. Weatherley should voluntarily choose to go into hiding?"

"You have something in your mind when you ask me a question like this!" she said. "What should I know about it at all? What makes you ask me?"

Then Arnold took his courage into both hands. Her eyes seemed to be compelling him.

"What I am going to say," he began, "may sound very foolish to you. I cannot help it. I only hope that you will not be angry with me."

Her eyes met his steadily.

"No," she murmured, "I will not be angry — I promise you that. It is better that I should know exactly what is in your mind. At present I do not understand."

His manner acquired a new earnestness. He forgot his luncheon and leaned across the table towards her.

"Fenella," he said, "try and consider how these things of which I am going to speak must have presented themselves to me. Try, if you can, and put yourself in my position for a few minutes. Before that evening on which Mr. Weatherley asked me to come to your house, nothing in the shape of an adventure had ever happened to me. I had had my troubles, but they were ordinary ones, such as the whole world knows of. From the day when I went to school to the day when I had to leave college hurriedly, lost my father, and came up to London a pauper, life with me was entirely an obvious affair. From the night I crossed the threshold of your house, things were different."

There was a cloud upon her face. She began to drum with her slim forefingers upon the tablecloth.

"I think that I would rather you did not go on," she said.

He shook his head.

"I must," he declared, fervently. "These things have been in my mind too long. It is not well for our friendship that I should have such thoughts and leave them unuttered. On that very first evening – the first time I ever saw you – you behaved, in a way, strangely. You took me into your little sitting-room and I could see that you were in trouble. Something was happening, or you were afraid that it was going to happen. You sent me to the window to look out and see if any one were watching the house. You remember all that?"

"Yes," she murmured, "I remember."

"There was some one watching it," Arnold went on. "I told you. I saw your lips quiver with fear. Then your husband came in and took you away. You left me there in the room alone. I was to wait for you. While I was there, one of the men, who had been watching, stole up through your garden to the very window. I saw his face. I saw his hand upon the windowsill with that strange ring upon his finger. You have not forgotten?"

"Forgotten!" she repeated. "As though that were possible!"

"Very well," Arnold continued. "Now let me ask you to remember another evening, only last week, the night I dined with your brother. I brought you home from the *Empire* and we found that your sitting-room had been entered from that same window. The door was locked and we all thought that burglars must be there. I climbed in at the window from the garden. You know what I found."

All the time she seemed to have been making an effort to listen to him unconcernedly. At this point, however, she broke down. She abandoned her attempt at continuing her luncheon. She looked up at him and he could see that she was trembling.

"Don't go on!" she begged; "please don't!"

"I must," he insisted. "These things have taken possession of me. I cannot sleep or rest for thinking of them."

"For my sake," she implored, "try and forget!"

He shook his head.

"It isn't possible," he said simply. "I am not made like that. Even if you hate me for it, I must go on. You know what I found in your sitting-room that night."

"But this is cruel!" she murmured.

"I found a dead man, a man who, to all appearance, had been murdered in there. Not only that, but there must have been people close at hand who were connected with him in some way, or who were responsible for the crime. We left the room for five minutes, and when we came back he had disappeared. All that we can judge as to what became of him is that that same night a dead man was left in a taxicab, not far away, by an unknown man whom as yet the police have failed to find."

"But this is all too horrible!" she murmured. "Why, do you remind me of it?"

"Because I must," he went on. "Listen. There are other things. This man Starling, for instance, whom I met at your house, and who is suspected of the murder of Rosario — both your brother and you seem to be trying to shield him. I don't understand it; I can't understand it. Your brother talked to me strangely the night I dined with him, but half the time I felt that he was not serious. I do not for a moment believe that he would stoop to any undignified or criminal action. I believe in him as I do in you. Yet if Starling is guilty, why do you both protect him?"

"Is there anything else?" she faltered.

"There is the final thing," he reminded her; "the reason why I have mentioned these matters to you at all — I mean the disappearance of Mr. Weatherley. Supposing he does not come back, how am I to keep silent, knowing all that I know, knowing that he was living in a house surrounded by mysteries? I hate my suspicions. They are like ugly shadows which follow me about. I like and admire your brother, and you — you know —"

He could not finish his sentence. She raised her eyes and he saw that they were full of tears.

"Help me," he begged. "You can if you will. Give me your confidence and I will tell you something which I think that even you do not know."

"Something concerned with these happenings?"

"Something concerned with them," he assented. "I will tell you when and by whom the body of that man was removed from your sitting-room."

She sat looking at him like a woman turned to stone. There was incredulity in her eyes, incredulity and horror.

"You cannot know that!" she faltered.

"I do know it," he asserted.

"Why have you kept this a secret from me?" she asked.

"I do not know," he answered. "Somehow or other, when I have been with you I have felt more anxious to talk of other things. Then there was another reason which made me anxious to forget the whole affair if I could. I had some knowledge of one of the men who were concerned in taking him away."

The waiter was busy now with the removal of their luncheon. To Arnold, the necessary exchange of commonplaces was an immense relief. It was several minutes before they were alone again. Then she leaned across towards him. She had lit a cigarette now, and, although she was very thoughtful, she seemed more at her ease.

"Listen," she began. "I do not ask you to tell me anything more about that night — I do not wish to hear anything. Tell me instead exactly what it is that you want from me!"

"I want nothing more nor less," he answered gently, "than permission to be your friend and to possess a little more of your confidence. I want you to end this mystery which surrounds the things of which I have spoken."

"And supposing," she said thoughtfully, "supposing I find that my obligations to other people forbid me to discuss these matters any more with you?"

"I can only hope," he answered, "that you will not feel like that. Remember that these things must have some bearing upon the disappearance of Mr. Weatherley."

She rose to her feet with a little shrug of the shoulders and walked up and down the room for several moments, smoking and humming a light tune to herself. Arnold watched her, struggling all the time against the reluctant admiration with which she always inspired him. She seemed to read in his eyes what was passing in his mind, for when at last she came to a standstill she stood by his side and laughed at him, with faintly upraised eyebrows, the cigarette smoke curling from her lips.

"And it was for a luncheon such as this," she protested, "that I wore my new muslin gown and came all the way from the country. I expected compliments at least. Perhaps I even hoped," she whispered, leaning a little towards him, with a smile upon her lips, — half mirthful, half provocative, — "that I might have turned for a moment that wonderfully hard head of yours."

Arnold rose abruptly to his feet.

"You treat men as though they were puppets," he muttered.

"And you speak of puppets," she murmured, "as though theirs was a most undesirable existence. Have you never tried to be a puppet, Arnold?"

He stepped a little further back still and gripped the back of the chair, but she kept close to him.

"I am to have no other answer from you, then, but this foolery?" he demanded, roughly.

"Why, yes!" she replied, graciously. "I have an answer ready for you. You are so abrupt. Listen to what I propose. We will go together to your office and see whether it is true that Mr. Weatherley has not returned. If he has really disappeared, and I think that anything which I can tell you will help, perhaps then I will do as you ask. It depends a great deal upon what you find in those papers. Shall we go now, or would you like to stay here a little longer?"

"We will go at once," he said firmly.

She sighed, and passed out of the door which he had thrown open.

"It is I who am a heroine," she declared. "I am coming down to Tooley Street with you. I am coming to brave the smells and the fog and the heat."

He handed her into the car. He had sufficiently recovered his self-control to smile.

"In other words," he remarked, "you mean to be there when I open the safe!"

# CHAPTER XXVII

## THE LETTERS IN THE SAFE

The arrival of Arnold, accompanied by Mrs. Weatherley, created a mild sensation in Tooley Street. Mr. Jarvis, fussier than ever, and blinking continually behind his gold-rimmed spectacles, followed them into the private office.

"You have heard nothing of Mr. Weatherley?" Arnold asked.

"Not a word," the cashier answered. "We have rung up several more places and have tried the hospitals again. We were all hoping that Mrs. Weatherley had brought us some news."

She shook her head.

"Mr. Weatherley left home exceedingly early this morning," she announced. "I believe that it was before half-past seven. Except that he called at the house in Hampstead for the letters, I have not heard of him since."

"It is most mysterious," Mr. Jarvis declared. "The governor — I beg your pardon, Mr. Weatherley — is a gentleman of most punctual habits. There are several matters of business which he knew awaited his decision today. You will excuse me, madam, if I ask whether Mr. Weatherley seemed in his usual health when he left this morning?"

Fenella smiled faintly.

"Have I not already told you," she said, "that he left the cottage in the country, where we spent the week-end, before half-past seven this morning? Naturally, therefore, I did not see him. The servants, however, noticed nothing unusual. Last night Mr. Chetwode here was with us, and he can tell you what was apparent to all of us. Mr. Weatherley seemed then in excellent health and spirits."

Mr. Jarvis had the air of a man hopelessly bewildered. Excellent servant though he was, nature had not bestowed upon him those gifts which enable a man to meet a crisis firmly.

"Can you suggest anything that we ought to do, madam?" he asked Mrs. Weatherley.

"I think," she replied, "that Mr. Chetwode has something to tell you."

Arnold took the key of the safe from his pocket and turned to the cashier.

"A few days ago, Mr. Jarvis," he said slowly, "Mr. Weatherley placed certain documents in that safe and gave me the key. My instructions from him were to open and examine them with you, if he should be, for any unexplained cause, absent from business."

Mr. Jarvis looked blankly incredulous.

"Goodness gracious!" he murmured weakly. "Why, that looks almost as though he expected something of the sort to happen."

"I think," Arnold continued, "that as it is now past three o'clock, and Mr. Weatherley is still absent, we had better open the safe."

He crossed the room as he spoke, fitted the key in the lock, and swung the door open. Mrs. Weatherley and the cashier looked over his shoulder. There were only the two letters there. One was addressed to Messrs. Turnbull & James, Solicitors; the other jointly to Mr. Jarvis and Mr. Arnold Chetwode. "There is nothing there for me?" Mrs. Weatherley asked, incredulously.

"There is nothing at all," Arnold replied; "unless there may be an enclosure. Mr. Jarvis, will you open this envelope?"

Mr. Jarvis took it to the desk and broke the seal with trembling fingers. He smoothed the letter out, switched on the electric reading light, and they all read it at the same time. It was written in Mr. Weatherley's familiar hand, every letter of which was perfectly distinct and legible.

> *To Jarvis and Chetwode.*
> This is a record of certain instructions which I wish carried out in the event of my unexplained absence from business at any time.
> Firstly — The business is to continue exactly as usual, and my absence to be alluded to as little as possible. It can be understood that I am away on the Continent or elsewhere, on a business voyage.
> Secondly — I have deposited a power of attorney at my solicitors, made out in the joint names of Henry Jarvis and Arnold Chetwode. This will enable you both to make and receive contracts on behalf of the firm. As regards financial affairs, Messrs. Neville, the accountants, have already the authority to sign cheques, and a representative from their firm will be in attendance each day, or according to your request. My letter to Messrs. Turnbull & James empowers them to make such payments as are necessary, on the joint application of you two, Henry Jarvis and Arnold Chetwode, to whom I address this letter.
> Thirdly — I have the most implicit confidence in Henry Jarvis, who has been in my employ for so many years, and I beg him to understand that I associate with him one so much his junior, for certain reasons into which I beg that he will not inquire.
> Fourthly — I repeat that I desire as little publicity as possible to be given to my absence, and that no money be spent on advertisements, or any other form of search. If within two years from the date of the opening of this letter, I have not been heard from further, I desire that the usual steps be taken to presume my decease. My will and all further particulars are with Messrs. Turnbull & James.
> Fifthly — I desire you to pay to my wife the sum of five hundred pounds

monthly. All other matters concerning my private estate, etc. are embodied in
the letter to Messrs. Turnbull & James.

They all finished reading the letter about the same time. Mr. Jarvis'
bewilderment grew deeper and deeper.

"This is the most extraordinary document I ever read in my life!" he
exclaimed. "Why, it seems as though he had gone away somewhere of his
own accord. After all, it can't be an accident, or anything of that sort."

Neither Arnold nor Mrs. Weatherley made any immediate reply. She
pointed to the letter.

"When did he write this?" she asked.

"Last Thursday," Arnold replied; "less than a week ago."

She sighed softly.

"Really, it is most mysterious," she said. "I wonder whether he can have
gone out of his mind suddenly, or anything of that sort."

"I have never," Mr. Jarvis declared, "known Mr. Weatherley to display so
much acumen and zest in business as during the last few days. Some of his
transactions have been most profitable. Every one in the place has remarked
upon it."

Mrs. Weatherley took up the lace parasol which she had laid upon the
office table.

"It is all most bewildering," she pronounced. "I think that it is no use
my staying here any longer. I will leave you two to talk of it together. You
have doubtless much business to arrange."

"Are you going back to Bourne End or to Hampstead?" Arnold asked.

She hesitated.

"Really, I am not quite sure," she replied, meeting his gaze without
flinching. "I am beginning to find the heat in town insufferable. I think, perhaps, that I shall go to Bourne End."

"In that case," Arnold said, "will you allow me to see you there tonight?"

"Tonight?" she repeated, as though in surprise.

"Without a doubt."

She did not answer him for a moment. Meanwhile, the telephone rang,
and Mr. Jarvis was presently engrossed in a business conversation with a customer. Arnold lowered his voice a little.

"Our discussion at luncheon was only postponed," he reminded her.
"We have seen these documents. We know now that Mr. Weatherley had
some reason to fear an interruption to his everyday life. Directly or indi-
rectly, that interruption is connected with certain things of which you and I
have spoken together. I am going to ask you, therefore, to keep your promise.

I am going to ask you to tell me everything that you know."

"Are you not afraid," she asked, "that I shall consider you a very inquisitive young man?"

"I am afraid of nothing of the sort," Arnold replied. "Mr. Weatherley's disappearance is too serious a matter for me to take such trifles into account."

She pointed to the letter which still lay upon the table.

"Is it not his expressed wish that you should make no effort towards solving the reasons for his disappearance?"

"There is no reason," Arnold answered, doggedly, "why one should not attempt to understand them."

Mr. Jarvis had finished his telephoning. Fenella went up to him with outstretched hand.

"Mr. Jarvis," she said, "there is nothing more I can do here. I am very much upset. Will you take me out to my car, please? I know that you will do the very best you can without Mr. Weatherley, and I am glad that you have Mr. Chetwode to help you. I would come down myself sometimes," she added, "but I am sure that I should only be in the way. Good afternoon, Mr. Chetwode."

"You have not answered my question," he persisted.

She looked at him as a great lady would look at a presuming servant.

"I see no necessity," she replied. "I am too much upset to receive visitors today. If you are ready, Mr. Jarvis."

She left the room without even a backward glance, closely followed by the cashier. Arnold stood looking after the retreating figures for a moment, then he turned away with a hard little laugh. Once more he read and re-read Mr. Weatherley's letter. Before he had finished, Mr. Jarvis came bustling back into the room.

"Well!" he exclaimed, dramatically. "Well!"

Arnold looked across at him.

"It's a queer business, isn't it?" he remarked.

"Queer business, indeed!" Mr. Jarvis repeated, sitting down and wiping his forehead. "It's the most extraordinary thing I ever heard of in my life. One doesn't read about such things even in books. Mrs. Weatherley seems to take it quite calmly, but the more I think of it, the more confused I become. What are we to do? Shall we go to the police or write to the newspapers? Can't you suggest something?"

Arnold finally laid down the letter, which he now knew pretty well by heart.

"It seems to me, Mr. Jarvis," he said, "that the thing for us to do is to obey orders. Mr. Weatherley expressly writes that he wishes us to take his absence, so far as possible, as a matter of course, and to look after the business. The very fact that he puts it like that makes it quite clear to me that he intends to return. My idea is that we should follow the lines of his letter strictly."

"You are quite right, Chetwode," Mr. Jarvis decided. "I feel exactly that way about the matter myself. We'll go right ahead with those orders now, then, and we can have a chat about the matter again after business hours, if you don't mind. It's hard to reconcile oneself to taking this so easily, but I suppose it's the only thing to do. I'll get out in the warehouse now. You had better send that note round to Turnbull's by express messenger, and ring up Yardley's about the American contracts."

Mr. Jarvis bustled away. Arnold himself found plenty to do. The business of Messrs. Weatherley & Company must go on, whatever happened. He set himself sedulously to make his mind a complete blank. It was not until the offices were closed, and he turned at last westwards, that he permitted himself even to realize this strange thing that had happened. On that first walk was born an impulse which remained with him for many weeks afterwards. He found himself always scanning the faces of the streams of people whom he was continually passing, on foot and in vehicles, half expecting that somewhere among them he would catch a glimpse of the features of the lost Mr. Weatherley.

# CHAPTER XXVIII

## TALK OF TREASURE SHIPS

In the twilight of the long spring evening, Ruth sat waiting in the bare room which had been Arnold's habitation during these days of his struggle against poverty. She was sitting on the couch, drawn up as usual to the window, her elbows upon her knees, her hands supporting her delicate, thoughtful face. Already the color which the sunshine had brought seemed to have been drained from her cheeks. Her eyes were unnaturally bright, her expression seemed to have borrowed something of that wistful earnestness of one of the earlier Madonnas, seeking with pathetic strenuousness to discover the germs of a truth which was as yet unborn. The clouds, which hung low over the other side of the river, were tinged with an unusual coloring, smoke-stained as they hovered over the chimneys. They grew clearer and more full of amber color as they floated slowly southwards. Through the open window came the ceaseless roar of the city, the undernote of grinding, commonplace life, seeking always to stifle and enchain the thoughts which would escape. Before her was spread out a telegram. She had read it many times, until every word was familiar to her. It was from Arnold, and she had received it several hours ago.

Please be prepared to go out with me directly I return this evening. All well. Love. Arnold.

It was past eight o'clock before her vigil was at an end. She listened to his step upon the stairs, and, as he entered, looked at him with all the eagerness of a wistful child, tremulously anxious to read his expression. A little wave of tenderness swept in upon him. He forgot in a moment the anxieties and worries of the day, and greeted her gayly.

"You got my telegram?"

"You extravagant person!" she answered. "Yes, I have been ready for quite a long time."

He laughed.

"To tell you the truth, I didn't even pay for the telegram. As I had to stay late, I took the liberty of sending it through the firm's accounts. You see, I have become quite an important person in Tooley Street all of a sudden. I'll tell you about it presently. Now hold on tightly to your stick. I'm much too impatient to go down the steps one by one. I'm going to carry you all the way."

"But where to?" she asked.

"Leave it to me," he laughed. "There are all sorts of surprises for you. The lady with the wand has been busy."

He carried her downstairs, where, to her surprise, she found a taxicab waiting.

"But, Arnold," she exclaimed, "how could you think of such extravagance! You know I can walk quite easily a little distance, if I take your arm."

"I'll tell you all about it at dinner-time," he replied.

"Dinner-time?" she cried. "Dinner at this hour?"

"Why not? It's quite the fashionable hour, I can assure you, and, to tell you the truth, I am half starved."

She resigned herself with a sigh of content. After all, it was so delightful to drift like this with some one infinitely stronger to take the responsibility for everything. They drove to a large and popular restaurant close at hand, where Arnold ordered the dinner, with frequent corrections from Ruth, who sat with a menu-card in her hand. A band was playing the music of the moment. It was all very commonplace, but to Ruth it was like a living chapter out of her book of dreams. Even there, though, the shadow pursued. She could bear the silence no longer. She dropped her voice a little. The place was crowded and there were people at the next table.

"Before I touch anything, Arnold, tell me this. Is there any news of Isaac?"

"None at all," he replied. "It all seemed very alarming to us, but it seems to be fizzling out. There is only quite a small paragraph in the evening paper. You can read it, if you like."

He drew the *Evening News* from his pocket and passed it to her. The paragraph to which he pointed was headed —

### ESCAPE OF AN ANARCHIST FROM ADAM STREET.

Up to the time of going to press, the man Isaac Lalonde, whom the police failed to arrest last night on a charge not at present precisely stated, has not been apprehended. The police are reticent about the matter, but it is believed that the missing man was connected with a dangerous band of anarchists who have lately come to this country.

"Poor Isaac!" she murmured, with a little shiver. "Do you know, I remember him years ago, when he was the kindest-hearted man breathing. He went to Russia to visit some of his mother's relatives, and when he came back everything was changed. He saw injustice everywhere, and it seemed almost to unbalance his mind. The very sight of the west-end, the crowds coming out of the theatres, the shops in Bond Street, seemed to send him half mad. And it all started, Arnold, with real pity for the poor. It isn't a personal matter with him at any time."

THE END